11

Contents

1 Once he's aware that **winter** has begun, it has already passed. — 003

2 And so begins the **all-girls battle** (with boys, too). ———— 023

3 Unexpectedly, what **Iroha Isshiki**'s absence brings is... ———— 047

4 And so begins the **boys' emotional roller coaster** (with girls, too). ———— 067

5 Suddenly, **Shizuka Hiratsuka** lectures about the present continuous and the past. ———— 089

6 He fails to reach the **"something real"** he's after and continues to get it wrong. ———— 121

7 **Haruno Yukinoshita**'s eyes are hopelessly clear. ———— 143

Interlude ———— 166

8 **Yui Yuigahama**'s gaze is always gentle and warm. ———— 171

9 **Spring** is made and begins to bud underneath the snow. ——— 197

Translation Notes ———— 209

MY YOUTH R♥MANTIC C☺MEDY iS WRØNG, AS I EXPECTED

Wataru Watari
Illustration **Ponkan⑧**

VOLUME
11

YEN
ON
NEW YORK

MY YOUTH ROMANTIC COMEDY IS WRONG, AS I EXPECTED Vol. 11

WATARU WATARI

Illustration by Ponkan⑧

Translation by Jennifer Ward

Cover art by Ponkan⑧

YAHARI ORE NO SEISHUN LOVE COME WA MACHIGATTEIRU.

Vol. 11 by Wataru WATARI

© 2011 Wataru WATARI

Illustration by PONKAN⑧

All rights reserved.

Original Japanese edition published by SHOGAKUKAN.

English translation rights in the United States of America, Canada, the United Kingdom, Ireland, Australia and New Zealand arranged with SHOGAKUKAN through Tuttle-Mori Agency, Inc.

English translation © 2021 by Yen Press, LLC

Yen On

150 West 30th Street, 19th Floor

New York, NY 10001

Visit us at yenpress.com

facebook.com/yenpress

twitter.com/yenpress

yenpress.tumblr.com

instagram.com/yenpress

First Yen On Edition: May 2021

Yen On is an imprint of Yen Press, LLC.

The Yen On name and logo are trademarks of Yen Press, LLC.

The publisher is not responsible for websites (or their content) that are not owned by the publisher.

Library of Congress Cataloging-in-Publication Data

Names: Watari, Wataru, author. | Ponkan 8, illustrator.

Title: My youth romantic comedy is wrong, as I expected / Wataru Watari ; illustration by Ponkan 8.

Other titles: Yahari ore no seishun love come wa machigatteiru. English

Description: New York : Yen On, 2016–

Identifiers: LCCN 2016005816 | ISBN 9780316312295 (v. 1 : pbk.) | ISBN 9780316396011 (v. 2 : pbk.) |
    ISBN 9780316318068 (v. 3 : pbk.) | ISBN 9780316318075 (v. 4 : pbk.) | ISBN 9780316318082 (v. 5 : pbk.) |
    ISBN 9780316411868 (v. 6 : pbk.) | ISBN 9781975384166 (v. 6.5 : pbk.) | ISBN 9781975384128 (v. 7 : pbk.) |
    ISBN 9781975384159 (v. 7.5 : pbk.) | ISBN 9781975384135 (v. 8 : pbk.) | ISBN 9781975384142 (v. 9 : pbk.) |
    ISBN 9781975384111 (v. 10 : pbk.) | ISBN 9781975384173 (v. 10.5 : pbk.) | ISBN 9781975324988 (v. 11 : pbk.)

Subjects: | CYAC: Optimism—Fiction. | School—Fiction.

Classification: LCC PZ7.1.W396 My 2016 | DDC [Fic]—dc23

LC record available at http://lccn.loc.gov/2016005816

ISBNs: 978-1-9753-2498-8 (paperback)
        978-1-9753-3363-8 (ebook)

10 9 8 7 6 5 4 3 2 1

LSC-C

Printed in the United States of America

MY YOUTH R♥MANTIC C☺MEDY iS WRØNG, AS I EXPECTED

eleven

Cast of Characters

Hachiman Hikigaya........... The main character. High school second-year. Twisted personality.

Yukino Yukinoshita........... Captain of the Service Club. Perfectionist.

Yui Yuigahama.................. Hachiman's classmate. Tends to worry about what other people think.

Saika Totsuka.................. In tennis club. Very cute. A boy, though.

Saki Kawasaki.................. Hachiman's classmate. Sort of a delinquent type.

Hayato Hayama.................. Hachiman's classmate. Popular. In the soccer club.

Kakeru Tobe.................... Hachiman's classmate. An excitable character and member of Hayama's clique.

Yumiko Miura.................. Hachiman's classmate. Reigns over the girls in class as queen bee.

Iroha Isshiki..................... Manager of the soccer club. First-year student who was elected student council president.

Kaori Orimoto................... Went to Hachiman's middle school. Student at Kaihin High School.

Shizuka Hiratsuka............. Japanese teacher. Guidance counselor.

Haruno Yukinoshita........... Yukino's older sister. In university.

Komachi Hikigaya............. Hachiman's little sister. In her third year in middle school.

Once he's aware that **winter** has begun, it has already passed.

It happened a little ways into February.

The winter was still biting cold, rattling and creaking the windows of the classroom with every gust of the dry north wind.

Once the end-of-day short homeroom was over, the cold would only get worse, by all appearances. My seat was close to the hallway side, so I was not chosen to be blessed by the heater, and the draft came in through the cracked-open door. The lick of cold flicking up my neck sent a shiver through me.

But when I looked to the window, the sun still maintained a fair height in the sky. The days were gradually getting longer.

It would soon be the first day of spring, by the lunar calendar. Of course it comes every year, but when it's this cold, you think, *Spring?! What the hell are you talking about? Man, the only place spring has sprung is inside your head.*

But they also say, "If winter comes, can spring be far behind?"

And the mood of spring had been gradually building in the classroom after school.

According to the lunar calendar, the day of Keichitsu was less than a month away.

Maybe it was just because the heat was on, but the class was buzzing a little sooner than the calendar would indicate, just like bugs, frogs, and snakes waking from hibernation.

The heater was right by the window seats, so the lucky kids warmed by it were full of energy. That day, they could be heard talking loudly and drawing attention, as they always did.

"Man, I wanna eat something sweet!" Tobe said while mussing up the hair at the back of his neck.

Ooka and Yamato slapped their knees as if they'd just been thinking the same thing, and they pointed at him. "Yeah, man."

"Totally, man."

The three of them exchanged looks—*glance, glance, glance, glance.*

"It's like...don'cha want somethin' seasonal?" Tobe said with unnecessary gravity, and the three of them all looked at each other smugly and glance-glanced over at the girls.

...Hmm. I was thinking spring was close, but it seems we're still in the middle of winter after all! Not even the crickets are awake.

But as cold as the weather was, Miura's reaction was far colder.

"...*Huh?*" She clicked her tongue, then gave Tobe and the guys the kind of dull look that would make even these three stooges think twice about speaking again. Ebina and Yuigahama smiled awkwardly.

"Oh yeah, Valentine's is coming up, huh...?" Hayama: ever the mediator.

Ooka and Yamato both nodded at him. "You'll be fine, Hayato, but we're basically screwed," Ooka said, as if this was a big deal, to which Yamato nodded gravely.

"Totally screwed."

Ooka sounded so serious. *Man, this virginal weather vane's twisted soul is truly awful. I love it,* I was thinking, when Tobe grinned that thoughtless smile of his and pat-patted Hayama's shoulder.

"Hey, but, like, Hayato generally doesn't accept chocolate."

"Are you kidding?! Why would you do that?!" Ooka cried, making Hayama smile wryly.

Oh, he must be trying to avoid trouble.

But I suspected that would be hard to accept for any girls who had a crush on Hayama. And the one at the top of that list, Miura, had turned away with frigid indifference as she listened to the guys' conversation in silence.

Noticing her reaction, Yuigahama nodded with understanding. "Ah."

But this time Ebina cut in with utter seriousness, apparently intending to put a halt to the discussion. "But it's kind of scary to take chocolate from someone you don't know… Wait. If he's not taking it, that means…top. So that means the bottom is Hikitani?"

The moment that was out of her mouth, Miura smacked her over the head.

How is she able to keep a straight face when she talks like that…?

Then, Miura shoved a packet of tissues at her. "Ebina, nosebleed."

"Oh, thanks, thanks." Stifling her inappropriate chuckles, Ebina blew her nose, and a gentle smile passed over Miura's face. The warmth among their group then wasn't just coming from the heater.

No—it was all over the classroom, not just with their clique and the three stooges. That giddiness had infected the whole room.

Societally speaking, it was almost Valentine's Day. For me, the day I get chocolate from my mom and sister.

Is Valentine's a day filled with blessed love? I think there's some room for doubt. For starters, its origins were extremely bloody. Not only is there the whole mess with the saint, it's also the day of that gang conflict. And if you ask a Chibanese, Valentine's means Bobby Valentine, and nobody cares about chocolate.

But of course my opinion doesn't matter; it's not going to change the way society in general sees it. In fact, if you try to lecture about confectionery industry conspiracies these days, you'll inevitably be branded as ignorant and uneducated.

Valentine's Day has already settled in as a unique element of the national culture, like Christmas. Even Halloween might soon enough take root as a Japanized tradition. It's not much different from summer festivals, the Bon dance, or the grave visits of the vernal and autumnal equinoxes.

In the end, it all comes down to whether you like it or hate it, and nobody questions if tradition or orthodoxy renders it invalid. If you want to reject Christmas or Valentine's, you have to loudly declare that you hate it.

Komachi will slip me some chocolate every year, so I don't hate it all that much. In fact, I eagerly await it, as Big Brother dearly loves his Komachi.

I had turned my mind to the joy of splurging for my sister, wondering how expensive the chocolates she'd give me would be this year, since she'd be demanding a return gift of equivalent value or higher, when a stir arose in the classroom.

"We're never going to make it now!"

"It'll be okay. We've still got time! Let's do our best! Don't give up!"

When I looked over, I saw in a different area of the class some girls from the second or third level in the hierarchy busying themselves with knitting needles, making scarves or sweaters or something. They were talking just like a light-novel author and an editor. *You're just not gonna make it in time, it's almost Valentine's Day, and you've still only done about ten percent.* Instead of trying to make it in time, it's more constructive and also more realistic to focus your efforts on extending the deadline!

Apparently, I wasn't the only one watching that tragic exchange.

Spinning her hair around a finger, Miura muttered half-heartedly, "…Well, homemade is kinda too much? I can kinda get why he wouldn't accept it."

Another girl sighed, too. "Too much…yeah, huh…" With her thin fingers poking out from her slightly overlong cardigan sleeves, Yuigahama combed through her pinkish-brown hair. She seemed embarrassed.

Seeing that expression suddenly reminded me of an incident some time ago, in another season.

—*Homemade, huh? Who was she trying to make that for?* I was thinking as my eyes wandered over, but then they met with hers. Our gazes both slid in opposite directions.

"Well, it's the thought that counts, more than the gift itself," I heard Hayama say, with a bit of wry chagrin in his tone.

"Yeah, totally, dude! Me too, man! I'd love to get something like that, y'know?" Tobe agreed, instantly smacking his knee.

But Ebina, sitting diagonally facing him, crossed her arms as her gaze shifted to the side. "But when it's homemade, it's really apparent when you cut corners. You've got to be fairly confident in your ability, or it can turn out badly. Wouldn't a store-bought item be a safer choice?" she said.

"Yeah, that's also, like, totally, dude!" Tobe immediately flip-flopped.

…C'mon, man, try a little harder.

"…Hmm, homemade, huh?" Miura repeated with disinterest, and their little group's pleasant chatter continued on loudly.

The divide that had been there was now gone.

Hayama was doing his best to be the Hayato Hayama everyone wanted, and Miura was, in her own way, trying to gradually close the distance between them. And with Tobe and Ebina, too—I guess they hadn't really changed, but with the passage of time, they'd managed to create a vibe that was very them.

And then there was Yuigahama, watching it all happily.

This scene in the restless classroom was still nevertheless gradually becoming warmer, just like the season gradually turning to spring. Seen from the sidelines, it was so perfect, I found it a little hard to watch.

$$\times \quad \times \quad \times$$

A cold, dry air filled the hallway to the special-use building. My lips were chapped, and my skin felt tight.

There had been condensation on the classroom windows, but the windows in this hallway were clear, and I had a good view of the school courtyard and its naked trees and the bare flower beds. It was a sort of dusty, olive-brown winter scenery of our latitude.

Chiba doesn't get much snow in the winter. Kanto in general isn't accustomed to snow, but I'm sure Chiba has some of the least. Last month when it was on the news that it was snowing in Tokyo, there wasn't even a sprinkle in Chiba then, either.

It's the lack of wintriness that makes it so chilly. I was really feeling the temperature drop between here and the classroom where I'd just been, and I tugged my scarf up around my neck.

It wasn't the nearby heater that had made that classroom, that place, seem warm. It was just being somewhere where the cracks were actually filled up.

Just as Hayama and his friends wished, there would be no dramatic ending, and they would welcome any and all endings peacefully and warmly. Just like the end of the world, and the end of life. It's through the efforts of people that happiness and peace are maintained, and I was reminded of that fact once again.

Maybe they understood from experience, too, after so many winters, that spring would come.

Not only will the spring be warm—a gentle parting awaits beyond, too. There is also the example of flowers and storms; life is naught but farewells.

Our classes will change, and all our social relationships will be constructed anew. Around this time next year will be the peak of entrance exam season, and we will no longer be coming to school. Everyone will be savoring this winter so as to peacefully welcome the end when it comes.

And there was legitimate warmth in that, but I found it rather chilly myself. I was walking along, quietly complaining under my scarf about the cold, when I heard the light patter of footsteps on the floor behind me.

As I was turning around, there was a clap on my shoulder. I looked to see Yuigahama pouting at me. "Why're you going without me...?" she asked.

"Uh, it's not like we said we were going together...," I said, a bit irritated. It just didn't make sense that she was acting this way.

Yuigahama's mouth dropped open, and then she combed through her hair like she was embarrassed. "...Oh, I thought you were waiting for me. Since you were in the classroom awhile..."

"No, that was just…" But even as I started to reply, I recalled why I'd stayed behind in the classroom. It was true Yuigahama had invited me countless times to walk to the clubroom together with her. Maybe I'd been waiting for her to come to me without even realizing it.

But I did hit on another reason, too. "Oh, I was just kinda checking how things were going with Hayama and Miura."

"Ohhh, yeah. It seems like they're okay now. What a relief," Yuigahama said with a slight sigh and nod. She went off a few steps ahead of me down the empty hallway, then turned back partway. "I kinda think it's nice. Everyone has stuff on their minds, but they're still making sure to treasure the moment. Like, no time like the present, and all…," she said, as if reflecting on each and every word, a peaceful smile on her face.

"Well, yeah. Maybe the present is the best time we have."

"Oh. You're not usually so positive, Hikki…"

"Remembering the past makes you want to die of regret, and thinking about the future makes you depressed from the anxiety, so it wins by process of elimination."

"I knew you were gonna make it sad!" Yuigahama puffed up her cheeks, shoulders slumping as she stalked on ahead. Then she grumbled quietly, "You always jump to saying things like that… You could consider the atmosphere."

"The atmosphere, huh…?"

Well, for example…this Valentine's Day atmosphere, I guess.

Oh, I can get that. I'd like to go along with the masses for once, too—lie to myself and let the seasonal festivities sweep me away and then blame any indiscretion on that. I'd love to get my hopes up and take advantage and leave it to someone else and wait.

But I don't think that's enough.

Just waiting is insincere. No matter what sort of answer or conclusion may await, you take a real step forward—with no lies, deception, or suspicion, and then afterward, you can properly remember and regret it.

So I would drink down this "mood" and try asking now.

"Oh yeah, so…" My voice sounded a bit hoarse when I spoke,

making Yuigahama turn around. With a tilt of her head and a look, she asked me to continue.

It was a little too much to look straight at her, so I angled my face away. "...Hey, are you free sometime soon?"

"Huh? Y-yeah. Um, probably... I guess I am generally free. Sorta." She flailed her hands like she was a little surprised, then rushed to pull out her cell phone. But then she froze and glanced over at the door to the clubroom. Then after that, she didn't say anything. Unlike before, her expression seemed somehow subdued.

I was a little surprised by that, but I didn't feel like I could ask why. So I said nothing at all. The air in the hallway was particularly cold and dry, and something felt wrong, like something was stuck to the back of my throat.

Maybe I shouldn't have asked here and now. Or maybe there was some other way of saying it, some smarter way of doing it. Or was the way I asked not casual enough? I just wasn't sure.

With my shoulders hunched and head lowered, unable to say anything else, I looked at Yuigahama. She was smiling with some discomfort, and it made my breath catch.

As if to fill the silence that had come between us, she said quickly, "I'll think about it a bit, so later, 'kay?"

"...O-okay."

Was this relief, or was it just my energy draining away? Or was it something else?

Whatever it was, my stomach was in a few more knots than it was before, and my reply came with a deep sigh. But Yuigahama didn't wait for it, pattering a few steps ahead to open the door of the clubroom.

×　×　×

The door was flung open. When I went inside, a soft, gentle air enveloped me.

Though there were far fewer people here than in the classroom, this place felt warmer, strangely enough. Or maybe it was because this special-use building gets more sun.

With the peaceful rays of the sun pouring down upon her, Yukino Yukinoshita was sitting in her usual seat. Looking up from the paperback in her hands, she gently combed back her long hair, and a soft smile came to her face. "Hello."

"Yahallo, Yukinon." Yuigahama shot up a hand as she replied, and I gave my usual lazy greeting.

"'Sup."

With that, we each sat down in our own chairs.

At some point, it had been decided this was the place I belonged. No one had declared it was, no one had forced me, and no one had questioned it. It was far more comfortable than I'd expected.

Because of this, it felt incredibly wrong to see someone there who wasn't one of the usual suspects.

"You're laaate!"

"Why are you here…?"

Leaning forward over her desk, swinging her legs back and forth as she complained, was the less-than-presidential student council president of Soubu High School: Iroha Isshiki. She gave me a very deliberate pout, then jerked her face away; every single move she made had manipulative intentions… And hey, she got here earlier than me or Yuigahama—is she as swift as the *Shimakaze*?

"I asked if she had some business, but she said she'd wait until you two were here, and she's been here the whole time," Yukinoshita said with a little whiff of a sigh. She shot Isshiki an exceptionally icy look. But nevertheless, she'd poured her a proper cup of tea and was offering her surprisingly legitimate hospitality—I wasn't sure if Isshiki's presence here meant membership, but it seemed they had some kind of relationship. There are many types of ships in the world—some people even build a collection!

And as for Isshiki, she maintained her devil-may-care attitude even under Yukinoshita's cold gaze. Turning her whole body toward me, she brought one hand to her mouth to murmur softly like she was imparting a secret, "Yukinoshita got really excited when I came in...but then she saw it was me, and she's been acting disappointed ever since."

Oh, I see... That's because whenever Isshiki shows up, it means trouble. But seriously. Why is she here? I was thinking as I heard a tiny *ahem*.

"...Isshiki?" I looked over to see a sweet smile on Yukinoshita's face.

Oh, I know this smile! This is Yukinon's intimidation face!

"Y-yes! I'm sorry—I did come for a reason!" Isshiki slipped around to prod me forward from behind, like some kind of conditioned reflex.

Hey, cut that out, I'm a little scared, too.

"H-hey, hey now. Does it have to do with the student council, Iroha-chan?" Yuigahama mediated, beckoning Isshiki.

"You're so nice, Yui!" Isshiki said, returning to her original position with a nonchalant expression.

When I gave Isshiki a look that asked her what she *was* here for, then, she replied with an even more nonchalant look as she did a little wave.

"Wellll, I've got more time on my hands than I thought I would, right?"

"Huh?" *I never know what she's talking about... We had a whole ton of work just the other day, thanks to* you...

Wait, does she mean she actually has nothing to do after all that? Is it like burnout? When you crunch for so long that when the pressure goes away, you don't know what to do with yourself? *...But I feel like I was the one burning out there. How about that, hmm?* With that thought, I shot her a persistent glare in an attempt to ascertain what she really meant.

Isshiki put her index finger to her chin and tilted her head cutely. "There's no school events right now, and the vice president and everyone else'll work super-hard to handle the minor stuff. And for the reports and stuff for the end of the fiscal year, I just have to do the stamping when they're done, so."

Oh. I'm not all that informed on student council work, but her story holds water. The third-years are right in the middle of university entrance exams, and the school administration is also heavily occupied with tests for prospective students.

Meaning not a lot of management for the rest of us, so she really might have nothing to do.

"So when we're not very busy, the student council decided not to have meetings," Isshiki continued.

Well, well, reasonable administration… Meanwhile, our club president requires attendance even when we have nothing to do. Extortion!

And as for said extortioner, she was nodding with a *hmm* as she gently touched her hand to her chin. "You have your club activities as well, don't you?" Yukinoshita said with a tilt of her head.

Isshiki blushed a bit bashfully and turned her face away. "…………… It's too cold for the soccer club right now."

Forget bashfulness—this is the kind of rationale you should just be flat ashamed of. Yukinoshita put a hand to her temple as if applying pressure to a headache.

Yuigahama also had a dry, mannerly smile on. "Ah, ah-ha-ha… So then what did you come for?" she asked.

Ahem. Isshiki cleared her throat, then spun around to face me. "Not like I care, but do you like sweets?"

"I think Hayama will gladly eat anything," I said, anticipating where this was going. I already had a grasp of Isshiki's motives and behavior. She puffed up her cheeks in apparent disappointment.

Yuigahama realized with a start. "Oh, but Hayato was saying he's not gonna accept any chocolates."

"Whaaat? Why nooot?" Isshiki whined.

"…I—I dunno?" Yuigahama tilted her head.

Yukinoshita let out a short sigh. "Because it would cause quarrels, obviously. Back in elementary school, the next day would always be very tense…"

"…Ahhh."

"…Ahhh. I think I get that."

Isshiki and Yuigahama both nodded. *Yeah, yeah, I get that, too! I get that!*

I'm sure the classroom the next day will wind up like *The Heart-Pounding ☆ All-Girls Witch Trial in Absentia! With added snitching!* and I can easily imagine it turning into a whole thing. Since much of "girl talk" amounts to bad-mouthing other girls (according to my personal research).

Whoa, scary. While I was thinking about it all, Isshiki, who I'd assume has lived her life being bashed in the dark underworld—I mean, civil society of girls—gave a faint sigh. "Fine, then you can answer as yourself this time. Do you like sweets?"

"What a weird way to ask…" *It's the same question as before, but it's too hard to answer honestly. I feel like I was just tossed in as an extra…* As I was thinking, there was a scrape of a chair. Looking over, I saw Yuigahama leaning forward enthusiastically.

"Hikki loves sweets!"

"He does." Meanwhile, Yukinoshita had a haughty, superior little smile on her face.

Isshiki seemed a bit overwhelmed by the two of them and responded somewhat evasively, "Dunno how I feel about you two answering instead of him, but…this is perfect, then!"

"Uh-huh…," I said. "Wait, what's perfect?"

"I was worrying about how sweet to make them, you know? 'Cause everybody's got their own preferences, riiight?" Isshiki continued, completely ignoring my question.

Yukinoshita tilted her head. "How sweet…? Isshiki, do you plan to make some yourself?"

"That's surprising," I said.

Isshiki huffed. "What's surprising? I'm good at making sweets." She puffed out her flat chest, while Yuigahama slumped forward.

"Awww, that's so nice! I wish I could do that, too, but I'm just no good at it…"

Hmm, the chest that's puffed toward me is still smaller than

Yuigahama's; it's throwing off my depth perception... Did they screw up on the perspective? Whatever, I'll submit a request for them to correct the animation when it comes out on Blu-ray!

Also, *no good* doesn't even begin to describe Yuigahama's culinary antiprowess, but compared with boobs, it's a minor issue.

"Yui. Cooking comes from the heart. What's needed for homemade baking is kindness and thoughtfulness. The fastest shortcut to improvement is considering the one you're cooking for." Isshiki comfortingly pat-patted the glum-looking Yuigahama on the shoulder, then stuck up a finger. With a mild smile, she offered her gentle encouragement. "You're giving it to boys, and they don't know the first thing about cooking, right? So homemade is the easy way out. You can mass-produce at low cost, and you can just tweak the finishing touches to customize for each individual. So it's easy to make something they'll go gaga for."

"You're being thoughtful about all the wrong things...," I said. "And your kindness is entirely directed at your wallet."

"But she isn't technically wrong," said Yukinoshita, "which makes it even worse..."

"It wouldn't make me very happy...," Yuigahama said.

Not even Isshiki was immune to all the criticism. She groaned, unable to respond, and then shoved it all to the side and forcibly changed the subject. "Well, I wasn't being serious. I mean, I was trying to do an imitation of him..." She looked over at me. "So anyway, what sort of sweets do you like? I was thinking it'll be helpful to know, for when I'm making obligatory chocolate."

"If you wanna know... This." What I took out from my bag was, of course, MAX Coffee. Why? Because this is very special stuff.

When I set my can down on the table, it received three skeptical looks.

Hey now, why so suspicious...? When you're giving something sweet, there's no Chibanese who will turn this baby down. Or so I would have liked to say, but they were really giving me the side-eye, huh...?

Staring at the can, Yuigahama muttered, "…I bet even I could make that."

"Hey, watch it. Don't you dare mock this drink. You better not be assuming that all you have to do is put sugar and condensed milk into coffee. Cut the crap, geez."

"Wait, are you actually mad?!"

Of course. This is far from just putting condensed milk into coffee. In fact, it's closer to putting coffee into condensed milk. There's no way you could get that rich sweetness if the ingredients were actually proportionate to their order on the label. This is no task for an amateur.

Isshiki touched her fingertip to her lip, then opened her mouth as if she were considering something. "Wait, though, that would take us over budget."

"I don't know how much you plan to make, but one serving at one hundred thirty yen is a pretty severe price to set it at…," Yukinoshita said with some exasperation, rubbing at her temple.

But her concerns were unfounded. "It's okay. With Max can, if you pick the right shop and buy in bulk, then it's even cheaper."

"How obsessed are you, Hikki…?"

"Well, when life gives you lemons, make lemonade with tons of sugar. The end of a lemon is the closest I'll ever get to sucking the golden teat anyway." A wry chuckle slipped out of me.

Yukinoshita swept the hair off her shoulders with a confident smile. "Oh, is that why you're so bitter?"

"Sure, whatever." I wasn't about to deny my lemony lot in life. "I'm still getting a sour deal, though. If I'm going to suck at something, I'd rather it taste sweet."

"I believe that's what they call 'sucking at life'…" Yukinoshita let out a long, deep sigh.

Oh, she is quite right indeed. I suck at life, too. From the above, you can surmise that life is a lemon, and thus makes for some really sour lemonade!

As I was entertaining such trivial thoughts, Isshiki snorted at me. "Agh. Well, not like anyone cares about that."

No one cares? Rude!

Isshiki tossed back her black tea in one go, set down her paper cup with a *tup*, and turned to me. "I wanted you to consider something I could give as obligatory chocolate."

"Obligatory chocolate, huh…?" Scratching my head, I did a pass over my memory, but no one's ever felt obligated to give me chocolate, so I don't really know what the standard is. The chocolate from my sister is the sincere kind, after all!

Such feelings must have shown on my face, as Isshiki gave me a nasty smirk. "Oh, are you one of those guys who's never gotten chocolate before? Don't boys compete over the number of chocolates they get? Getting nothing hurts your pride, you know?"

"Uh, it's not like I need any of that… Come on, is Valentine's Day a sport or what?"

"Highest score wins" is as simple and clear as you get, but the application of the rules in practice is all over the place. Especially when they come roaring at you with an offside trap like obligatory chocolate! That's like faking you got hit with a foul, an instant red card… That works, right? What's an offside, again? Ah, you got me; I don't really know anything about soccer.

Anyhow, despite my various arguments, Isshiki seemed to take them all as bravado and bluster, and she wouldn't listen at all. In fact, she gave me an uncomfortably warm look and sighed as if to say, *Good grief.* "Well, there's only one way to fix—"

"You don't need to worry about that." But Yukinoshita cut her off. Swishing her hair back, she smiled with calm composure. It was quite a contrast with Isshiki, whose mouth was innocently hanging open.

"Huh…? Wait, Yukinoshita—," Isshiki began.

But Yukinoshita wouldn't let her finish, a soft smile crossing her face. "Hikigaya doesn't have any friends to compete with."

"Oh, I see." I found myself nodding along with Isshiki until we looked like a couple of chickens. *I see—that's true. So loners are primitive communists for whom the principle of competition doesn't operate, huh? So primitive it's only one person…*

As I was preparing to ponder the principles of peace, Yuigahama puffed up her cheeks in a pout. "I don't think you have to worry… But, like, Hikki won't get *nothing*… Right?" she said, then flicked a hesitant look at me.

I nodded back at her with a casual smile.

"Huh…? Do you mean…?" Isshiki's gaze shifted between Yuigahama and me. Her bewildered eyes met mine.

A triumphant chuckle crawled its way out from deep within my throat. "Heh, that's right… I have Komachi!" *So I will actually get some! Yay! I really am glad I have a little sister! A sister's all you need!*

But Isshiki tilted her head with a blank expression. "Huh? Komachi? Who's that? The rice girl?"

"She's not rice," I said.

What, do they eat a lot of Akita Komachi–brand rice in the Isshiki household? My sister should be the beautiful mascot up there in the north. Or even down here in Chiba.

"Oh, Komachi-chan is Hikki's little sister," Yuigahama explained.

"Uh-huh, gotcha," Isshiki said, while her expression said she totally didn't care. "Didn't know you had a sister."

"Yeah." I do. A world-class sister. In fact, she's the little sister of the world.

My proud answer earned me a dubious stare from Isshiki. With her eyes narrowed to slits, she gave me a long, hard look, then cocked her head just slightly. "…Sister complex?"

"Pfft lol come on no way," I said in a hurry, but the others didn't exactly rush to my defense.

"…I think, maybe…I can't…deny it," Yuigahama said, and Yukinoshita nodded gravely.

Hey, back me up here.

Irohasu seemed quite satisfied by that reaction, nodding. Then she stuck up her index finger and touched it to her chin, tilting her head with a cutesy smile. "I knew it. You like younger girls, huh?"

"No not really actually," I said, again in a hurry.

It doesn't matter if they're older or younger: I have an almighty weakness to basically everyone.

When I brushed her off, Isshiki gave me a super-quiet *tsk*. "So then…" With a little *hem* to ensure her throat was in good working order, she gave me a glance with upturned eyes, then immediately looked away. She squeezed the chest of her uniform, her other hand trembling slightly as she fixed where her skirt had gone askew from her squirming. Her breath was hot; her eyes were moist.

And then, hesitantly, she opened her mouth. "Do you…hate younger girls?"

………*Hate them?! No! No! In fact, if I have to say, I love them!*

Yuigahama let out a short sigh and glanced at Isshiki with exasperation. "That's just about how you say it and your body language, isn't it…?"

"…Well, yeah." Yeah, I'm in agreement with that opinion. I have, as one might expect, gained a level of tolerance in this area.

Isshiki apparently didn't like that and shot me a slightly resentful look.

I couldn't help but smirk at her reaction.

I think Isshiki's gestures and manner of speaking are charming enough, as is Isshiki herself—it's just that for a number of reasons, they don't have much effect on me now. Not long ago, that would've easily made me light-headed. Definitely.

Of those many reasons, if I were to put the biggest one most plainly… "I love all little sisters, whether they're older or younger."

"That's even worse than having a sister complex! Or liking younger girls!" Yuigahama yelled with utter sorrow, and Isshiki nodded along as she cringed away from me.

What? Just imagining an older Komachi for a moment is very productive. Looking around to see if maybe someone else might agree, I found Yukinoshita tilting her head, arms folded, with a slightly dubious expression on her face.

"But what makes a girl count as 'younger' to you? Is it school year? Year of birth? Or if she was just born a few days later...? The definition here is vague. Shouldn't you decide that first?" Yukinoshita was muttering.

Yuigahama seemed to hear that, as she suddenly clapped. "Oh, but Hikki's really compatible with a slightly-older-sister type! Yeah! ...Probably. Definitely!" Her clenched fist was unusually tense.

Listen. I'm simply not fixated on such trivial matters. Not at all.

"...That doesn't really matter. Just one year's difference doesn't change much," I said.

Mainly in the realm of income! What's important is whether she can support me financially or not. And in that regard, my Komachi will do a perfect job taking care of me! She's got what it takes to be an excellent pet mom.

Isshiki's reply was a *hmuurg.* "What, really? Does Hayama think the same way?"

"Uh, I don't know what Hayama thinks."

"Buuuut before, you said that being younger put me at an advantage, didn't you?"

"Oh. Well, yeah..." Now that she mentioned it, the thought hit me. *Oh yeah, she is younger than me, huh? More or less...* But Isshiki doesn't show any sense of respect or reverence or honor or admiration or whatever, so it kind of kills that "younger girl" feeling...

And, like—she really takes me pretty lightly. My initials may be H2, but I hope I'm a little more of a heavyweight than hydrogen. Neither am I a baseball manga (which is a little light on the baseballness for a baseball manga), okay? In fact, I don't even consider that a baseball manga; that's a teen romantic comedy. It's such a masterpiece, I reread the whole series every year during summer vacation.

"But hey," I said, "I mean, you were born in April, and there's actually less than a year between us. I don't really get the impression that you're younger."

These days, I have the sense that you only just start to feel the difference when you're two or three years apart. Someone like Komachi or Haruno counts as having an age gap. If you're at the level of Miss Hiratsuka...yeah.

The age gap between me and Isshiki is actually eight months. And Yukinoshita and Isshiki are only three months apart.

Or so was my thought, but Isshiki must not have seen it this way, as she blinked.

"..."

"What...?" I asked her.

She started petting at her bangs as if trying to cover her reaction. "Oh, nothing... That's just a little surprising."

Meanwhile, Yuigahama, sitting opposite her, pushed her chair away from me with a super-loud scraping sound. "How do you know her birthday?! Yikes! Hikki, that's creepy... Ohhh, that's really creepy, actually..."

"...You're quite informed, aren't you?" And Yukinoshita remained unmoved, smiling like the sun. Like how the sun lances into your eyes, specifically.

"Uh, Isshiki brought it up herself before, and she was manipulatively and pointlessly bringing attention to it..."

"Pointless?! I-it's not pointless! And it's not manipulative, either—in fact, you're being way more manipulative here!" Isshiki shot to her feet, jabbing her index finger at me.

Hey, I'm not being manipulative, and Isshiki's the one you'd normally call manipulative... "I have a really great memory, okay...? And look, if you've done what you came for, then go back to the student council room or the soccer club or whatever," I said. Isshiki stuck out her lower lip grumpily but still got up to leave the clubroom, albeit reluctantly. *This girl and her bag of tricks... Yeah, yeah, very manipulative, uh-huh.*

Yukinoshita, Yuigahama, and I were all watching her go with chagrined smiles, when there was a knock at the door of the Service Club.

And so begins the **all-girls battle** (with boys, too).

After the light knock, we spent a moment staring at the door.

Isshiki, who'd been on her way out of the clubroom, looked at us and then back at the door again before quietly returning to her original seat. Well, it'd be awkward to walk out right then and bump into the visitor.

Eventually, animated voices sounded from the other side of the thin wall.

"It's not like I need to ask these guys for help…"

"Come on, why not? And it's not like I'm any good at this, either."

The first voice beyond the door was familiar and sharp, while the second was gentle but carried some force beneath it.

Then there was another knock, slightly more rhythmic this time.

"Come in," Yukinoshita called out.

The door opened with a mild rattle, and Ebina's face popped in through the crack. "Hello, hellooo! Do you have some time?"

"Hina? Oh, come on in!" Yuigahama beckoned her, and Ebina nodded back.

Mm-hmm, yeah, get her in here fast, keeps the wind from blowing in. My seat is close to the door, after all…

"Pardon meee." With that polite remark, Ebina came in, with Miura following her silently, her face turned away.

"Did you need something?" Yukinoshita asked them.

Miura looked over at Isshiki. "Why's she here?" she mumbled reluctantly.

"Um, I'd like to ask the same thing…or, like, something." Isshiki replied with a giggle, and Miura glared back while irritably twirling her hair.

Hmm, I dunno about this…

But Yuigahama seemed to pick up on the tension and jumped in to rescue the situation. "Oh, ummm, is it hard to talk with so many people?"

"No, it's not that…," Miura said, but she was still acting pretty brusque. In the current situation, we'd have a hard time getting her to talk to us.

"We can make Isshiki leave," I said.

"Huh?! Why?!" Isshiki wailed.

Uh, I mean, it's not like you're a member of the club… Why are you even taking it for granted that you should be here?

Ebina interceded, patting Miura's shoulder. "Hey now, Yumiko. Look, it all depends on how you word it. It's okay if you don't get into specifics. Right?"

"Yes… I'm sure some things are difficult to say… So that's fine." Yukinoshita's eyes flicked toward me in a wordless question, and I nodded back.

"Well, we can just hear what she has to say, right?" I said. "And if we still don't get what she's saying, then we can just ask about it separately."

"Yeah, that's right," Yuigahama agreed. "…And hey, you know, Iroha-chan's opinion might be helpful, too."

Isshiki was pouting again, apparently unhappy to be sidelined here, but she nodded reluctantly anyway. Yuigahama smiled, apparently relieved by her response. She was taking care to ensure both sides were happy, and I felt bad about that.

"Well, then. Let's start over and hear what you have to say," Yukinoshita said, bringing us back.

Miura gave Isshiki a long, hard look but then turned away, examining her hair for split ends as she spoke. "...So, like...I wanna try making chocolate myself or whatever... Um, since next year is entrance exams and stuff... You know, like a last hurrah in high school or whatever." Miura's voice was brimming with shyness and embarrassment, her cheeks growing redder and redder as her voice got increasingly quiet.

But there was a forlornness behind it, too—or maybe I was just seeing what I wanted to.

This time next year, we wouldn't have to come to school.

It would be right in the middle of entrance exam season—probably smack on exam day for a private university. So this was functionally the last Valentine's Day of high school. Most likely, the Valentine's Days in our futures would mean something completely different.

Like, once you get into university or start a career, the holiday loses a lot of its impact. I bet those wild ups and downs over whether you got chocolate vanish once you're an adult. It's like how when you're little, snowfall is fun and special, and that little snow icon on the weather forecast is exciting. But now, what comes to mind is the hassle: *Ugh, getting to school's gonna be a headache* or *It's so cold* or *I'll get wet.*

"...So, like, I guess I was just thinking I could give it a shot." Miura twirled her hair around her finger as if trying to distract us from the pink tinge on her cheeks. As her hair swished downward, I could agree with just a bit of what she said.

Depending on how you looked at it, this was going to be the final Valentine's Day of our lives.

But apparently, most of us couldn't fully sympathize. Being still in her first year, it seemed Isshiki wasn't really feeling it. She was just giving the standard "Huh, okay," while Yukinoshita had her hand on her chin with a thoughtful *hmm*.

As for Yuigahama, her cheeks were puffed out in a pout. She gave Miura a bit of a reproachful look. "...But, Yumiko, you said homemade is too much."

"…I—I mean." That silenced Miura, and with an *urk*, she sneakily found something else to look at. But Yuigahama wasn't letting her get away, and her head turned to follow Miura's.

While Yuigahama was quietly groaning, Ebina cut in to mediate. "Come on, guys! There's no problem, right? I think making it yourself is nice."

"Huh? You're doing it, too, Hina?" Blinking, Yuigahama looked at Ebina.

"Uh-huh. Well, I was thinking I might as well do it with Yumiko. If she's learning, so can I."

"Huh, that's kinda surprising…"

"Is it? Look, it's good to know this stuff if you wanna offer snacks to artists at Comiket."

Listening to their conversation, something felt off to me. "Hmm…"

…Snacks for artists, snacks, huh. Hmm? Curious, I glanced at Ebina, and she returned the look.

Her gaze seemed to be asking me if I had a problem. I responded with just a tiny shake of my head.

When you're offering a gift or a token to someone who isn't a friend or acquaintance, you generally shy away from homemade items. And Ebina would doubtless be aware of that. But if she was saying she wanted to learn how to make obligatory chocolate anyway, then this had to be evidence there was someone she was at least slightly interested in.

…You did it, Tobe. You're making a tiny bit of progress. Except I don't know if she's actually thinking of Tobe; hell, I don't even know who Tobe is. Who is Tobe?

A flicker of warmth had stirred in my heart when her eyebrows twitched up. Then, with a meaningful chuckle, her slash goggles—er, glasses flashed. "Homemade really is great! Hikitani, you and Hayama should share some guy chocolate, too!"

"I'm not doing that…"

Ahhh, Ebina really is Ebina, huh…in every sense. What the heck is this whole culture around friendship chocolate anyway? What is "guy chocolate" even supposed to be? Might be a good name for a cartoon character.

"But he's not gonna accept it, remember?" I pointed out.

"You're a guy! So you're in the clear!"

The initial assumption here is already out of the question.

There's no point in listening to Ebina… And Miura, who was normally responsible for keeping her in check, was just twirling her hair and pressing her lips together…

As I continued to ignore even more of Ebina's preaching about guy chocolate or gay chocolate or whatever, off to the side, Isshiki was *hnnn-n*ing as she folded her arms.

"Ah, that's right. He's already gone on record saying he won't take any, so that's gonna make it harder."

Mm-hmm, but, uh, that's not the issue here. Hayama and I are both boys, you know… Actually, since chocolate from a guy wouldn't have girls attempting to settle the score with me, I feel like he'd just accept it like normal with a charming smile… Whoa, seems like there'd be another kind of scoring going on! But on that score, *scoring* is out of the question. Final score: 0/10. On that idea anyway.

"I wonder what I should do…," Isshiki muttered.

"Agh… Yeah, seriously," Miura agreed, and they both sighed in unison, then both looked up at the same time. Their gazes clashed, and I could almost hear the crackle of sparks flying.

Aw man, this is scary…

✕   ✕   ✕

At the vending machine in front of the school store on the first floor, I clicked the MAX Coffee button.

I pulled it out and stood, then heaved a sigh.

That quiet battle crackling away between Isshiki and Miura was wearing me thin. So thin, in fact, that I was starting to wonder if that American urban legend of Slender Man was referring to me.

On the way to the washroom, I'd stopped by the vending machine, and after injecting some caffeine into my tired body, I was about to head back to the clubroom, sipping away at the Max can as I trudged up the stairs, when I caught sight of a figure lurking in front of the door.

With each fidget and glance she made, her bluish-black ponytail did a hop-hop here and a hop-hop there, here a hop, there a hop, everywhere a hop-hop.

She was acting so suspiciously, I asked almost on instinct, "...Huh? What's up?"

Her ponytail jumped. Slowly and timidly, her face turned to me.

She was eyeing me with blatant apprehension, like a wildcat you've stumbled upon in the middle of the woods, and her manner gave me this knee-jerk urge to click my tongue and beckon to her with a Max can. But you're not supposed to feed wild animals.

And you should give it a name before you feed it! Um...yeah, guess we're good with Kawa-something, right? Heeeere, Kawa-something! I said in my mind as I asked what she was up to. "You need something?"

Kawa-something let out a relieved-sounding sigh, then beckoned me down past the clubroom, to the corner of the hallway. *Oh yeah! It's Saki Kawasaki, huh? I knew that.*

While making little glances over at the clubroom, Kawasaki asked, "C-can we talk?"

"Uh, you could come in. It's cold here." She clearly had some kind of business with the Service Club, so frankly, I wanted to hurry into the heated clubroom.

But she paused pensively for a moment, then waved her hands. "Huh... No, here's good! We can stay out here! Um, there was just something I kind of wanted to ask Yukinoshita..."

Uh, then ask her directly...? "Yukinoshita's inside. Just come in. It's chilly here—you'll get sick."

There must have been a window open in one of the rooms for ventilation; the special-use building was filled with icy air. It was crawling up from the floor, and the sound of rattling window glass that came with every gust of wind felt like it was carrying the cold all the way to my ears.

"I'm whatever… It's fine, though…" Kawasaki jerked her face away.

Uh, but I'm not fine… It'd be a disaster if I caught a cold at this time of year and gave it to Komachi, and she'd have a tough time recovering.

As for how we people of Chiba get over colds, the best thing is to start with a bowl of ramen with the extra-thick broth at Naritake with extra condiments and a big blob of chopped garlic, drink a *waaarm* MAX Coffee, and go to bed. Then, you'll have to go to the doctor the next day. And so I have come to believe that preventing a cold is another reason you should just stay home all the time.

Besides, Kawasaki also has someone in her family studying for exams. If Kawasaki's little brother Taishi were to catch that cold and pass it on to Komachi, I would have to dirty my hands with blood and sin…

"Just come in already." My hostility toward vermin like Taishi made the words come out more harshly than I intended.

Kawasaki wilted just slightly, head hanging. "I-if you're gonna insist…"

I'm glad I have your understanding. I want to keep Komachi safe from the risk of more colds as much as possible after all.

"Well, we can't have you getting sick," I said as I opened the door to the clubroom and prompted Kawasaki to go inside.

She looked back at me with a dazed expression. "…O-okay," she replied with a weakness that belied her scary appearance, then walked in with soft footsteps.

She comes off like a delinquent at first glance, but she's just a meek, good girl, huh? I thought as I followed her.

"Welcome back, Hikki… Wait, Saki?" Yuigahama turned to me and then tilted her head curiously. Then her whole upper body tilted along with it.

All eyes in the room gathered on Kawasaki, who replied uncomfortably, "Oh, yeah…"

Yukinoshita gave her a puzzled look, while Isshiki shrank away in fright. *No, no, no, Kawa-something here looks scary, but she's a total sweetheart, all right?*

Ebina, on the other hand, addressed her with energy and a smile. "Oh, it's Saki-Saki. Hello, hello!"

"Don't call me Saki-Saki," Kawasaki shot back.

In an attempt to mollify her, Yuigahama brought her a chair. "We don't see you here often, Saki… Wait, it's your first time, huh?"

They must have become friends (or something close to it) since the school field trip, if Yuigahama was calling her Saki. I could hardly remember Saki Kawa-something's name myself, so I was touched that someone had. My eyes teared up a little. I must be more prone to that these days; every Sunday when they're in trouble on *PreCure*, just seeing the girls stand up again makes me cry. Yep, that's me.

Yes, yes, it's nice that the girls are getting along. It's a lovely thing.

As this heartwarming sight left my chest all toasty in the cold, Yukinoshita was setting out tea in a paper cup. "So did you need something from us?" she asked.

"Th-thanks…um…," Kawasaki began, but she didn't quite seem like she'd be out with it.

Oh yeah, didn't she say she had something to talk to Yukinoshita about? While Kawasaki was moaning and struggling to begin, I heard the *tap, tap, tap* of nails clicking on a desk.

Looking over, I saw a very displeased Miura there. Kawasaki didn't seem to like her attitude, as she gave Miura an icy glare.

Miura returned in kind. "Like, I'm still not done talking, though?"

"What? You're just drinking tea."

I retract my previous statement. Kawasaki really is scary…

Neither Kawasaki nor Miura would yield, glaring daggers at one another. *Ohhh, you two still don't get along, huh…?*

Isshiki was frozen as she watched their stare-down.

Then Ebina cut into the stalemate. "C'mon now, Yumiko, what's the problem? You've got something you wanted to talk about, too, right, Saki-Saki? I can listen if you want."

"Though we'll be the ones helping her...," Yukinoshita muttered.

"Anyway, just talk to us," Ebina prompted, apparently not at all listening to Yukinoshita's grumbling.

Kawasaki's eyes moved between me, Yuigahama, and Yukinoshita. She let out a soft sigh before finally saying, "Um, it's about chocolate..."

Miura snorted. "Hmph. What, you're giving chocolate to someone, too? That's *so* funny."

"What?"

"What?"

The two of them had yet another stare-down.

"...*Too?*" said Kawasaki. "Can you quit projecting on me? I don't care about that stuff like *you*, and I'm not interested."

"What?"

"What?"

...Stop it! Let's all get along!

Seeing Kawasaki and Miura, Yukinoshita sighed and shook her head with dramatic chagrin.

You've got a big personality, too, y'know..., I thought. Hmm, but, well, lately that jagged-hearted Yukinon-ness, sharp edges hurting everything that touched her, had also settled down.

Watching the stubborn stare-off between Miura and Kawasaki, Isshiki muttered in my direction, "You know a lot of weirdos, huh...?"

"What?"

"What?"

As the anger of both girls turned on her, Isshiki made a swift retreat behind my back. *Come on, stop walking into minefields like that... This is like watching a video compilation of cats falling off things... I mean, even I'm a little scared of these two, you know!*

Anyway, let's move on. That's the only way to quickly escape from this.

"So what was this about chocolate?" I asked.

"My sister heard about Valentine's at preschool, and she said she wants to try making some...," said Kawasaki. "Isn't there, like, a kind that even small children can make?"

"Something a kid can make…" Yukinoshita nodded with a *hmm*.

Ebina tilted her head. "Oh? But, Saki-Saki, I thought you were good at domestic things."

Oh yeah, I did seem to recall that Kawasaki had a lot of younger siblings and busy parents, so she often took over household responsibilities. I remembered the unexpectedly domestic picture of her carrying shopping bags with green onions poking out of them. *Meaning she'd be a good cook, too, right?* I thought, looking at her.

She turned away awkwardly. "…Um, the stuff I make is kind of plain. I doubt a little kid would have much fun with it."

"By the way, may I ask what sort of things you're good at cooking, Kawasaki?" Yukinoshita asked.

After a stretch of silence, Kawasaki said quietly and with much hesitation, "S-sweet…"

Sweet. For whatever reason, my mind first jumped to sugar decorations, but that wasn't exactly too plain for kids to enjoy. When I was little, Komachi and I would fight over the sugar Santa on the Christmas cake… Though it didn't take long for me to realize those things don't actually taste great, and both of us stopped eating it, and then Dad was always in charge of its disposal.

But Kawasaki was not talking about sugar decorations. All attention was on her as we waited to hear the rest.

With everyone's eyes on her, Kawasaki looked down like she was embarrassed and said in an extremely quiet voice, "Sweet potatoes… boiled sweet potatoes."

…She's right; that is bland.

Kawasaki's specialty being basically boiled potatoes was such a bland choice, its blandness far surpassed expectations and momentarily silenced the whole clubroom. The brutal honesty of everyone's reaction made Kawasaki a little teary-eyed. She was pretty embarrassed.

Noticing this, Yuigahama jerked her head up and put extra cheer in her voice. "It's okay! Look, I can't cook at all, so I'm still impressed. Right, Yukinon?" She turned the question to Yukinoshita.

Yukinoshita nodded, expression serious. "That's right. Potato is a good name for a cat, so there is something cute to it."

"That's a weird way to encourage her!" Yuigahama looked at her with an expression of shock.

Indeed. That is not encouragement at all.

And what do cats have to do with baking? Well, I suppose they do like to make biscuits and turn into a loaf. But if you try to roll them out, they'll give you a grumpy look—which is supercute. Maybe she does have a point. Still, don't try to roll them out—a long-haired cat will wind up absorbing dust and stuff like a mop, so you need to watch out for that!

Well, never mind about cats. Right now, this is about Kawasaki. Yukinoshita's bizarre defense must have been particularly embarrassing for Kawasaki, as she was trembling like a newly adopted kitten. *I'm incredibly sorry; she just sucks at comforting people...*

What I offered probably wasn't enough to be a consolation, but I did clear my throat to say, "Well, as long as you can cook it right."

"Agh, well, that's true. Still, it *is* bland...," Isshiki followed up, though she sounded a bit confused. But there was no edge of derision or mockery there.

"Yeah, it's cool! It's your thing, Saki-Saki!" Ebina stuck up her thumbs with an Ebi-Ebi smile.

The compliments must have made Kawasaki uncomfortable in another way, as now she was fidgeting and twisting around. And then she froze. Following her gaze, I saw her attention was on Miura. Apparently, she was worried what her recent opponent would say.

But Miura just gave Kawasaki a long look, then turned away in disinterest. She didn't even appear to be talking to her as she said, "Didn't know you could cook."

"Huh? Oh, um, well..."

"Hmm..." Though she was twirling her hair around her fingertip, there was some respect in her tone. Well, Miura can't cook herself, far as I can tell... Someone as feminine as her might admire those skills.

"If you have basic cooking ability, Kawasaki, then if we just gave you a menu to work with, you could take care of the rest, right?" After pondering the matter, Yukinoshita put a hand to her chin and tilted her head.

"M-me too! I want to learn, too! If a little kid can do it, I can, too!" Yuigahama flung her hand up.

But Yukinoshita lowered her gaze sadly. "...I don't know about that."

"C'mon, Yukinon, can't you spare my feelings a little?!"

"I mean, she's not saying it's impossible. I think she *was* sparing your feelings," I said.

"Just how useless do you think I am?!"

You're not very self-aware...

With Yuigahama, I feel like the problem isn't so much her choice of menu or cooking style as it is her useless attempts to add extra flavor or tweaks. Way back when she and Yukinoshita cooked together, I seem to recall it turned out fairly edible in the end after all. Not to say there's no issues with Yukinoshita's teaching methods...

It seemed Miura and Ebina had gotten tired of discussing Kawasaki's issue. "Hey, weren't we talking about me?" Miura interjected with a pout.

"Yeah, yeah. Don't forget about us!" Ebina pouted along with her.

Isshiki also popped up a dainty hand. "Oh, then I'd like to join in, too, just for reference."

Yukinoshita breathed a little sigh. "I don't mind...," she said, then glanced over at me.

"...Well, we can just say we'll think about it, right?" I said. "They'll be doing the actual work themselves."

"Of course... All right. I'm going to get together what we need, so if you could allow me a little time...," Yukinoshita said with a look at Miura, Ebina, and Kawasaki in turn, and the three girls all nodded back at her in unison.

×   ×   ×

Miura and the others had left a little while ago. In the now finally peaceful clubroom, Yukinoshita quietly sighed. "Today has been rather exhausting…"

As we brought our new cups of black tea to our lips, we sighed, too. We'd gotten an unusual number of visitors. Three in one day—no, four, if you included Isshiki—may have been a new record.

Compared with how it had been before, we were doing brisk business.

This room had hardly anything—it was basically just a closet, and I'd thought it was too big—but there was actually some life in it now. Though the once-scattered chairs were all pointed in different directions, they'd come to draw a wobbly sort of ring around the long table in the middle where the tea set was.

The clubroom had changed a lot since then.

The heater on low, the tea set and the blanket, and the stack of paperback books. The number of chairs and their positions. The amount of sunlight slanting in, and the coats hanging on the wall.

The cold, late-spring colors of this room had turned to warmer hues without my realizing it.

I couldn't say if this was because of the changing of seasons or something else. The air here seemed to lull you to sleep, and my eyes wandered out the window.

The weather report had said there was a big cold front or something coming in a few days, and the wind was blowing hard again that day.

Even with the girls' chatter over it, I could clearly hear the rattling and creaking of the window glass. And soon another sound joined it—the loud scrape of the door sliding open, followed by a loud yell.

"Isshiki!"

"Hyerk!"

Isshiki flinched, and then she looked over toward the door with intense trepidation. There, Miss Hiratsuka was looming intimidatingly, scowling and angry.

"Miss Hiratsuka, please knock…," Yukinoshita said with a sigh, pressing her temple.

"Oh, my bad. I was in a bit of a rush," Miss Hiratsuka answered with a quirk of a smile as she strode briskly into the clubroom. "…Isshiki." Going to stand beside the student council president, she folded her arms in a forbidding manner. "What happened to your work?"

"Uhhhh…" Isshiki was at a loss for words, her eyes swimming around. And then her wandering gaze met with mine.

"Hey, didn't you say you didn't have anything to do?" I asked.

Isshiki primly turned away and sulked. "…I don't."

Miss Hiratsuka breathed an exaggerated sigh. "It's true that student council business is going smoothly, but you have other work to do. I told you to come up with a farewell address for the graduation ceremony and bring it to me, didn't I?"

The graduation ceremony… Is it already that time? I thought. But the ceremony was supposed to be at the start of the second week of March. Wasn't there still time?

Apparently, Isshiki was of the same mind, as she made a cute *ah-ha-ha ☆ oh nooo!* sort of laugh. "B-but we have still a month…"

"You fool! That carelessness will be your downfall!" Miss Hiratsuka warned her severely, but Isshiki just shrugged.

Indeed. Don't assume you have a month—no, no.

This is true with work, summer vacation, or anything else. The moment you think you have time, that's right when you lose any buffer you had.

As the saying goes, time and tide wait for no man. You'll be thinking, *We can still save it, we can still save it, we can save it save it please don't make us corporate slave it!* when you wind up in a situation where you definitely cannot save it—it's a rare occurrence that often happens.

Why must deadlines come so quickly?

"I mean, when we're in February, you can't say we have one month. There's fewer days in the month, and with entrance exams and whatnot on top of that, the staff won't have time, either. February schedules are extra tight," Miss Hiratsuka said flatly.

"Yes! I'll do it! I'll do my best! I'll manage! That's why I've come here to consult them about it! I've come here to ask about last year!" Isshiki answered with wonderful enthusiasm.

But, uh, don't I recall that you came here to ask about chocolate…?

Not like it's important, but there are no words less trustworthy than *I'll do my best* or *I'll manage*.

You must not believe a corporate slave when they say either of those things. Source: my dad. He says that stuff a lot when he's taking work calls at home, but then after he hangs up, he's like, "That's impossible, jackass!"

Of course, Miss Hiratsuka also saw right through Isshiki's foolish response, combing back her long hair uneasily as her expression turned grim. "Listen, you can't be like that. You have to be fully independent next year. You can't be getting help from your elders forever, all right?"

Yukinoshita, cup still in hand, nodded in agreement. "Of course."

"Hmm, I think it'll be tough… But she is the president…" Yuigahama gave Isshiki a troubled smile.

In search of allies, Isshiki inched her chair over to me. With moist and trusting eyes, she came to tug at my sleeve.

I really am weak to people who make requests of me like that.

Komachi often tries to use tears to get her way when she's in trouble, but an elite big brother of my level will side with a little sister basically unconditionally. It's just what's expected of a big brother who wouldn't mind destroying a world or two for his little sister's sake.

I have no choice. I'll talk my way out of this somehow and fix this for her…, I thought, opening my mouth.

But Yukinoshita cut me off. "Hikigaya, don't indulge her."

"I mean, but she is saying she basically came here asking for help…," I said.

Isshiki leaned forward. "Yeah! You listened to the others who came here for help, *riiight?*"

"But I feel like Iroha-chan's thing is a little different from Yumiko's and Saki's…" Yuigahama seemed to worry over it with a little *hmm*.

Miss Hiratsuka blinked. "Oh, there were others here asking for advice?"

"Yep!" Isshiki piped up. "There were! A bunch of them, actually, so I was also helping with that, kinda…"

"That's not your job." Miss Hiratsuka instantly shot her down, and Isshiki gritted her teeth.

"Urk."

Isshiki, you fool. If you're going to avoid a Miss Hiratsuka interrogation, there's no use in trying to say the right thing flat-out. No matter how you think about it, what Miss Hiratsuka says is going to be even more flat-out right. I'd even say there's nothing flat-out right about Isshiki. Just flat—well, that's not technically true. But maybe a little. Really, the "just flat" is a certain Miss Someone-else-shita.

At the end of the day, a sound argument is a weapon to be used against other people, not something to listen to. Therefore, the correct choice is to ignore it or deflect.

Let me show you how it's done…

"Well, um," I began, "they came for advice on girl stuff, so of course, it's best to have more girls. Not like I'd know. It's just, with Valentine's Day coming up and all."

Valentine's Day. When I used those magic words, Miss Hiratsuka froze on the spot. Then her eyes turned to the window, suddenly distant. "I see—Valentine's Day, eh…? Ah, memories…"

With a mildly self-deprecating sigh, the teacher finally turned her gaze back to us. She gave us a long look, then quietly repeated once more, "Valentine's Day, eh?" The earlier humor in her tone was all gone, replaced by a touch of sorrow.

Clearing her throat and checking her voice, Miss Hiratsuka started over. "If you've had a rush of consults, then the matter of the farewell address can wait a bit. Couldn't hurt to have Isshiki help you from time to time."

"Uh, well, we don't really need her, though...," I said.

"Hey, rude!" Isshiki spun around to shoot me an indignant look, but I stared back at her icily. *I mean, you just increase our workload...*

Then Yuigahama came in to mediate. "H-hey, now... It's okay. If she can help us, then that'll be good for us, too..."

"Will it, though?"

"Come on, what do you take me for...?" Isshiki grumbled at me, but I ignored her and looked at Yukinoshita.

"If Yuigahama is all right with it, then I don't mind...," Yukinoshita said.

Miss Hiratsuka clapped her hands sharply. "Then it's settled. Isshiki can work on the farewell address on her own. Besides, everyone is counting on you guys now. I'd say that's a ringing endorsement of everything this club has done this year."

"You sure we're not just being treated like the errand club...?" I asked.

It was true there were a lot more people coming to us for help than before. That also meant our workload had increased considerably. The problem was that we were getting nothing out of it. This was way worse than unpaid overtime. What is this? Is this like overtime under the white-collar exemption? I've been gaining so many service skills, I could hold my own working at some exploitative sweatshop of an office job.

Miss Hiratsuka's response to my remark was a glare, then a wink. "But you're still helping people. Having someone there to give you a little push from behind is very important. It's not a bad thing for Isshiki to take that on as well."

"Yeah, I'll learn from their example!" Isshiki's response was positively full of energy, but I could hear her thoughts behind the blatantly self-satisfied smile: *Yaaay, I got a deadline extension.*

"...Although you're rubbing off on her in the worst ways. Anyway, make sure to get this done." And with that, Miss Hiratsuka smiled wryly, gave Isshiki a gentle pat on the head, then fluttered her hand in a wave as she left the clubroom.

We all watched her go, then breathed little sighs.

"Now we have a problem…," Yukinoshita muttered, arms folded.

Then Isshiki, whose arms were also crossed, sighed gravely. "Definitely. Miura's starting to get serious."

"I meant the number of requests…"

"Ha-ha," Yuigahama said, watching their exchange with a forced smile. "But you know, I can kind of understand Hayato's feelings…"

Hayama's feelings? Where'd that come from…? With a look, I asked what she meant.

Yuigahama seemed to be thinking aloud as she answered. "Oh, you know…it's like, um… Maybe he's trying to take a lot of things into account, like not accepting chocolates openly and stuff…" That was a very Yuigahama way of showing consideration.

Listening, Isshiki also nodded. "Oh, that's kinda like you, Yui. Like, you're so nice."

"Oh…you think…? Ah-ha-ha… Like me, huh…?" Yuigahama laughed with some embarrassment, and then her expression wilted slightly.

I don't think receiving a compliment had embarrassed her. Maybe it was just because of the suffocating feeling that comes from being kind and considerate—just like Hayato Hayama. When you think about it, Yuigahama is friends with Hayama, Miura, and Isshiki. She's struggled before, like when she was stuck between them that time at Destiny Land, and she was an immediate witness to it again now.

It'd be a lot easier if I could just be like, *Man, that sucks, I'm sorry…* But I couldn't be so callous and distant from this.

The desire to keep a close eye on all the social relationships around you is hard to understand. But I can sympathize with it—with the feelings that lead you to that conclusion, at any rate.

Yukinoshita is probably the same. I could see the concern on her face as Yuigahama turned glum.

For example, if you're able to come up with a solution like Haya-ma's, it might all come undone somewhere along the line.

Of his own will, he chooses to be the Hayato Hayama everyone desires, to play his part perfectly.

He uncompromisingly makes the highest grade of compromise; he pours his body and soul into putting them both on life support.

There can surely be no insincerity as sincere as that.

There isn't much the unkind can do for the sake of such "kind" people—at most, you can just quietly grumble the same old complaints to yourself.

"…Well, then you just have to have an excuse, right? One that would satisfy Hayama," I said.

"Hmmm?" Isshiki tilted her head so hard her whole upper body went with it. She had no idea what I was getting at.

That gesture is very cute, but it's an irritating response, Isshiki…

"Like a situation where the most natural thing would be for him to take it; then he'll accept it, maybe," I rephrased myself.

Isshiki was mushing her lips together with this skeptical look like maybe she got it, and maybe she didn't.

Then Yukinoshita put her cup down with a *clink* and turned her quiet eyes to me. "In other words, you mean it will work as long as you have an *excuse?*" Yukinoshita enunciated the word in English. "Yes, if you were to give him chocolates in a somewhat *closed* environment, then Hayama could avoid dealing with any disputes."

"Yeah, *closed*, that," I said. I didn't care if it was *Crows* or *Worst* or *QP* or what, but basically, we just had to create a situation where Hayama wouldn't have to be concerned about people watching, where it wouldn't damage his public image.

But still, Isshiki and Yuigahama both had question marks over their heads, like this didn't make sense to them. Yuigahama in particu-lar seemed confused by the English. "*Closet…?*"

What the heck is a closet environment? Doraemon's living space?

"Like for example…," I said. "If you say it's not for Valentine's but you ask him to try taste-testing it, then Hayama'll have some. Probably. Not like I know."

"…Ohhh, so then we just have to make them together?" Yuigahama murmured with a deep sigh. Something resembling relief flickered across her face.

Mm-hmm. I'm relieved, too, that you got my drift.

"Well, yeah. If Isshiki, Miura, and Hayama are all cooking together and they tell him to try some, then it'd be hard for him to say no." Though in this case, with Miura and Isshiki feeding him chocolate, he might be biting off more than he can chew…

When I looked over at the three girls for a response to my suggestion, the most suspicious of the crew voiced an admiring *ohhh*.

"I see… I think I get it! Sooo I just have to drag him somewhere away from anyone who could get in my way."

"Yes, but maybe watch how you word it," I chided Isshiki.

Yukinoshita giggled. "But that's the most important point. You really are a genius when it comes to avoiding attention and pulling dastardly tricks."

"Yeah, you watch how you word things, too, okay?" *Sometimes it's worth considering positive reinforcement,* I was thinking, when Yuigahama suddenly slapped her knee and surged to her feet.

"So then let's all do it together! Like with us, too."

"…Indeed," Yukinoshita agreed. "If I can teach everyone on the spot, then I won't have to come up with a menu suggestion for each individual, too."

"Ohhh, that's a great idea. Gathering up everyone who came here with requests to do sort of an event thing and, like, kinda teach each other. So then, we can get you to teach us, right, Yukinoshita?" Isshiki inched her whole chair up to Yukinoshita's side.

Yukinoshita was pondering and *hmm*ing when Isshiki took her hand and squeezed it, tilted her head, and gave her a wheedling, coquettish smile.

"Y-yes… I wouldn't mind that, I suppose…"

This was Yukinoshita, who we're all familiar with for being incredibly weak to physical contact and intimacy. And if you're sincerely asking for her help, too, she'll instantly crumble. Even if Isshiki's body language wasn't cultivated as naturally as Yuigahama's, it was still highly effective on Yukinoshita.

Yukinoshita cleared her throat lightly, then glanced over questioningly at me. "I think if I'm just helping, that would be fine, but…what do you think?"

"Uh, don't ask me… I mean, you'll be the one teaching them, so if that's easier for you, then sure." And besides, Yuigahama was excited about it, too, so there was no reason to refuse at this point.

"I see. Well then, we have to figure out what this will be so that we can begin making arrangements…" Yukinoshita put her hand to her chin and started to think.

Then Isshiki, sitting beside her, suddenly dialed someone on her phone. "Oh, Vice President. I'm ordering you to submit a proposal. Something like *Cooking class event!* …What? Uh, yeah anyhoo, just get this green-lit, book the venue, and type up the notice, 'kay?"

The voice I could hear faintly coming from the receiver did not sound happy about this, but Isshiki started giving orders in a low voice with added tongue clicking. But anyway, "get it green-lit and book the venue…"? She isn't gonna start saying things like *We've got to double-time it, or they'll be booked out!* soon, is she?

"Hey, hey, Yukinon, what about meee?" Yuigahama's chair scraped as she came up to Yukinoshita's side, too, examining her face.

Yukinoshita paused a moment to consider. "As for you…" Then she laid a heavy hand on Yuigahama's shoulder and said gently, as if speaking to a small child, "Let's have you do it with me."

"You don't trust me at all?! Urk… Oh, then…what about Hikki?" She spun around to ask me.

But I doubted there was much I could do to help here. "I can't cook or anything," I answered.

Yukinoshita laughed a little. "I don't mind. You can just taste-test and offer your opinion."

I'd heard those words at some point before. But the tone and sound of her voice were different from that time. Yuigahama, sitting beside her, seemed to remember something, and she smothered a giggle.

"...Leave that to me; it's my specialty," I said, while thinking back on what I'd answered that time. The three of us just sort of exchanged looks, then broke into chuckles.

Isshiki, still on the phone, must have been curious about our quiet snickers, as her gaze shifted over to us. *Why're you laughing?* she asked with her eyes, which I answered with a *It's nothing* shake of my head.

There's no point in explaining something like this. Some things you understand because you've spent the time together, shared enough memories, and found the significance of it.

My gesture made Isshiki a little skeptical, but eventually, it seemed her discussion with the vice president was settled, and she moved to end it. "Yep, yeeeep, yeeep, thanks very much."

It sounded like the vice president was complaining on the other end, but Isshiki ignored him and hung up. The call done, she rose to her feet.

"Right, the student council will handle the details, so you handle the cooking class." She muttered quietly, "Since I did barge in on you," and gave us a snappy salute, then made to leave. She was probably headed off to start arranging for said cooking class.

There was nothing in her manner that seemed unreliable, like before.

She was a bit forceful in her methods, but I figured this was another kind of growth for Isshiki. Well, maybe *growth* was a little strong, but she'd learned how to manage. She was treating the vice president the same way she did Tobe, after all...

"Then we'll be counting on you, Isshiki," said Yukinoshita.

"Yeah! Let's do our best, Iroha-chan!" Yuigahama added.

When Isshiki bobbed her head in a bow at the door, Yukinoshita gave a genuine, kind smile, while Yuigahama cheerily raised a hand. I nodded back at Isshiki and saw her off.

As I watched Isshiki quietly slide the door to the clubroom shut, the thought hit me.

…Huh, she's actually doing her job this time, so there's nothing much for me to do. When she's not being a handful anymore, I almost feel left out.

Unexpectedly, what **Iroha Isshiki**'s absence brings is...

When someone tells you not to sweat the details, that's anxiety inducing in its own way.

For the few days after that wave of consults and Isshiki's proposal, there was a somewhat uneasy air in the clubroom.

Arriving after school, I read my book, drank tea, occasionally nibbled on some snacks with the tea, and glanced at the door periodically. That was how I'd been spending my time. And that day was more of the same.

This restless feeling was a lot like watching *My First Errand*. I'd always gotten such so much work dumped on me before, so I was totally on edge. *Oh dear, will Isshiki be able to do it herself?*

Mm, yes. That has to be it. It's, you know—a dad thing.

If not, I'll start to suspect that I might actually like work, and then I'll have an identity crisis…

We'd fallen into a sort of routine: Whenever we got a request or consultation or something, it always led to an avalanche of work. But this time, things were looking a bit different.

It reminds me a bit of the extended torture that comes when you've been told the deadline or submission date, but you haven't yet been told what exactly it is you're supposed to do. And then Iroha Isshiki being the one to bring this to us was adding to the anxiety. I felt like the protagonist of a magical girl anime. *Oh no! What's gonna happen to me now?!* I was sighing deeply when I heard another sigh opposite me.

When I glanced over, I saw Yukinoshita's head rise from her paperback to look at the door.

It seemed she shared similar anxieties. Or maybe she had a crush on Isshiki? I think IroYuki could be a thing!

As I was entertaining such thoughts, a giggle came from Yuigahama. "You guys have been looking at the door a lot," she said with a little smile. "If it's about Iroha-chan, I don't think you have to worry that much…"

"I'm not worried about Isshiki."

"No one has said a word about Isshiki."

Yukinoshita's and my response came at almost the same time. Yukinoshita jerked her face away, too.

My mind actually was on Isshiki, and probably Yukinoshita was thinking the same thing, but it was just too embarrassing that Yuigahama could read us so easily. I couldn't help but snap back.

But Yuigahama apparently could see through that contrarian retort, too, as she gave a teasing grin. "Ohhh, really?"

"Yes, really." With Yuigahama examining her face, this time Yukinoshita turned her whole body away. Her cheeks and the ears peeking out from her hair were pink.

Yuigahama sighed happily. If only that had been enough to satisfy her.

Instead, Yuigahama looked over at me with her eyebrows draw together thoughtfully, head tilted. "Hmm? …But, Hikki, you're nice to Iroha-chan."

As soon as Yukinoshita heard that, she fixed me with a piercing look, expression stern. "Indeed. You indulge her too much. I really have to wonder about that."

Hey? Would you stop immediately narrowing your target down to me?

"I'm really not…," I answered, but Yuigahama and Yukinoshita were both staring at me suspiciously. *Uh, why aren't they saying anything…?*

I don't even really get why I was making excuses and protesting, *No, it's not like that, really!* But I cleared my throat with a *gafum gafum hekapomf* and opened my mouth. "I'm just worried because she might drop everything on us out of nowhere. I don't want to deal with her abandoned projects when it's already too late to fix them. It'd be way more efficient for me to be involved from the start," I said. I thought that was pretty on the mark, if I do say so myself, for something I'd come up with on the spur of the moment. In fact, that impulsivity was why I was sure it was the truth.

This is a bad habit of mine.

If you can't let someone else handle something, it means you don't believe in them.

A person who does that could never understand trust. And there's much less reason for them to discover that far crueler "something" that resembles trust.

It's presumptuous, foolish even, for such a person to be worried about another.

I remembered what I'd been told back in that café, with the cold wind blowing. Can anyone really answer that question?

Pondering this made my mouth stop moving and created a little silence. When I noticed it, I quickly added, "So what I'm worried about is my own future, more than Isshiki. I don't wanna get stuck with more work."

"That makes me far more concerned about your future than anything else..." Yukinoshita pressed her forehead and breathed a deep sigh.

"Well, that's also a very Hikki-like answer, so..." Yuigahama responded with a strained smile that was part exasperation, part awkward feelings.

Well, Yukinoshita isn't exactly kind to Isshiki. Nor am I.

If anyone is, it's Yuigahama, at least in how she believes Isshiki will actually do what she says. She's acknowledged Isshiki and doesn't waste her time worrying about her or getting in her business. In that area, I'd say she's distinctly different from me and Yukinoshita.

But with Yukinoshita, well... Isshiki has discovered the Yuki-no-resistance side of her, the side that instantly caves to wheedling and touchy-feely attacks...

When I considered that, I couldn't not say it. I gave Yukinoshita a critical look. "I mean, if we're talking about indulging her, then you're pretty bad, too."

"Me? I've always thought I was rather strict with her, though..." Yukinoshita tilted her head with a puzzled look.

But Yuigahama got what I was trying to say and folded her arms with a groan. "Hmm... I guess there's a sort of kindness to it. I mean, you really like taking care of people, Yukinon."

I'd expect nothing less from Gahama. Amazingahama. She gets it.

"Yeah. After all, she often takes care of you, too, Yuigahama."

"Huh? N-no she doesn't! I'm not depending on her! Not that much anyway!" Yuigahama loudly tried to argue back, chair scraping as she leaped to her feet, but she was cut off by a smile from Yukinoshita, who was beside her.

"Oh, so you weren't aware of it yourself?" Yukinoshita smiled brightly at her.

"C-c'mon, I'm not *totally* oblivious..." Yuigahama blushed as she muttered that under her breath, then dejectedly sat back down again. At the same time, she also sat up straighter and quietly laid her hands on her lap.

Yes, self-awareness is important.

But still, the way Yukinoshita takes care of Yuigahama is slightly different from the way she takes care of Isshiki.

With Yuigahama, she just lets Yuigahama do what she wants—or more like Yukinoshita is just totally at her mercy. But with Isshiki, I get the impression Yukinoshita takes care of her in a more active way. It's a little more distant—what struck me was how Yukinoshita herself seemed aware she was in a more or less superior position.

If Yukinoshita and Yuigahama had a relationship like a cat and puppy, then perhaps I could call Isshiki and Yukinoshita like a mother cat and kitten? Though Isshiki isn't very catlike; at heart, she's actually more like a ferocious and powerful stoat.

…Well, I also get the sense that Yukinoshita gets taken care of a lot, too, so there's problems on both ends, I guess.

Ah yes, it's lovely to see pretty girls getting along. Or to be more precise, it's really scary when pretty girls are getting in fights… Things can get so intense, like with Miura and Kawasaki. I wouldn't just be freaking, I'd be leaking—and I might even wind up squeaking like a Chibull alien. Or not.

Anyway, you could say Isshiki had a pretty decent relationship with the Service Club.

As I was pondering these matters, Yuigahama appeared convinced. "Well, maybe Iroha-chan really enjoys people taking care of her. It's cute. Must be nice…" She said that last part in a murmur, flopped forward over her desk. Well, Yuigahama does have a pretty firm head on her shoulders sometimes, and I don't get the impression she'd choose to rely on someone else. Though the two seem to come from similar places at first glance, they're actually sort of polar opposites, aren't they…? Maybe Yuigahama would feel envious.

But just one Isshiki is enough.

I dunno how I feel about Yuigahama becoming like Isshiki, and more than one of her would be a real handful. *Like, she's fine the way she is, I guess, and I'd say maybe it's best for her to stay that way… Mm-hmm…* I almost said all that incoherent nonsense aloud, but I managed to clear my throat with a *gefum gefum kapatoon coconut* and swallowed the remark.

My exceedingly unnatural throat-clearing sound made Yuigahama, still flopped over her desk, roll her head toward me.

The hairs that had escaped from her bun dropped back, her bangs swishing downward to partially cover her eyes. Her trembling, glossy lips were slightly parted, and a sigh slipped out.

Captured by her gaze from below, whatever I was planning to say immediately vanished. "Uh, I mean, the whole cuteness factor is, like, whatever, and it's not like that's the only thing cute about her any-way...," I said, scratching my head in embarrassment, and I dropped my face to the page of the paperback I wasn't even reading. That non-sensical string wasn't even words. Shoulda kept my mouth shut...

As I was mentally beating myself up, I heard a little giggle. Looking over, I saw Yuigahama had pushed herself up, and she was smiling. "...Yeah, that's right."

Her answer made me strangely relieved, and what I said next came out normally. "Besides, I bet she likes this place because she's got nice older girls who will give her attention. I mean, lately she's been getting here even earlier than me."

Yukinoshita put a hand to her mouth, *hmm*ing with a thoughtful expression. "I don't know if she likes it here or not. But...I do wish she would let us know beforehand when she comes. We run out of tea more quickly, and I also have to arrange for extra snacks. Worst of all, it means less time to relax and read." She breathed a dramatic sigh. But despite her complaining, her relaxed expression was soft, even pleased.

You could compare her to a mean old lady who's wildly smitten with her grandchild. Or how you complain about a cat. *I bought her a bed, but instead of sleeping there, she uses the cardboard box it came from! Good grief!* I could kind of imagine Yukinoshita and Isshiki's interac-tions when they were alone.

Yukinoshita would act disinterested in Isshiki, and yet she'd worry about her and put out tea, taking care of her in various ways. Mean-while, Isshiki would be smirking to herself, pleased about getting away with her crimes, even as trust was taking root in the depths of her heart. What the heck, that works; I think IroYuki could be a thing.

As Yukinoshita was sighing and complaining about Isshiki, Yuiga-hama was watching her with unfocused eyes. "Maybe I'll come a lit-tle earlier, too, huh...?" she muttered, and I could hear something like envy in her tone.

Yukinoshita's eyebrows twitched upward in an accusatory manner. "...This is a real club, you know, so coming early is the expectation."

"Oh, yeah, but I get into talking with Yumiko, then I just wind up late, y'know?" Yuigahama laughed to avoid the issue as she combed at her bun, but there was no smile on the other girl's face.

"...I see," Yukinoshita replied briefly, then slowly and quietly dropped her eyes to the book in her hands.

It seemed she was sulking a little. Well, Yuigahama's behavior could be taken as choosing Miura over Yukinoshita. What a Jellynon, huh? Another peaceful day in the clubroom.

And if I was noticing this, there was no way Yuigahama wouldn't. She adjusted her posture and shuffled over a little with her chair, too. "But maybe I'll actually try to come a bit earlier, huh? I really like it when the three of us are relaxing here together... I love it, actually."

Maybe that shortened distance made it easier for her words to reach Yukinoshita. Yukinoshita let out a short sigh, then briefly examined Yuigahama's expression. Although there wasn't much to be gained doing that. After all, their expressions were about the same.

Their eyes matched: downturned slightly with a hint of shyness and pink cheeks.

"...I'll pour us some more tea," Yukinoshita said.

"Oh, really? Then I'll put out some more snacks!" Yuigahama said as she started fishing around in her bag.

Yeah, but you're the one eating most of those snacks... You sure snacks aren't your true love here...? But the sarcastic remark never left my mouth.

What came out instead was a sigh that was half chuckle.

"Hikigaya," Yukinoshita said.

I held out my Japanese-style cup. "Yeah."

Warm steam, followed by the scent of black tea. And then the sweet aroma of cookies.

"Here, Hikki."

"Oh, thanks."

Yuigahama slid the plate she'd piled with snacks over to me, and I snatched one and munched on it. And then, after I took a sip of tea and complained that was a bit too hot, a relaxed sigh slid out of me. It happened to be the moment the other two sighed, too.

We automatically looked at each other.

Well.

More often than not, these are the times when visitors show up.

That prediction was proved true with a light rapping on the door. When Yukinoshita called to the visitor to come in, they responded by slowly opening the door.

"Sorry to make you guys waaait!" Iroha Isshiki said as she made her first appearance in the clubroom in a long while.

×　×　×

As Yukinoshita was preparing another cup of tea for the newcomer, Isshiki handed us all some printouts.

"Okay, so I made a lot of decisions on this stuff, so I'll explain about it now."

"Yes. Please do," Yukinoshita answered as she offered tea in a paper cup. She added in two stick sugars while she was at it. Isshiki accepted them calmly and with thanks… Yukinoshita's thoughtfulness is impressive, but Isshiki is also pretty amazing for having her so well trained.

"Anyway, about the schedule and the location…"

As I was busy being surprised, Isshiki began her explanation. While she talked, I read from the printout I'd received.

My eyes happened to catch on the date. "We're not doing it on Valentine's Day?"

Considering where the conversation about how to give Hayato Hayama chocolate had been going, I'd totally assumed the event would be on Valentine's. But the schedule had the event a few days earlier than that.

Yukinoshita seemed to put two and two together, her eyes rising from her printout to look at me. "Valentine's Day is also the day of entrance exams, so I'd assume we wouldn't receive permission from the supervising teacher."

"Oh, that's right, and there's no school that day, too." Yuigahama was following the logic, and Isshiki nodded back at her.

"Wellll, that's part of it, but also, I'm sure some people will have plans on the day of. If we want a lot of people to participate, it'd help the most to have the event beforehand, y'know?"

"I see…" That was indeed a convincing rationale.

Since Valentine's Day is the day of entrance exams, then I would also of course be spending the whole day chanting and praying for Komachi to pass. I mean I'd even do scapulimancy, *tsujiura* fortune cookies, or that *kukatachi* trial-by-ordeal thing… Actually, no, I'm not going to stick my hand in boiling water.

With my head all full of thoughts of Komachi, I kind of didn't care about the event anymore.

If her entrance exams are on Valentine's Day, then she won't have made chocolates, huh…? And, like, if she stayed up all night to make chocolates filled with love right before entrance exams, even I might get mad enough to give her a smack and then gently embrace her…

Ahhh, my Komachi chocolate, my Koma-choco is drifting into the distance…

As I was groaning to myself, Isshiki was solemnly continuing her explanation. "Are you okay to come in for the event around five PM, Yukinoshita? Him and Yui can come a little later, though."

"I'm fine with that," said Yukinoshita.

"We'll come over with Yukinon. Right, Hikki?" I heard Yuigahama's voice in the distance.

"Yeah, sure, whatever…" *If I can't get chocolate from Komachi, then it doesn't even matter…*

My mood had gone dusty and dry, my body powdery filth ready to be blown away by the wind. I was just like an ARMS with the core knocked out of it. Well, Komachi is my core, you know. What can you do.

As I leaned against the backrest of my chair, burned out and pale, I felt Isshiki, seated diagonally opposite me, shoot me a dull, cold look. "You don't seem to care about this very much…"

Yuigahama laughed her off. "Ah-ha-ha! Well, when Hikki gets like this, it's basically always for the same reason. It's okay."

"Yes, I think I can imagine what it is. You can just leave him be, and it will be fine," Yukinoshita said, sounding utterly exasperated.

"Huhhh, is that right…?" Isshiki replied, making sure we all knew she didn't actually care, then continued her explanation. "The student council will arrange for all the ingredients and cooking implements, so there's no problem there. For aprons and stuff, it'll be, like, BYO, though."

Yukinoshita, who had been listening with her hand on her chin, looked up. "Could you show me your list of cooking implements after this, just in case? I'd like to make sure nothing is missing."

"Whatever you want!" While it was unclear if she understood or not, Isshiki scribbled off a note on her own paper. When she was done, she spun her pen around like a magic wand and looked over at Yuigahama. "This is who we have to call up, more or less, so, um, can I ask you to let Miura and Ebina know about this? I don't have their numbers for whatever reason."

"Okay, gotcha," Yuigahama responded calmly.

But I was momentarily frozen.

O-oh…could you, uh, stop giving me these weird little glimpses at girl society…? They see each other and talk fairly often, but they never message each other? Yikes… The scary thing about girls is that you might never be able to tell you're not friends with them during a conversation with them…

…Well, Isshiki and Miura don't seem particularly close, so I guess that's normal. As expected of the Queen—she hates it when anyone isn't straightforward!

"Oh, also, that Kawa…Kawa… That kind-of-scary girl as well, I'd like to ask someone to contact her, too," Isshiki said.

"Yeah, I'll message Saki," Yuigahama answered.

But I was frozen for a moment.

O-oh…so Isshiki doesn't actually remember her name, either… Just what I'd expect from Kawa-something. But you can't say that to her face, Irohasu! Not at the face! At the body!

Isshiki was checking over the printout again. "Guess that's it... Ah! Oh yeah!" she said suddenly. "If there's anyone else you want to invite, please let me know, and I'll make adjustments on the numbers, 'kay?"

"Oh, so we can bring more people?" said Yuigahama.

"Yeah. Like Tobe wasn't invited, but apparently he's still coming," Isshiki said in a highly disparaging tone with an added snort.

You're pretty awful to Tobe, aren't you? We're really on the same page there.

"Oh, I guess he heard about it from Yumiko or Hayato, ah-ha-ha..." Yuigahama laughed uncomfortably.

But Tobe's coming, too, huh? Well, if Tobe was coming to an event with all these girls, that'd make it less stressful for Hayama to join in. Tobe's a surprisingly considerate guy, so maybe he heard about it somewhere and decided to come right over. Tobe's obnoxious, but he's a good guy...

After considering this point, snippets of the discussion popped up in my mind again.

Tobe, boys, girls, Hayama... We can invite other people?

So then, that means..., I thought, carefully putting the pieces in their places. Whereupon, they gradually began to coalesce into a singular image.

In other words...

...that meant...

............*Doesn't that mean I can invite Totsuka, too?*

"Okay, leave contacting people to me!" I cried out the moment I arrived at that conclusion.

Isshiki's shoulders jumped in surprise, and then her head slowly turned toward me with an expression of disgust. "You're awfully enthusiastic all of a sudden..."

"Ah-ha-ha." Yuigahama laughed her off. "Well, when Hikki gets like this, it's basically always for the same reason. It's okay."

"Yes, I think I can imagine what it is. You can just leave him be, and it will be fine," Yukinoshita said, sounding utterly exasperated.

"Huhhh, is that right...?" Isshiki replied, making sure we all knew she didn't actually care.

Oh, good, these two catch on so quickly. Wait—they've just given up on me, haven't they...?

"Yukinoshitaaa, I want to ask about the menu—I was *thinking* it'd be a good idea to decide on a few candidates. If we don't, then we won't be able to order the ingredients." Isshiki was just ignoring me now and moving on with the discussion as she pulled some booklets on baking and making chocolates out of her bag and dropped them on the table. Yukinoshita nodded, picked up one of the booklets, and started flipping through it.

"You have lots here, but what would be best...? French chocolate cake, German Sacher torte, chocolate truffles...though I wouldn't mind picking the safe option and going with cookies. Obviously, we can't do pure chocolates, and we'll have to make it easy enough for beginners..." *Hmm*ing as she considered, Yukinoshita flipped another page. Well, under the category of "chocolate-based sweets," there are lots of different kinds.

I'm fairly uninformed in that arena, so it'd be best for me to avoid butting in unnecessarily. I'm so uninformed, you could say a Sacher torte was a Sachatel and I'd believe you.

But at times like these, there are some people in the world who will speak without fear, their own level of knowledge be damned. And Yuigahama is one of those people.

Yuigahama's hand shot straight up, and without waiting to be called on, she declared enthusiastically, "Ohhh, yeah! Or like chocolate fondue! This is like a choco-pa! It'll be fun!"

"Cho...copa...? Huh, what...?" This must have been the first Yukinoshita had ever heard the term, as she was tilting her head with a dubious expression.

Well, guessing based off remarks Yuigahama has made before, this "choco-pa" thing had to be an abbreviation for a "chocolate party," or a party where you have chocolate fondue. I've just about got my level two in the Gahamanese Proficiency Exam. I could get a high score on the YUEIC.

Yukinoshita still had a question mark hovering over her head, but Isshiki seemed impressed. "*Wellll*, if we're all hanging out together, then maybe yeah, huhhh? Maybe that could be an option."

Is it an option…? But man. With your *tako*-pa or *nabe*-pa or curry-pa and turning everything into a party, you're seriously jooshy polly yey party people every day…

"But this is supposed to be a cooking event, so…" Though she seemed to struggle against some internal resistance, Isshiki made a little X with her fingers. Yuigahama's head hung as she whined.

Yukinoshita, who'd been watching their exchange, nodded. "So it would be best to teach the basics after all… Something simple with visual appeal…" Skimming over the cookbooks, Yukinoshita's eyes paused on a certain section, a page with an ad. A line saying something about a "new product" leaped out at me.

"They have these things all together as a kit, so you don't need to measure the ingredients. It seems simple," said Yukinoshita.

"Ohhh, I bet even I could handle that," Yuigahama said.

Instantly, my voice choked in my throat. *Hey, wait, what? What are you talking about…?*

"…"

"Don't go all quiet!" Yuigahama's pained wail broke the moment of silence.

Once the echoes had faded, Yukinoshita gently stroked Yuigahama's shoulder and spoke as kindly as possible. "Yuigahama, for this, would it be possible to put your efforts into the wrapping instead?"

"Stop being all considerate!" I could hear the lamentations in Yuigahama's heart.

Uh, wrapping is important, though. Like, a blue ribbon around your chest will accentuate it in a way that's sure to get everyone talking about you! Your popularity will explode!

As I was pondering this, Isshiki breathed a little sigh. "Agh, I don't think a kit will change how it tastes, and you won't be able to tell at a glance... Anyway, this is for an event, so let's steer away from kits."

"Well, the kits would be more expensive," Yukinoshita agreed.

"Yes. Well, I do plan to charge a participation fee to cover costs, just in case, but you can never be too cheap."

"...Huh? You're charging for this?" My feelings showed clearly in my voice. It was probably showing on my face, too, since Isshiki seemed a bit weirded out.

"Why so shocked...? It's a few hundred yen... And, like, you guys don't have to pay. Since you'll be helping out."

"Then that's okay...," I said.

"Yes," said Yukinoshita. "If you're charging, we may have more leeway in the budget than I thought... For now, could you let me see what the budget is? I'll come up with some candidates based on your numbers, and I'll write you up a rough estimate for the cost of ingredients."

"Yes, please do," Isshiki said, pulling a printout from a plastic folder. It looked like a trial balance sheet for the event.

Yukinoshita checked over it, then began reconsidering menu options.

All the requests we'd gotten had some fairly strenuous conditions. It was no wonder she was having trouble.

We needed something you could give to your friends but also wouldn't be embarrassing to give your crush, something that would also be a generally useful recipe and fun for a kid to make.

And then the most unreasonable ask was the one Yukinoshita had been muttering all this time, like someone in a delirium. "Something even Yuigahama can make... Something even Yuigahama can make..."

"That's so mean, Yukinon!"

Though Yukinoshita seemed a bit distracted by Yuigahama's

wailing, she continued flipping through the cookbooks with Yuigahama basically clinging to her the whole time.

Yukinoshita pulled some options, noting down the necessary ingredients and the amounts. Yuigahama remained latched on to her, peering in from the side to watch. Then she broke into a happy grin.

Curious about the giggling beside her, Yukinoshita shot the other girl a grumpy look. "...What?"

"...Oh, nothing!" Yuigahama hurriedly waved her hands to cover her reaction, then lowered them and said quietly, "...I just thought... this feels kinda nostalgic." She seemed awkward as she looked at Yukinoshita.

"...It does," Yukinoshita replied briefly. But the gaze she returned to Yuigahama lasted far longer than those words.

Eventually, Yuigahama gave a shy laugh and shifted her chair closer so that both of them were lined up in front of me.

Then Yuigahama asked me quietly, searchingly, "...Right?"

The angle of her head as she looked at me from that distance seemed so innocent, I found myself cracking a smile. "I guess." My reply was also brief as I looked away.

It hadn't even been a year since then, but already that day felt so nostalgic—nothing had begun in that room, and yet the change had definitely happened.

"Thanks, Iroha-chan," said Yuigahama.

"Huh? Oh, yeah, it's nothing... Y-you're welcome?" The sudden thanks seemed to confuse Isshiki, as her head flip-flopped.

Yuigahama giggled. Then, once her laughter settled, she let out a satisfied breath. "The year is almost over, but I'm glad we'll be able to do something fun at the end..."

"Well, this year's only just started," I said.

"The correct term is this *fiscal* year," Yukinoshita added, which made Yuigahama a little sulky.

As for Isshiki, she was a little bewildered. "Whoa, you two are so anal about this..."

But despite this exchange, the matter was resolved enough for Isshiki. She swept her gaze over us and let out a long sigh before standing up. "Right, then. Thank you very much for the tea. Well, I'll leave it to you."

"Oh, yeah. We'll be counting on you at the event!" Yuigahama replied.

"Well then, I'll see you again soon. I'll submit the estimate," Yukinoshita said, and Isshiki bowed and left the clubroom.

Once the three of us were alone again, I could feel that earlier nostalgia more keenly.

I was probably feeling that way because a lot of things had changed. Because somewhere along the line, an identity had been lost. Because I understood that I would never have the same thing again.

That's why it was nostalgic.

If something has indeed been set into motion, it's sure to eventually stop. Everything that begins will eventually end.

Yukinoshita looked at Yuigahama's pure smile as if it was something precious, even though the two of them were just having an ordinary, trivial conversation.

That was all it was, but strangely, it felt like something was caught in my chest.

×   ×   ×

When you get into the bath in wintertime, you just can't avoid the tendency to soak for a good long while.

Maybe it was all the full-speed pedaling along the miserably dreary, long road at night, but I couldn't help but sink in all the way as I let out a deep, deep sigh. I got out just before my head started to swim, then shoved my legs straight into the *kotatsu* so I didn't catch a chill and flopped down there.

The things I'd been avoiding thinking about were showing up on my face, and it felt like the ground was shifting under my feet.

And that made me roll around restlessly and kick a soft ball of fur.

The family cat, Kamakura, wriggled his way out from inside the *kotatsu*. He shot me a withering look, then started to groom himself with his tongue. Eventually, he seemed to notice something, and his ears perked up, turning to the door. At just about the same moment, there was a click as the front door opened.

Komachi was home. I heard the sound of footsteps coming up the stairs, and then the living room door opened. "I'm hooome!"

"Hey, welcome back."

Komachi dropped her bag and was moving to take off her coat when Kamakura rubbed against her legs, pestering her with a request to pick him up. "Hey, no! You'll get fur on my uniform."

Komachi smoothly avoided the cat, so I picked up Kamakura instead. *Here, here, I'll give you attention. You can't be bothering Komachi when she's tired.*

Whether he understood my thoughts or not, Kamakura began flailing in my grasp. *Geez, get a clue, cat…*

Hey, you, Mr. Kamakura, don't you think this reaction is a bit excessive? Why're you pressing your paws into my face, huh…?

With the cat shoving at my face, I looked over at Komachi to see her standing on one leg as she tugged off her knee socks.

Though the heat was on, the floor had to be chilly. I gave her a mom look. *Don't let yourself get too cold, all right?*

She must have noticed my expression, as she tilted her head with a question in her eyes. "Oh, Komachi's gonna go fill up the bath."

"Oh. Got it. But I had one just now, so there's already water."

"Yeah. So Komachi's gonna go fill the bath."

"Uh, like I said. I just had one, so it's already full."

"Yeah, so." Komachi repeated the same thing again with a deadpan expression.

…Hey? What's that supposed to mean? I gave her an accusatory look.

Komachi waved her hands. "No, no, no, there's no way I could go in water you already used. I mean, you've kinda flavored the broth. No way, no way."

"Can you not talk about me like I'm tonkotsu ramen?"

Will the day eventually come when Wakame-chan talks to Katsuo like this…? The Isono family bathwater would probably taste really good.

Wait, has she been refilling the tub after I bathe all this time? Are you truly so hard on your brother? Though when I bathe after Komachi, I always savor the Komachi broth… Okay, yeah, I see her point.

When she was little, we called her the smart, cute Komaachika, but these days, I suppose even Komachi-chan has one foot firmly in puberty now, huh…?

As I was shedding an emotional tear at how big my little sister's gotten, something sparkly shone in the corners of Komachi's eyes—*Awww, does she feel the same?!*—and then it was followed up by an exhausted-sounding yawn.

"Then Komachi's gonna go have a bath," she said.

"Yeah, take it easy. Go to bed after."

"Yeah, yeah," she replied, yawning through the words. She seemed pretty tired.

Well, I guess it wasn't long until her actual exams.

All I could do for her was to not bathe before her from this day on, and to pray. The most I could do otherwise would be to warm her futon and her shoes. Oh no, she's gonna hate me again! But if this were the Sengoku era, I'd be a success!

This is no time for Valentine's, huh…?

It'd be best not to tell Komachi about the cooking event. No point in causing her unnecessary worry or regret. She'd have her hands full with entrance exams. Once those were over, it'd be a good idea to give her a big show of appreciation.

Meaning right now, I had to avoid causing her trouble, worry, or concern as much as possible!

I couldn't get in the way when she was working so hard on her own.

Doing your best with your own strength, of your own will, is the first step to success. By standing up and walking on your own two feet, you gain an understanding of what it means to walk with another person.

Komachi's growing further and further away from her big brother and becoming an adult, huh? It's a complicated feeling. Lonely, but also lonely... but still a little lonely, too.

I was so lonely, I buried my face in the stomach fur of the cat in my arms.

Aghhhh... How much longer will I get chocolate from Komachi, I wonder... I wish I could get chocolate from Komachi my whole life.

Who cares about guy chocolate or gay chocolate? I want K-chocolate.

...Can I have...some Komachoco?

And so begins the **boys' emotional roller coaster** (with girls, too).

A few days had passed since the surge of consults had hit us.

The Service Club hadn't done anything resembling work during that time, just giving Isshiki tidbits of advice when she occasionally came in to check things with us.

On the other hand, Isshiki was taking care of her job, as far as I could tell, and I caught sight of her after school many times in a continuous flurry of activity.

By the way, I also frequently sighted the vice president carrying a huge stack of documents while hanging his head and sighing, and Miss Secretary encouraging him.

You screwing around? Do your job, Vice Prez. Having a reputation for generally looking at guys with a harsh eye, hello, that's me.

Anyway, it seemed the whole student council was busy with work on the day of, too. It was quite a bit different from that Christmas event.

The community center near the station was filled with young chattering voices. This was earlier than the arrival time on the schedule, but we were helping out with the event that day anyway—well, Yukinoshita was at least.

And so I'd trudged my way over to the community center. I actually hadn't been there since Christmas, but nothing was going to change over such a short span of time. I parked my bicycle on the racks, and then three of us just strolled right into the community center like a trio of pros.

Inside, Isshiki and the other members of the student council were hard at work, bustling all over in preparation for the event.

As I was observing from the entrance, Isshiki noticed us and ambled on over. She was carrying a stack of papers in her arms. "Oh, heeey, it's you guys! You're early."

"Uh-huh," I replied casually instead of a proper greeting, and then Yukinoshita and Yuigahama behind me also popped their heads out.

"Hello, Isshiki."

"Yahallooo! I was wondering if there was something we could help out with," Yuigahama said.

Isshiki cocked her head. "Hmm. What can you help with…? Oh. Then here, please help me put these around. You can just stick them up by the entrance, so it's, like, the details are basically up to you," she said and handed over some hastily made B2-sized posters.

Well, I call them "posters," but they were just handwritten notices scratched out in various colors of fat marker. Aside from the text announcing the event, someone had drawn graffiti-esque illustrations on them, things like hearts and chocolates and emotes. It'd be more accurate to call them jumbo-sized hand-drawn pop signs.

But the shabby, slapdash work wasn't the problem.

The problem was the words written on them.

No experience necessary! No quotas! At-home atmosphere! Get the know-how and experience to become independent in the future!

This was not just a company run by black-hearted executives, but Black Company RX… An "at-home atmosphere" just means you're extra brutal on anyone but your own cronies.

"I wouldn't mind, if it's just putting up some posters, but…," Yukinoshita said anxiously.

Isshiki lifted her head to look into thin air as she touched her chin, pausing to think a bit. "Ahhh… Oh no, it's kinda crazy in there right now, so I'll put up posters, too."

She had to think to come up with that? She just wants to slack off, doesn't she...? I was thinking, when of course, my other two associates were of exactly the same mind.

"...Ah, ah-ha-ha. Th-that's kinda a sketchy reason."

"We don't mind if you go back in, Isshiki."

Yuigahama had her forced smile on full power, while Yukinoshita's icy smile was downright arctic.

"I-it's not like that; I'm not slacking, okay? And, like, there isn't much work to do for this event anyway..."

When I gave her a questioning look like, *Why not...?* Isshiki blew out a tired *phew*.

"The boy-girl ratio in the student council is about fifty-fifty? And Miss Secretary and Vice Prez are kinda close, right? And then there's also, um... Uh, well, just a ton of reasons! ☆" Isshiki equivocated for a while, then smiled cutely to get out of everything. It's the most irritating thing in the world when someone drops what they were saying halfway through, but that was adorable, so she's in the clear!

"...?" Yukinoshita tilted her head with a questioning look.

But the info Isshiki had just provided was enough to tell Yuigahama the general situation. "Ah, ahhh...I get it."

I basically got it, too.

The hard thing was not the work itself; it was the social relationships. There's lots of workplaces like that out there. I've quit part-time jobs for those reasons. I mean, it's really too much. When the store manager is dating a high school girl, and then she cheats on him with the pretty-boy university kid they just hired, and then the manager starts bullying him for it—that kind of workplace environment is just brutal...

...Well, you get that stuff in any community. It's basically everywhere. It's so common, and everyone knows it.

But still, nobody knows the best answer.

I was about to start thinking about the problem I wasn't looking at and the answers that wouldn't come—when I felt a prod at my back.

"So let's hurry and put them up! Slowly, if possible!" said Isshiki.

"You're one hundred percent just trying to buy time here, aren't you? Whatever. But it's cold outside, so I wanna get this done fast." When I looked through the single glass door that separated us from the outside, the cold air came to surround me, and I did a full-body shiver.

I looked up at the sky; the light of day still remained, telling me there was still some time until nightfall.

When I sighed, my breath rose white in the air, and my eyes followed it up until it vanished.

×   ×   ×

We spread out the posters flat and came up with the general area of where to stick them. The wind had died down, compared with the past few days, and that kept the thin papers from flipping up.

As we were doing that, Isshiki, who'd gone over to the convenience store across the street to buy some Scotch tape, came back with a plastic bag hanging from one hand.

"It really is cold, huh? Here you go." What she pulled out from the bag was black tea in a plastic bottle. She must have bought it while she was at the store. She handed one each to Yukinoshita and Yuigahama.

"Thanks."

"Oh, it's warm!"

Accepting the drinks, Yukinoshita wrapped both hands around her bottle to hold it, while Yuigahama touched hers to her cheek to capture the meager warmth from it.

"Here, and you too."

"Oh." What she gave me was a Max can. …*She actually gets it.*

I popped the tab, took a gulp, and instinctively let out a deep sigh.

The sky was utterly clear and bright, with nothing moving in it. With the weather like this, the night was gonna get a lot colder.

Now that I thought about it, it seemed strange that it got colder on sunny days. But maybe it's not so strange.

If you know about radiative cooling, the idea is easier to accept. Or maybe, if you've already accepted the more nebulous idea that winter is just cold, you probably wouldn't even find it strange in the first place.

Human intuition is unreliable; intuition is just perception, memory, and delusion put together.

But whether the sky was sunny or cloudy, it was still cold. So I squeezed the Max can tight to warm my hands and went to work.

First, we stuck a poster up on the glass at the entrance of the community center.

"Here."

"Thanks." I took a poster from Yuigahama. There was Scotch tape stuck on the four corners, so I just had to press this against the wall and smack the taped parts to make it stick. Done and done.

Let's put it a little higher so you can see it... I stretched a little with a *hup* and stuck it on. "This good?" I turned back to ask.

Yukinoshita, watching me from a few steps farther away, gave a little shake of her head. "It's askew."

"It is? Isn't this right?" I examined the poster I'd just put up again, but it didn't really seem crooked. When I cocked my head with a dubious expression, Yukinoshita breathed a short sigh.

"Perhaps it looks fine to you, given your skewed perspectives on things."

"Oh, I can definitely believe that... Hey, but you're not exactly unskewed yourself. And if it's all a matter of perspective, how do you know which is which?" I asked as I glanced her way again.

Yukinoshita swept the hair off her shoulders and gave me a look. "There is no absolute standard of righteousness—only what someone has decided is right. Here and now, that would be what I say. So just listen to me and tilt it slightly to the left."

"Speaking of twisted perspectives... So is this good?"

"Well, good enough."

After getting the all clear from Yukinoshita, I went to do the same with another sheet, carrying the posters to tack one on the bulletin board that faced the street, and once again figured out a position for it.

So Yukinoshita accompanied me, and this time Yuigahama trotted over, too, coming to stand beside her. For some reason, Isshiki joined us, lining up beside the other girls.

"Hikki, a little higher! Higher!"

"That's too far up. Bring it down a little."

"Huh? But shouldn't you do something about the left side first?"

…Okay, guys, one person to give instructions is enough.

With people telling me to go up and down and left, right, left, right and stuff to put up the poster, I was suddenly remembering the Konami code, like I was back in elementary school. Although I guess that's forgotten knowledge on the playground these days.

"Looks good. Guess I'll put up one more." I gave the poster a couple of little smacks, pushing it in firmly as I turned around and saw Isshiki, canned cocoa in her hands covered by overlong sleeves, shaking her head.

"Well, I guess that's good enough. It's not like that many people are coming, so this is just, like, a landmark, or just in case."

Is that how it is…? Well, maybe this is enough when it's just a small gathering of friends and acquaintances. Besides, landmarks are actually pretty important. The world is more convenient these days, and you can just search wherever you want to go on your phone, but you do still sometimes wonder if you're in the right place and then just go home out of fear of embarrassment… Landmarks are important! This is one of the reasons I often abandoned interviews for part-time jobs!

Anyway, I wonder what sort of people will come to this… This time around, I honestly hadn't been involved with anything aside from helping out that day, so I didn't know what the plan was.

Miura and Ebina came to consult with us, and Kawasaki, too, so they'll come for sure, and they should be bringing Hayama to taste-test… As I was thinking this, some familiar figures approached from the other side of the street.

Noticing them, Yuigahama waved widely. "Oh, it's them. Yahallooo!"

After waiting for the light to change, Ebina trotted over. "Hello, hellooo! Thanks for today."

Running up by her side was Tobe. "Yo, yoooo!"

What's with that greeting? Is he gonna show off his Walk the Dog like we're in elementary school? Maybe he always got like this for events, but he was even more excitable than usual. He went straight into a loud conversation with Ebina and Yuigahama.

He's obnoxious, but that's nothing new, I thought. Meanwhile, Miura, following behind him, seemed comparatively quiet. She was constantly glancing over at the person beside her, reshouldering her bag, and fiddling with her hair, and she seemed nervous.

Well, no wonder. She was about to make chocolate and give it to him.

I don't know what she'd said to invite him, but it seemed she'd convinced Hayama to come.

Anyway, we'd made it past hurdle number one. Next, if Miura did a good job with her cooking, then her request would be no problem. Relieved for the moment, I picked up the Max can I'd left on the stairs at my feet and took a sip.

That was when I heard the patter of footsteps. In a heartbeat, Iroha Isshiki was right there in front of us.

"Ohhh, Hayama! Thanks *so* much for coming today!" she said, immediately coming up by his side. Miura glared death at her over Hayama's shoulder, but Isshiki smiled brightly and ignored her.

Ah, a new hurdle has appeared for Miura…

"Hey, Iroha. Oh…was it okay for me to come, too? I've never done any baking or anything, so I don't feel like I'll be all that useful." Caught between Miura and Isshiki, Hayama had this uncomfortable, confused smile on his face as he scratched his cheek.

Miura gave his shoulder a little bump. "It's not like you have to worry about that stuff? I mean, like, if you let us know what you think, that's enough…," she said shyly to keep him where he was, while Isshiki spoke sweetly to drag him in.

"Yeah! We'll be counting on you for taste-testing!"

Hayama had his trademark breezy smile. "Okay, then might as well go in."

"Yes, we have to start getting ready," said Yukinoshita. She and

Yuigahama nodded to each other, and Ebina and Tobe followed after them into the community center.

With Miura and Isshiki guarding either side, Hayama went after them.

Looks like he's in for a bad time, ah-ha-ha-ha, I thought, watching it in a detached manner. Not my problem. I was taking another sip of my Max can, when my eyes happened to meet with Hayama's.

"Hey," he said, then prompted Miura and Isshiki with a look to go on ahead. Though they both seemed nonplussed, they headed toward the entrance hall.

Hayama watched them go with a gentle smile, then glanced at me. "You're on taste-testing, too, Hikigaya?"

"Basically," I replied bluntly.

Hayama narrowed his eyes. "…I see." And then, as if he couldn't hold it back, a tiny giggle slipped out of him.

"What…?"

That all-knowing look in his eyes, and that vaguely pitying smile. And the way he was talking—all of it reminded me of confronting a certain someone else. It was getting on my nerves, and I couldn't completely hide it in my reply.

But Hayama just shrugged with a light shake of his head. His expression was gentle, and the strangely mature air of a moment ago was gone. "Oh, no. I just thought you were a good choice."

"Huh?"

"You like sweets, right?" he teased as he pointed to the Max can in my hands.

Well, it is *true that I'm often drinking these…*

"That's why," he added quietly. With that, he started off again at a brisk pace toward the entrance hall where Miura and Isshiki were waiting.

That was close! I thought for a second I might swoon! "Oh no, Hayama knows my favorite drink! Yeek!" Yeah, that definitely wouldn't happen.

…In fact, I didn't feel very good at all. I had to force a lame joke in there, or I might actually think too much. Hayama was probably the same, which was why he'd deliberately teased me to avoid the issue.

I knocked back the rest of my half-drunk Max can in one go and clenched the steel can in my fist, although I knew I wasn't strong enough to crush it.

Well, the postering was over.

I won't know the situation inside the community center without looking, but I guess I can't just stand out here and watch. I've got to pick something small to do.

And so, the next work begins…

×   ×   ×

Though I'd mentally braced myself for some kind of involuntary labor, I hadn't anticipated it would be manual involuntary labor.

Various cardboard boxes, large and small, were sitting right there *bam* in the middle of the entrance hall. Inside was the baking chocolate, sugar, baking powder, and the other stuff the student council had ordered.

My job for the moment was to carry all this to the kitchen on the second floor.

It was good that they'd requested delivery from the supplier and had them carry it in, but I wished they could've tried a little harder and carried it up to the second floor while they were at it… Well, at least they didn't make me go out and buy it.

"Awright, then I'll take this right up." Tobe rolled up the sleeves of his uniform dress shirt and hefted the cardboard box. I went next, and then the vice president. The crew choice here was clearly selected by Iroha Isshiki… Also known as: The Association of Victims of Iroha Isshiki. Hayato Hayama is of course exempted.

Carrying the boxes filled with ingredients, we heaved and hoed our way up the stairs.

"Duuude, this is actually really heavy, huh?" Tobe was perky in the lead, but as we approached the halfway point of the staircase, the weight of his box was getting to him. He adjusted his grip with a *hyup*.

Then the vice president, following behind me, said apologetically, "Sorry, we don't have many boys, so this honestly helps."

"Oh, I don't mind, though…," I said.

"For sure, dude. I'm used to this kinda thing." Tobe did this wide sweep of his head in our direction, like he was getting his hair out of his face, and grinned.

God, you're annoying. And that's dangerous. Eyes forward, come on. You'll fall and get hurt. And you need to cut your hair.

But Tobe's an easy mark, getting yanked around on Isshiki's whims. And I felt like the vice president was getting grief from her, too—maybe it was his timid-looking face. So this was like, you know—the three of us combined made the Worldly Sufferer Series. Seems like we could become a weapon for defeating vampires.

With some straining and groaning, the three of us finally arrived at our goal, the kitchen. Still carrying his box, Tobe skillfully opened the sliding door with his elbow.

Yuigahama and Yukinoshita were inside, having laid out the cooking implements and set up each table. The student council was directing Miura, Ebina, and Hayama to help with the other tables.

First, I went over to Isshiki, Yuigahama, and Yukinoshita to ask where this box went.

"Thanks!" Yuigahama said as I set down my load with a *thump*.

Yukinoshita came over to inspect the boxes. "Good. Isshiki, have the ingredients been divided up?" Yukinoshita asked her.

"Yep, yep. We just have to toss 'em all over each table, and we're good," Isshiki replied as she counted the boxes one, two, three and nodded. "Looks like they're all here. Then let's open 'em up and get it all set out everywhere quick," she ordered, and the vice president, still with a box in his arms, whisked himself straight over to the table where Miss Secretary was.

Tobe and I squatted down on the spot first to start opening the boxes. The sound of cardboard popping and metal clanking brought home the sense that something was actually starting.

The one feeling this the most had to be Tobe. He kept tugging at the hair at the back of his head, and he seemed to be in high spirits. "Man, I love stuff like this. Hey, Irohasu, you're like a real student council president now, huh?"

"Yep, I sure am. But I'm still team manager. Once it gets warmer, I'll make sure to go to practice!"

Uh, you should go to practice even when it's cold…

Hearing Isshiki's cheery response, Tobe gave her a thumbs-up, a wink, and a smile. Maaan, he's obnoxious.

So we opened the boxes no problem and pulled out variety packs of baking chocolate, the main ingredient for the day.

Seeing it, Tobe seemed to remember something, "Man, this looks so good, dude. Now I want some."

"Huh?" Isshiki shot him a cold look.

But Tobe did not stop talking. In fact, he took a little breath and then braced himself with a look of determination.

He stood up and checked all around nearby, then tried to wave us together into a circle.

"What? Are we having a secret meeting?" Yuigahama stuck her head in with deep interest.

"I can't really leave my task now, though…" Yukinoshita looked bothered, but she capitulated when Yuigahama dragged her over.

And so we formed a huddle. He's not gonna say *Gather round for a round of cheers, whoo!* or anything, right…?

My misgivings, however, proved unfounded. Tobe just tugged at the hair at the back of his neck and twirled it around his fingers, being all shy as he opened his mouth. *Hey, that's not cute.*

"Ah, well, like…they're making chocolate stuff today, right? So I was thinking maybe I could turn it around in a way and be the one to go for it instead, but… You don't have nothin'?"

"You don't have nothin'?" Look, this isn't an ad for Ajigonomi…and I'm not your mom.

And that isn't "turning it around" at all—you're always making a go for it, and she blocks or ignores everything. If you're going to "turn it around," then learn how to back off. What is this, like "if pushing doesn't work, then just try pulling…"? Oh, no! Boys are rarely so forceful these days; it gets my heart pounding!

But it seemed I was the only one with a pattering heart. The reaction from the girls was lacking.

"…Uh-huh, so you want to try to push her directly to give you chocolate?" I was forced to sum it up in brief, since nobody would give the guy a response.

Tobe pointed a finger at me. "Yeah, dude! Well, basically?"

Isshiki made an *eugh* face. "I don't know who you're after, but that'll have the opposite effect. Shilling for chocolate is high-key creepy. Please just keep quiet."

"O-okay…"

Irohasu is brutal… Struck silent, Tobe looked around at all of us, seeking someone to defend him.

The one to respond to his hopes was Yukinoshita. She put her hand to her cheek and tilted her head, then offered a conclusion she seemed to have considered very seriously.

"But there's a logic to what Isshiki is saying, isn't there…? Someone scampering around in the corner of your eye, constantly piping up… It's obnoxious."

"…" Even Tobe was left speechless after such a thorough thrashing.

So then why is Irohasu leaning her shoulder against our dear Miss Yukinoshita, playing cute and going "Riiight?"

This is just sad, I was thinking, when Yuigahama groaned.

"H-hmm… But you know, if you act like you totally don't want it at all, she won't know what to do, so I dunno…"

"Right, dude?!" Tobe's mood did a 180 as he regained his cheer, snapping his fingers.

But Isshiki's verbal assault wasn't over. "No, no, no. What Yui is saying is for when a girl already plans to give you some. This doesn't apply to you." She waved her hands to make her point.

That would take the wind out of anyone's sails, even Tobe's. "Dude…"

But the odds weren't totally zero, as far as I could tell. I don't have any clear evidence of anything, but if Ebina was showing up here with the intention of making something, that was a bit different from before. Of course, she could just be tagging along with Miura. That wasn't for me to know.

I think all that nebulous uncertainty was what made it effective.

"Well, if everyone's working on making stuff, then you'll wind up getting to taste-test for her, right? Not like I know. Anyway, take this over there," I said, shoving the remaining box at Tobe.

At first, his mouth just hung open, but then he figured out what I was trying to say and clapped his hands. "Yeah! That's it, dude!" Tobe jabbed a finger at me with some relief, then hefted the cardboard box up to his shoulder and quickly scampered off to the table where Ebina and their crowd was.

He may be a good guy, but god is everything he does obnoxious.

Where the heck is Tobe from…? He says *dude* way too much.

$$\times \quad \times \quad \times$$

We spent some more time setting up the cooking event, and then it was just about time to start.

Isshiki, Yukinoshita, and Yuigahama were having a meeting on what they were going to make. I didn't chime in, but with nothing else to do, I just listened and stared off into space.

And then, mingling with the sound of their discussion, I faintly heard the chattering and carrying on from outside the kitchen. Glancing over at the clock, I saw it was almost time for everyone else to be showing up.

So that voice is Kawa-something… No, there's too many voices for it to be her. Or are there multiple Kawa-somethings, and I just never knew? No wonder I can't remember their names…

I kept my eyes firmly on the door so that I would be able to receive the visitor, no matter which Kawa-something came, be it Kawashima, Kawaguchi, Kawagoe, Kawanakajima, Sendai, or Sendai…

Then, the door rattled open.

And standing there was Tama-something.

"Hey, Iroha-chan. Oh, this is great! Especially since the last event was so well received, you know. I was so delighted to receive your *offer* just as I was thinking that, moving forward, I would like to build a rigorous *partnership* and continue building upon our *cooperative enterprise*," he said, dropping enough fancy English that I doubt Isshiki even understood half of it.

"Yeah, thanks for your help." Despite his long address, Isshiki didn't comment on any of it.

The student council president of Kaihin High School, Tamanawa… Still making those jabs the moment he enters the ring, huh…? The guy's got a golden left arm for high-speed pottery wheel spins; maybe he's just the one we need to aim for glory.

What's more, he brought friends. Some familiar faces from the joint Christmas event came into the kitchen one after another—probably the student council from his school. That irritating hairpin and that aggravating preppy cardigan around the shoulders looked familiar.

"This event is also a *business opportunity*, right? *Forward planning* by utilizing *crowdfunding* to raise money before taking it to the next level could be an option."

"I'm in *agreeance* with that."

"If we can construct a *methodology* that will restore *incentives*, we might gain traction with *early adapters*."

"When the *USA* was a *free market*, children would sell *lemonade* to nurture a sense for economics—maybe this is *similar*."

"Yeah, that's one *case study*, huh?"

In the context of their conversation, even the word *lemonade* sounded mysteriously pretentious. When they say it, would even a *lifeguard* guzzling *coffee with milk* sound fancy?

"Still have no idea what they're talking about…," I muttered.

Yukinoshita let out a short sigh. "That's because your brain isn't engaged. Pupils wide, lips purple, and when someone talks to you, there's not much response…"

"Sounds like my brain is completely off."

If my pupils are wide, then that means I'm dead, actually… Anyway, those guys haven't changed much. Well, people don't change so easily. Honestly, if one or two failures was enough to stop them, they would never have gotten that bad in the first place. If I thought of this as a form of sticking to your guns, it didn't seem so bad.

Mm-hmm, I kinda hope Tamanawa and his crowd stay like that forever, I was thinking, when someone popped out from behind the group.

"Oh, it's Hikigaya. So you did come!"

"Y-yeah."

The one talking to me in the same old casual manner, ignoring all social barriers, was Kaori Orimoto. Slipping on out of the Kaihin circle, she strolled up to me.

And then she leaned around to see behind me.

"Oh, hi." Orimoto bowed with her head only, and Yuigahama seemed a bit flustered as she returned it.

"H-hi…"

Yukinoshita just acknowledged Orimoto with a casual look, arms still folded.

What's with the tension…?

Oh yeah, they've never had the chance to actually talk. They only know the other exists, basically. It wasn't like I wanted them to be friends, but I really would have preferred to avoid this awkward vibe.

Isshiki was better able to converse with Orimoto, and she was known to at least convincingly pretend to get along with her, so I shot her a pleading look. *Irohasuuuu, save me, Irohasuuuu.* What I got back was a throat-clearing noise.

It was a deeper noise, a *hem, gefum* in a more full-sounding voice. *Surprisingly uncute for Isshiki,* I thought, and then I saw it was

Tamanawa. Orimoto coming over to talk to us must have alerted Tamanawa to my presence. His expression was displeased. "Ah, I see they've come, too…," he said.

"Ohhh, didn't I mention?" Isshiki touched a slim finger to her glossy lips and tilted her head.

She is a master of playing dumb…

"H-hmm…I'm not sure. I don't think there were *logs* of any *e-mail-based* exchanges…"

With the groaning Tamanawa in the corner of her eye, Isshiki turned to me and stuck out her tongue mischievously. *What the hell, that's cute?*

Isshiki's amazing act did the trick, and Tamanawa gave up on pressing her further. All he said was "Hmm, hmm, uhhh, er" and then left with the Kaihin crowd in tow, heading in the opposite direction.

"Well, see you." Orimoto raised a casual hand and dashed off to join them.

Watching her go, I whispered to Isshiki, who had this fake-looking smile on, "So what's going on with those guys…?"

"Best scenario is calling this a joint event and then reeling in funds from Kaihin, too, right? And that's a score for me, since I'll save myself the cost of the obligatory chocolate for them!"

"O-okay…" *Iroha Isshiki, you never let me down… Seriously, won't she get stabbed one day? Is she gonna be okay?* With some worry, I gave her a disparaging look.

Isshiki seemed a little embarrassed, blushing as she cleared her throat. "Ahem. Besides, we are charging for the event just in case, so budget-wise, we're in the black for this. Well, if you subtract all expenses, then it's a wash. Barely makes the BEP, but we're about net zero, though."

"You…kinda lost me, Iroha-chan…" Yuigahama held her head in her hands and moaned.

Well, there's some overlap between your pretentious types and business wannabes… By the way, "it's a wash" and "barely making the break-even point" both mean "net zero"!

Isshiki must have pulled some strings to invest student council funds in this though, huh? She'd probably made those posters so she could have some concrete record of our activities. Having the documentation is always convenient for filing time! She'd really gained a good sense for business, for better or worse. The fee for participants was also a pretty cheap sale price, and I am not the one called sale-immune. Sale prism power, make up!

Bringing in another school means two times the budget, and collecting fees for participation makes is a triple-bang, increasing the acquired funds Quiz Derby–style.

Well, accusations of using student council funds for personal reasons or embezzlement aren't exactly something you can excuse... I had no idea about the fiscal management in that area, so I would close my eyes on this one. Most of all, inside me lives the corporate slave mind-set: *It's not really my money, so whatever.*

Even just listening to this talk was giving me a headache, but this was what had brought the event to life, so Isshiki's endeavors were not entirely misguided.

It seemed I wasn't the only one feeling this was headache-worthy, as Yukinoshita also had a hand at her temple, sighing deeply. "Leaving aside the ethics of your approach... You've been surprisingly capable with this, Isshiki..."

"She has been. She has things together pretty good, you know? Even if she can be a little inconsistent."

"Ah, I think I kinda get that." Yuigahama answered that gentle-fluffy voice with a strained smile. Indeed, she was quite right.

...Gentle-fluffy?

That voice had a softness to it that didn't belong to Yukinoshita or Yuigahama, a tone that somehow drew you into drowsiness. My head jerked around to look.

Bangs snapped in a hairpin, shiny forehead, and a fluffy-gentle air around her with every sway of her braids—and her Megu☆rin-bright smile.

"Oh! Shiromeguri!"

"H-hello..."

Yuigahama's call of surprise and Yukinoshita's somewhat-confused greeting came at the same time. They both blinked.

"Yeah! Good to see you!" Meguri Shiromeguri, the previous student council president, waved her hand in front of her modest chest as she returned their greetings.

"Um, why are you here…?" Her sudden entrance had hit me with the Megurin Effect (mainly used for healing and relaxation, big sister elemental), but I somehow managed to ask that.

Meguri clapped her hands and cocked her head an inch, looking pleased. "I was invited…so here I am." With a fluffy *eh-he*, she activated the Megu-Megu-Megurin ☆ Megurish Effect (main effects are resurrection and detox, also confers big sister element, and you also gain the added status effect of seeing the occasional mature air and innocent gestures. The opponent dies).

Still with that fuzzy-wafty tone, Meguri slid a step forward and took Isshiki's hand in a gentle grip. "I got invited! I'm doing the address at the graduation ceremony, you know, so I ran into Isshiki when I came to school for that, and that's when she made the offer."

Oh-ho, so Isshiki was the one to invite her. She didn't seem to enjoy engaging with Meguri all that much, though…, I thought, looking at Isshiki.

She jerked her face away, muttering in a super-quiet voice, "… Well, once you have a certain number of participants, the unit cost goes down." It seemed her words didn't quite reach Meguri.

Meguri actually seemed pleased Isshiki had invited her, swinging Isshiki's hand back and forth in her grasp. With each swing, Isshiki twisted around like she was embarrassed.

"I already got into university on a recommendation, so I have nothing to do, you know!" said Meguri. "My friends all seem busy with entrance exams… So I brought along the members who had the time."

"Oh, I see…" After replying to her, I suddenly realized something felt off. *Members? That's an odd way to put it…* It's like something pressured her to say that instead of *suspects*, resulting in that strange wording.

When I gave Meguri a questioning look, she spun around to face behind her. "Right?" she called back, and then *poof*, a bunch of kids were there. *What the heck, are these nin-nin ninjas or what?* Pulling up my vague and dim memories, I found I did know them, more or less. They had that distinct glasses-y vibe—meaning they had to be the glasses-wearing former members of the student council.

They must have been worried about the succeeding student council after all—given what had happened that led to Isshiki becoming student council president. And the student council was probably a special place to Meguri.

Meguri finally released Isshiki and next laid her hands gently on Yukinoshita's and Yuigahama's shoulders. Then she surveyed our faces fondly. "Things are a little different from what I expected, but still…I'm glad I got to show up to a student council job again like this and be able to speak with you, Yukinoshita, Yuigahama…and Hikigaya."

"Oh…me too!" Yuigahama replied with a soft, squishy smile. She must have been hit by the Megurin Effect, too. Though Yukinoshita didn't reply, her face was slightly downturned, her ears red.

Now that I thought about it, for the members of the Service Club, the only senior we knew was Meguri.

…Oh no, if I see Meguri at the graduation ceremony making her speech, I might cry. I'm even starting to tear up right now. I may have a reputation for being super-weak to younger girls, but older girls are also a weak point of mine.

I'm glad I have her to look up to, I was thinking, feeling fluffy and gentle, as Meguri observed us and nodded.

Then she pumped a little fist like she was trying to get us energized. "Okay, then let's do our best today, too! Whoo!"

Nobody responded to her, either. The admirable attitude Isshiki had shown earlier had evaporated, and she was giving Meguri an apathetic look.

But Meguri was not at all fazed by the cold reception, happy to take the time she needed as she stuck her fist up again. "Whoo!"

"…Wh-whoo." *If I don't respond, she'll keep going again and again…*

The pressure from the old student council members waiting behind her is intense... Glancing around to see what I should be doing, I raised my hand not too far, just about the height of a cat's swipe. Seeing our reply, Meguri made a satisfied-sounding *hmf.*

Then she glanced at the clock on the wall, drawing my eye over, too. Just about everyone had arrived, and we were also done setting out the ingredients and cooking implements. Kawasaki and her sister were a little late, but they'd be coming soon.

Then it's about time to start, I was thinking, when Meguri tilted her head with a *hmm.*

"Haru's a little late, huh?"

"Yeah. I don't think this place is too hard to find, though." Isshiki nodded back at Meguri.

But I was unable to nod—I'd just heard an ominous word.

Haru here didn't particularly refer to a hostess who works at a hot spring. There was only one person Meguri would call by that name.

Shifting my gaze to the side, I saw Yukinoshita's eyebrows drawing into a scowl. Yuigahama also must have basically figured it out, as she was staring at the door.

Eventually, there was a rattle.

The door wasn't very well fitted, so it was extra-noisy as it slid open. Fine, willowy fingers reached into that opening, and then the door was wrenched loudly.

Next came the click of her heel against the floor. Slowly, with firm step after step, she entered the room and came to stand before us. "Hya-hallooo! Sorry, am I late?"

"And sooo, this is our bonus instructor today, our very special senior Haru!" Isshiki said in a cutesy-sweet tone.

"Hi, hi, I'm the very special senior Haru." Haruno Yukinoshita's bright-red coat fluttered as she raised a hand in casual greeting and joined Isshiki's little joke.

"Oh, Haru. It's been a long time," Meguri said as she ambled up to the other girl.

"…We saw each other just the other day, didn't we, Meguri?" Haruno said with exasperation as she gave her a little poke in the forehead.

"Your cooking is so good! I'm looking forward to it."

"Well, I was asked to do it, so I'll make some. As a kind big sister figure, I can't refuse requests from people looking to me for help, you know?"

Kind? You mean kinda scary? 'Cause I'm actually feeling nothing but terror…

The two of them went straight from greetings into some idle chitchat. I took that opportunity to beckon Isshiki over with little waves. "Hey, why'd you invite her?" I asked quietly.

"I mean, she's a total veteran at this, right?" Isshiki said as if it were entirely obvious, apparently baffled.

Yes, you are quite correct in that assessment. She's not just a total veteran; she's an undefeated champion. And also the most fearsome and terrible.

"But I was enough, though…" Yukinoshita held her own elbows in a loose grip as she averted her eyes from Haruno, who was standing opposite her.

"Well, your teaching methods aside, you are a great cook," I said.

"…Not that great." The compliment must have surprised her, as she went silent for a moment before immediately jerking her face away.

Uh, that wasn't a compliment. I'm saying you're a bad teacher.

"*I'm* looking forward to having you teach me, Yukinon!" Yuigahama said, glomping Yukinoshita. That seemed to cheer Yukinoshita a little, as she cleared her throat a bit bashfully.

…Well, having someone aside from Yukinoshita who could give instructions would allow her to give more attention to Yuigahama, so it wasn't really a bad thing.

But I was still wondering why Isshiki had expressly invited Haruno.

First of all, if you considered the number of people participating in the event, it wasn't like there was a huge crowd to teach, and Isshiki had professed to knowing what she was doing, too. And there had to be some other girls with experience in baking and chocolate making, too.

"It didn't have to be her, did it? Yukinoshita is way better than some rando off the street, you know." I indirectly probed for the reason why Isshiki had reached out to Haruno specifically.

"Well, I do think Yukinoshita is a supergood cook, which is why I asked for her help." But Isshiki paused there and shifted her gaze awkwardly. "It's just, well, um…I kinda wondered if she'd make things that'd be a hit with boys."

"Very good point…"

Yukinoshita really is a great cook, but she's lacking in service spirit, or just lacking in fanservice. Specifically in the chest area. By contrast, Yuigahama has a lot of service, but her basic skills are catastrophic… Oh, I'm sure Yukinoshita's work would be solid and safe, but when it comes to something that would be a "hit with boys," as Isshiki put it—something to show off her girlish charms—I couldn't offer quite as strong an endorsement.

And Haruno Yukinoshita would steal the hearts of anyone, boy or girl, in that area. Nay—she would take them in her grasp and crush them. I don't know anyone more skilled when it comes to seeing through the cracks in people's hearts.

On top of that, her basic specs are even higher than Yukinoshita's. I'm sure she'd make a thorough demonstration of her abilities, artifices, and wiles with cooking, too. She's so good, I bet she could win over not just humans, but fairies, too.

I had to make jokes to myself, or my anxiety would be off the charts.

Every single thing Haruno Yukinoshita does means both nothing and everything.

If she was showing up here today, she had to be here for a reason. There was no way she'd come over just because a student from her old school had asked.

She was always like that.

Just like her name, she exposes things under the light of the sun.

Even though she doesn't reveal a single thing about herself.

Suddenly, **Shizuka Hiratsuka** lectures about the present continuous and the past.

There were no particularly large obstacles to getting started or anything unique to the proceedings that we could see, and we took our time moving things along.

When it was coming to the time to start, we just sort of looked at each other and got the sense we should hop to it or something. Isshiki casually announced it was happening, and everyone began a flurry of cooking.

I wasn't part of the culinary side of this, so there wasn't really anything for me to do. My main job (such as it was) was support, backup, assistance, help—but to be blunt, I was unemployed.

By contrast, Yukinoshita was putting her nose right to the grindstone.

At the table ahead of me, the trio of Yukinoshita, Yuigahama, and Miura all examined the cooking tools before them with utmost seriousness.

"First, we cut up the chocolate and heat it in a water bath," said Yukinoshita. "This will depend on what you're making, but this stage will be necessary."

"That all?" Miura asked, sounding underwhelmed.

"…Basically, yes. But the important part comes after that," Yukinoshita answered as she chopped up the chocolate chunks into finer pieces with rhythmical strikes of the blade. Yuigahama gave an appreciative "Ohhh" at how smooth her movements were.

Uh, I don't think it's time to be impressed yet, though…

Next, Miura imitated Yukinoshita. She was a bit timid with the cooking knife, but she broke up the chocolate in her own way. And no, Yuigahama was still not permitted to touch a knife. This was nonnegotiable.

Once the chocolate was mostly chopped, Miura straightened up again with some satisfaction. *Uh, it's still totally not done, though...*

But she was apparently pleased with her results. "Huh... This is pretty easy," she crowed, her face breaking into a proud smile that seemed to say, *How d'you like that?*

But she was immediately confronted with protests from both sides.

"You have no idea, Yumiko!" Yuigahama said, bluntly and passionately.

"None at all." Yukinoshita's remark came with a cold smile.

But neither seemed to clear Miura's impression that this task was surprisingly easy, as she cocked her head. "Huh? Is there something hard?" she asked.

Yuigahama puffed out her chest with a smug chuckle. "The hard part comes next! A water bath doesn't mean to put it in water. You kinda go *brrrr*. Y'know, like *brrrr*."

She was probably talking about whipping and tempering, and I could make a joke about her whipping herself into a panic over this. But I won't.

Meanwhile, Yuigahama's sound effects must have been giving Yukinoshita a bit of a headache, as touched her hand to her temple and said with a sigh, "Once you've melted chocolate, you can't just let it harden again. The fat will separate and turn white, which doesn't look or taste good. And there's a lot of work involved in the process after this stage."

Man, Yukinoshita's response was on a whole different level... This is like the difference between a whale and an F2Per here.

Between Yuigahama's energy and Yukinoshita's logic, Miura was overwhelmed into reconsidering.

"Hmm. Uh-huh... So what's next?" she asked in the typical Miura way, but her attitude was more commendable. At the very least, you could see she was trying to learn. And that brought a little smile to Yukinoshita's face.

"First, the water bath and tempering. The next steps will depend on what we make, so... Well, we have a lot of people, so how about we try French chocolate cake?"

"French chocolate cake! I didn't know you could even make it at home!" said Yuigahama.

"It's nothing that difficult... I'm using unsweetened chocolate, but I think you two can go with what you like."

Yuigahama's eyes were shining with respect, while Miura was giving her a look like, *Huh, not bad.* Yukinoshita smiled wryly.

Well, I was a bit uneasy about Yuigahama, but if Yukinoshita was with her, it probably wouldn't end in disaster.

Okay, then how about the others? I thought, looking over to a table to the side, and there I saw Isshiki, cooking at her own pace.

From what I could see, things with her were going well.

She'd already finished melting her chocolate into a smooth and lustrous paste, while in another bowl, she'd beaten meringue to fluffiness. Just seeing how smoothly she was managing it, I could tell she knew what she was doing.

Next, Isshiki dropped a teaspoon of something that looked like Western liquor into the bowl and mixed it up a little more. After she scooped up a tad with a spoon, her lips closed over it as she took a taste.

She nommed the spoon in her mouth for a while, then tilted her head with a *hmm.* It seemed she was not satisfied, and she started adding in this and that: sugar, whipped cream, and cocoa powder and such.

"You're actually good at this, huh...?" Maybe I shouldn't have said so, but I was so surprised that it just slipped out.

That drew a glare from Isshiki. "Didn't I tell you?"

"Oh, no... I was just impressed. You're working pretty hard at this." Thinking about everything she was doing to get Hayama to eat her cooking, I had to appreciate how single-minded she was about it. Well, I was also getting hints of her nefarious scheming to save money on the cost of obligatory chocolate. But still. Maybe it was just the school uniform/apron combo talking, but even her scheming seemed transformed into charming determination, mysteriously enough. And let me tell you this right here: An apron over a uniform hits you harder than an apron over nothing at all! The one that hits hardest is Komachi in a tank top and shorts and an apron, though.

So I'd been thinking as I'd made that remark.

Isshiki blinked, mouth dropping open. But then she quickly put both hands in front of her and backed away. "What, are you trying to hit on me? Like this sweet talk will work just because we're making sweets? Well, you can bet your 'sweet' bippy that's not gonna work, so go over your strategy again and come back later, sorry." With a polite bow of her head, she thoroughly rejected me.

I'm not trying to hit on you, though, and I'm not coming back later…

Iroha Isshiki seriously hasn't changed one bit. Unless she's gotten more cunning and tenacious. She's really something, I thought, sighing half in exasperation, half in awe. And that was when a spoon popped up in front of my face.

"Hyup!" Isshiki went, and the spoon skimmed my cheek to stick into my mouth. It was so sudden, I flailed and made muffled noises of distress as my eyes rolled back and forth in my head, and in my flickering field of vision, Isshiki smiled enchantingly.

"You don't like sweets, like this?" Swinging her spoon, she tilted her head and looked at me through her lashes. She was smiling proudly like a child who'd succeeded in mischief, despite the way she was girlishly and provocatively puffing out her chest. That mismatch was just what made her so terribly charming.

"…I don't hate it." I'm sure there wasn't that much sugar, but it was sweet enough to make my tongue tingle. *Wait, you were just using this spoon, weren't you…? It's really bad for my heart when you do stuff like that to me, so don't…*

They say sugar is good for fatigue, but it seems the effect reverses when it's coupled with emotional strain. A wave of exhaustion knocked a sigh out of me, and Isshiki sighed, too.

"Agh. It's not like I asked for your opinion on the taste, though." She was pretending she didn't care, but the look she flicked in my direction gave me the sense she might be waiting for a response.

Taking the time to reflect on the lingering sweetness in my mouth, I digested what Isshiki was trying to say. "That still doesn't change my answer…"

"…Oh." Isshiki gazed into the bowl in her arms as if she was pondering something and nodded to herself. Then she jerked her chin up again. "This has been useful. Okay, I'm going off for a bit. Hayamaaaa!" And before she even finished saying that, she pattered off with a bright smile on her face.

As I watched her go, I wiped some chocolate off my cheek with one finger and brought it to my mouth. The scent of cocoa and rum wafted up my nostrils.

"It's too sweet…" As I grumbled to myself about the flavor again, under the sound of my own voice, I heard the ticking sound of metal hitting metal.

That particular sound has a coldness to it that sends a shiver up your spine. *This doesn't bode well*, I thought as I turned around to see Yukinoshita with a bowl in hand, stirring its contents with a spoon.

"…Oh yes, wasn't your job to taste-test, Hikigaya? You haven't been the slightest bit useful all this time, so I'd completely forgotten. I would very much like to hear your opinion of this," she said as she spun her spoon around to point the handle at me. There was a thick glob of black chocolate on the proffered utensil.

"That's got to be over ninety percent cacao. It's gonna be bitter…" I didn't need to eat it to know that. There was definitely no sugar or whipped cream added to this—maybe salted butter at most. The gleaming luster of the chocolate and the smell were both very cacao.

But Yukinoshita's eyes remained locked on me, with no indication she would back down. She slid another step forward, silently holding out the spoon to me. No way in hell was I taking it.

As we glared at one another, Yuigahama cut between us. "Ah, here! What about mine?!" she asked, offering a bowl of light-brown, sloshy fluid. It would be impertinent to even call it chocolate anymore; it wasn't even thick enough to call it chocolate sauce—it was so liquidy, I think I'd buy it if someone said it was Van Houten Milk Cocoa.

A sweet scent wafted up from the bowl thrust under my nose.

"I think you'll probably like this…" She smiled with an *ehe-heh* as she held the bowl out to me, and when I examined its contents once more, I got this weird sense of déjà vu. Along with the cloying sweetness was the faint scent of coffee. There was a whitish tinge to the light-brown fluid, and bubbles in it that indicated some viscosity…

It's kind of like MAX Coffee…

But Yuigahama was the one to make this… It's definitely not going to taste what it looks like… She's a jack-in-the-box when it comes to flavor. Wait, wasn't she making chocolate?

On one side, there was a dark mass that you could tell was bitter without even having to taste it. On the other side was a dark mass of unpredictable flavor. *So sweet and bitter, I feel like my head will spin!*

With both girls offering their work to me, I didn't know what to say. "H-hold on a second?"

As I was hesitating, there was a rattle as the door to the kitchen was flung open, and then the clicking of disgruntled heels across the floor.

The source of the sound came straight over to me, then blew a sigh like a gust escaping the depths of hell.

"Geez, it's so sweet in here…" The one muttering that as hatefully as if she'd just detected miasma could only be one person: Shizuka Hiratsuka-chan (single, thirtyish)!

Miss Hiratsuka seemed real unhappy about this, but there was no sweet atmosphere to be found here…

"Um, why are you here, Miss Hiratsuka?" Yukinoshita asked, confused.

"Hmm? Ah, Isshiki made a report to me. I came to check on things, just in case," the teacher replied with a tired sigh. And then when she looked into the bowls Yukinoshita and Yuigahama were holding, she chuckled low. "I forgot to mention it, but it's forbidden to bring chocolate to school."

"I don't remember that rule." Yuigahama tilted her head.

Miss Hiratsuka smiled wickedly. "There's no school rule. But it's forbidden anyway. It has nothing to do with your studies, and it's a distraction. A distraction! Why do you think I agreed to abolish obligatory chocolate from the staff room? Partly because it's a hassle, but also so we can make students taste the same bitterness. Emotions burn all the brighter when there are obstacles in the way. It's very purposeful."

She smiles so beautifully as she says the worst things! That's just what I love about her! But actually, I think some stories might begin with obligatory chocolate! I'd be very happy to solicit people who will take chocolate from Miss Hiratsuka, and also people who will take Miss Hiratsuka herself!

"Either way, there's no school on Valentine's due to entrance exams," Miss Hiratsuka said, and then a soft smile crossed her face as she added, "I'm messing with you." Her gaze turned to the bowls in Yukinoshita's and Yuigahama's grasps as she petted both their heads happily. "Well, good luck."

Yuigahama gave a confused *ummm* as she smiled awkwardly, while Yukinoshita jerked her face away. Miss Hiratsuka grinned back at them a little darkly, and she gave them both one last pat on their heads.

×   ×   ×

I wouldn't say it was thanks to Miss Hiratsuka, but the presence of an intruder changed the mood of the room a little. All the sugar in the air was slowly joined by a sense of peace as well.

And then someone else showed up—someone who was like a symbol of that peace.

Her bluish-black hair was cut to shoulder length and tied in two pigtails, and she was equipped with a perfectly fitted children's apron. I remembered her face clearly—with features like that, you knew she'd grow up to be beautiful.

Keika Kawasaki. Kawa-something's little sister.

After picking up Keika from preschool, Kawasaki arrived a little late with shopping bags in hand, and once she was done briskly getting her sister ready to cook, she sighed in satisfaction, then snapped a picture for the memories.

She must have been the one to put in the extra effort to tailor the apron to Keika's size. The appliqué and her name embroidered on it were very cute.

Once Kawasaki was done taking pictures, she seemed to realize she had yet to prepare herself. She beckoned me over to her with little waves. "U-um," she said hesitantly, "I'd like to leave for a bit to get ready…"

Hmm. I don't know what sort of "getting ready" she'd have to leave to do, but girls have their reasons. I'd already had it on good authority from Komachi that if you probe too deeply at times like these, she'll get mad at you. And besides, there were lots of people she didn't know here, plus all the dangerous cooking tools and such. She must have been worried about taking her eye off Keika.

"Ah, I'll be watching her, so don't worry," I said.

"O-okay, then…," Kawasaki said as she nodded back at me, then strode out of the kitchen.

I watched her go, then turned back to Keika.

She must have been tired from preschool or from getting those photo-of-a-lifetime shots taken by Kawasaki just now. Her eyelids were sagging, and she looked a little sleepy.

But then she looked up at me, blinked a few times, and opened her mouth wide. "It's Haa-chan!" She apparently remembered me, too, as she stretched her short arm as far as it would go to point up at my face.

"Yeah, that's right. I'm Haa-chan. Though actually it's Hachiman. Don't point at people, hey. Or you get the point of a stick."

With a huff, I squatted down so we could be on eye level. While I was at it, I pointed back at her and poked at her cheek. *Oh no, it's so soft…*

As I high-speed poked and mushed her cheek, a very confused Keika responded with a weird *auu, auu* sound like a seal in her confusion. …*Hmm, discipline complete. Now she'll think twice about pointing.*

Though I was satisfied, her cheek was so soft, I couldn't quite bring myself to pull away my finger. *Oh no, it really is so soft… Komachi was like this, once… Oh, I wonder if her cheeks are still soft now…?* I thought as I went in with even more soft poking.

Keika looked bothered, but then she went *ohhh* like she was struck with an idea. "Hya!"

Her attack went *boop* right into my cheek with zero hesitation.

"Ow... Hey, I said not to point. What if you got me in the eye?"

So I poked her some more to discipline her. Now she thought this was a game, shrieking in laughter and poking back at my cheek in revenge. *H-hmm... Maybe discipline has failed.*

So what do I do now? I was wondering as I poked Keika's cheek some more, and a cold voice came down on me from behind.

"...Hey, what're you doing?"

"Huh? Uh, nothing..."

When I turned around, there was Kawasaki in an apron. She had a bowl of chocolate chunks in her hands as she looked down at me with judgmental eyes. She blew a deep sigh, then opened her mouth, possibly struggling to find the words. "Listen, you watching her is a big help, but that sort of thing is, um..."

"No, no, wait. This isn't what it looks like." A dangerous, rotten-eyed man poking a cute little girl's cheek... From appearances alone, it's 100 percent criminal. If I were outside, I could even envision the incident being reported in the neighborhood newsletter, and the moms would laugh at me, *Isn't this you, cackle, cackle, cackle*, while I'd have nothing to say for myself and just go *Uhhh...* On top of that, the silent *But I trusted you...* in Kawasaki's eyes was weirdly painful, and it made my heart twinge with guilt.

"I'm just, um..." I stood up and raised my hands, showing I had no intention of resisting as I searched for the next string of excuses.

But then something stuck to my leg. Looking down, I found Keika hugging my waist. "I was keeping Haa-chan company."

"Uh-huh, well, yeah..." I'd meant to be the one keeping her company, but from another angle, it could be taken as the little girl messing with me. And given how her cuteness and the softness of her cheeks had utterly played me, I really couldn't say for sure that was wrong.

To have a man wrapped around her finger at this age—she's a force to be reckoned with...!

Well, it was clear there were high hopes for her in the future. Her older sister Saki Kawasaki was, as you can see, what most people would think of as beautiful. The problem is that at a glance, she comes off kinda delinquent-ish, even girl-gang-ish.

But there was nothing intimidating or scary about the way she looked at her sister. "...I see." A smile crossed Kawasaki's face, as if Keika's cherubic manner had knocked any hostility out of her, too.

Then Keika got the same big smile and, still stuck to my side, cocked her head adorably. "You wanna play, too, Saa-chan?"

"I-I'm not going to play! Come on, Kei-chan, come here." Kawasaki pulled Keika away from me and squeezed her tight in her own arms.

Uh, no need to be so cautious. I won't do anything, okay?

Anyway, it seemed like I could avoid causing an incident, police reports, or arrest. I let out a relieved breath.

But Kawasaki did not feel the same. Even as she petted Keika's head, her eyes were moving, scanning the kitchen as she said, "Was it really okay for me to bring her?"

I could see where she was coming from. Just about everyone there was a high schooler. And there were kids from another school, too, so Keika's presence was really odd. But this wasn't exactly a public event, and it wasn't as if we'd set any clear rules, either.

I glanced over at the table diagonally across from me. Haruno was there, chatting with Meguri. If Haruno was here, there was no point quibbling over who had the right to participate.

"Well, I'm sure it's fine. A bunch of other people are here, too," I said.

Kawasaki seemed convinced. "Yeah..."

Well, one of the reasons this event was being held at all was because she'd come to consult with us. I felt bad that we'd made the atmosphere uncomfortable for her, but I'd fulfill her request, at least... Not that I was doing anything myself directly.

As I was casting all around in search of the one who was going to be fulfilling that request, I heard the pitter-patter of hurried footsteps behind me.

"Ohhh, Saki. You made it!" came Yuigahama's cheerful call. Yukinoshita was following behind her. "And good to see you again, too, Keika-chan!" Yuigahama said as she squatted down to pet her head. Yuigahama and Yukinoshita had both met Keika for the Christmas event, so they knew her.

Yukinoshita approached Keika as well, but she just kept reaching out her slightly raised hand a bit, then pulling it back again. It seemed she couldn't quite figure out if it was okay to give her a pat or what. *She's so awkward*, I thought.

But she wasn't the only one.

After some waffling about how to greet them, a very embarrassed-looking Kawasaki murmured, "Um…thanks…for today…"

Whatever Keika thought about her sister's behavior, she was looking up at her with an open-mouthed expression. But then she straightened her posture and made a deep bow. "Thank you very much."

She must have learned it at preschool—she said it in a drawn-out tone, but you could feel a friendliness in her words that contrasted with her sister's curt manner, and seeing it made my face relax in a smile. Meanwhile, Yuigahama was going *yeek* as she squirmed around at the cuteness, and Kawasaki was getting a little misty-eyed over her sister's growth.

Yukinoshita's lips pulled into an affectionate smile, too. Pressing down the hem of her skirt with a stroke, she squatted down to meet Keika at eye level and said to her slowly, "Yes. And thank you for coming. All right, then what kind of sweets should we make?" she asked.

Keika looked up at Kawasaki, and Kawasaki nodded back. "Kei-chan, what sort of sweets do you want to eat?"

Keika briefly went blank, but then she suddenly opened her mouth to say, "Eel."

"O-okay… I see…" Those were the only words I could find. *I see… Eel, huh…?*

"Sorry, our family had eel recently, and she's been really into it ever since." Kawasaki looked down awkwardly.

But kids will often say pretty nonsensical things. She probably hadn't given it much thought, just said whatever had left an impression on her... There was no point in taking it seriously.

Or so I thought, but Miss Yukinoshita here has her hand on her chin and is thinking about it seriously...

"So then, Unagi Pie? I could make the pastry, but I'd have to do a little research into how they deal with the eel powder..."

"Whoa, you can just make those things?" I said.

"Yes," Yukinoshita answered as if it were obvious.

She can make anything off the rack at the convenience store, huh? And yet she can't do anything about her own rack...

"Would you like to give it a try?" Yukinoshita asked.

Face bright red, Kawasaki shook her head hard. "I-it's fine, whatever! Just teach me the normal stuff, something even she could make..."

"All right. So then perhaps something like truffles... I'll go get some additional ingredients," Yukinoshita said, and she went toward the teaching lectern at the front of the kitchen.

While waiting for her, figuring I was babysitting now, I looked over at Keika.

And then Yuigahama stole away my babysitting job. Heedless of how it made her skirt flap up, Yuigahama squatted down and got into an enthusiastic conversation with Keika. "Eel, huh, I get that! That makes me kinda want to try something like that, too!"

"Eel is so good! And, and there's sauce and rice with it, too."

"Right! Eel is really good, huh?"

"Yeah, the rice is good."

"Huh? The rice...?"

They didn't seem to be having the same conversation, but they both appeared to be enjoying themselves. With Yuigahama, I think she's serious about trying to make Unagi Pie, unfortunately.

But regardless, with Yukinoshita and Kawasaki there, Keika would be well managed. And it looked like it'd be a while before I was up for taste-testing, too.

I'll just go hang around somewhere until it's my turn on deck.

$$\times \quad \times \quad \times$$

Once Kawasaki and Keika had gotten started making chocolates under Yukinoshita's direction, my babysitting job was completely over. I was yet again fully unemployed. When you're out of work long enough, you wind up thinking maybe you'll go pick up rocks by the riverside to sell them or something. Or no, that's *The Man Without Talent*, huh?

As for Hayama, who was also there under the pretext of taste-testing like me, he was still firmly in Isshiki's and Miura's grasp, while the other guy doing his best to get a taste-testing job, Tobe, was being his loud self near Ebina and annoying everyone.

Haruno and Meguri had been chatting with Miss Hiratsuka the whole time. Both old and new members of student council were doing the rounds of all the tables, but Vice Prez and Miss Secretary were occasionally having smiley conversations. *Seriously, do your job, Vice Prez.*

With Tamanawa leading, the Kaihin crowd was having a round-table discussion at their square table. But seeing how their hands weren't doing any cooking, were they having another thought shower?

At this point, I really was the only one with nothing to do.

So I was just zoning out for the time being, watching from a spot where I wouldn't get in everyone's way, when in the corner of my eye, the door to the kitchen opened slightly.

The one with their hand on the draw must have been checking inside, as the door opened a little but then stopped.

What's this...? Maybe there's been a complaint from another group using the community center, saying we're too loud...?

It seemed I was the only one who noticed the door moving, so I was more or less compelled to go check on it.

I strode up to the door but then hesitated a second.

Yikes, what if it's some pretty young lady…? If she came in to belt out a string of complaints, I'd totally cave. But still, a corporate slave takes it for granted that someone is going to be angry with them. It's their job to get yelled at by people. Ah well. And I'm unpaid, too. No financial return. I'm at the point of no return. Sixth layer of the Abyss. Unpaid in Abyss.

Steeling myself, I pulled the door handle, and it rattled roughly open.

And there was someone I knew well.

He looked like he was coming back from his club, in a loose wind-breaker and baggy track pants. His sleeves were overlong, with only his fingertips peeking out of the cuffs, folded in front of his chest anxiously. Maybe it was just because of his general demeanor, but when he stood there with his back slightly hunched, even the nylon-y material of his jacket looked soft.

And when his eyes met with mine, he broke into a sparkly smile. "Hachiman!"

"T-Totsuka… You came."

"Yeah. I was at club for a little while, though, so I'm here late."

The one at the door was my classmate Saika Totsuka. I'd mentioned the event that day when our paths crossed at school, but I never expected he'd actually come.

"Oh, I'm so glad. I thought maybe I'd gotten the wrong place," he said, looking over at the Kaihin group. Oh, they must have been the only ones Totsuka had been able to see through the cracked-open door.

Mm-hmm, some things you can't see when you've got tunnel vision, huh?

Like for example, the presence of the one behind Totsuka at that moment.

"Hachimaaan!"

The one behind Totsuka was my… Just what is he to me, actually? Well, let's call him my gym class partner. My gym class partner, Yoshiteru Zaimokuza. I don't see him much at school, and I hadn't said a word to him about what we were doing that day, either, but I'd kinda had a feeling he'd come. Why? Because he's Zaimokuza. Don't think about it too hard.

"So what about you, Zaimokuza? What do you want? You're already leaving?" I asked.

Zaimokuza cleared his throat in a deliberate-sounding way. "Hapum, hapum. Not long ago, when I was with Sir Totsuka, Scholar Hiratsuka sent me on a quest. Therefore, I shan't yet return."

"She sent you on an errand? You're still not leaving?"

"Hark, I just *spake* to you I shan't yet return." Zaimokuza waved his hands vigorously in front of his chest as he replied with a speech affectation from who knows where (or when).

But anyway, what was this errand Miss Hiratsuka sent him on…? I was wondering, when Totsuka lowered the bag over his shoulder with a *huff*.

"Um, she told us to go get something…," Totsuka said as he began to rummage around inside the bag.

That was when Miss Hiratsuka noticed us and came over. "Oh, you're here. Did you run into any trouble picking them up?"

That moment, Totsuka found what he was after from inside the bag and let out a *phew* before giving it to the teacher with a bright smile. "No—here you go."

The rustling bundle he handed over was a bunch of the freezer bags they give you for taking things home when you buy food or groceries from an underground department store or a place like that. Miss Hiratsuka accepted the gleaming silver bags with a thanks to show her appreciation, then began to examine the contents.

"What's that?" I asked.

"Hmm? Oh, glad you asked. I'll open them up over there." Bringing the bags with her, Miss Hiratsuka strode briskly back to the window side of the cooking room, where she'd been before. Pulling out a nearby chair, she sat down with a thump. Humming and looking quite cheerful all the while, she began to lay out the contents of the freezer bags.

"You're all eating together afterward, right? So I was thinking I'd get you something, both for munching and for reference. But I wound up ordering too much. And then I ran into these two while I was out, so I asked them to grab them for me."

"Huh, I see," I said.

At this time of year, you can get famous brand-name chocolate from confectioneries, department stores, and even online. Miss Hiratsuka must have used one of those services, then sent Zaimokuza and Totsuka to go pick them up.

But it seemed she'd ordered more than just one or two—she opened a number of freezer bags with different shop names on them and pulled out the contents.

The spread of high-quality chocolates drew attention even from a distance, and I could feel eyes on us.

Among the various onlookers, Haruno jumped on it with the most enthusiasm. She and Meguri strolled over and checked each one with deep interest.

"Ohhh, Shizuka-chan, you splurged, huh? I'm not surprised to see Godiva, but you've even got Pierre Hermé and Jean-Paul Hévin... And then Emperor Hotel and New Otani, too... Oh, and there's even Sadaharu Aoki."

"Heh, I might have. Just a bit." Miss Hiratsuka must have been pleased that Haruno had recognized their value, as she preened a little.

My opinion was that chocolate was still just chocolate, but apparently, this was one of those things where if you knew, you knew. Of course, even I've heard of Godiva, but it seemed there were a bunch of other famous ones, too. Was that other stuff Haruno said French? Maybe? I dunno.

What'd she just say? Pi, Pie... Pierre Taki? Jean Pierre...Polnareff? I don't really know them, but anyway. Chocolates from famous places, I guess.

After opening the fancy packaging, Miss Hiratsuka lined up the chocolates into a display as dazzling as the show window of a jewelry store.

Meguri sighed. "Wow, they look so good..."

"Aha, I knew you'd have a discerning eye, too, Meguri," said Haruno. "These are really good. I recommend them."

"Wait, what are you acting so proud for? I'm the one who picked them," Miss Hiratsuka grumbled sourly at Haruno, who was puffing out her substantial chest and acting like a know-it-all.

Ahhh, Shizuka-chan is impressive as ever, loading all her stats into her hobbies… The car she drives seems super-expensive, too… Pouring all her money and passion into what she loves is so manly and cool.

I couldn't help but gaze at her with respect for her principle of focused opulence.

I wasn't the only one, though—Totsuka was staring at the teacher, too. "So you like sweets, Miss Hiratsuka?"

With Totsuka's sparkling eyes on her, Miss Hiratsuka was struck speechless. "…Y-yeah, kinda… Does it, uh, not make sense for me?" Her shoulders slumped.

"Oh, I—I didn't mean that… I—I think it suits you!" Totsuka hurriedly backpedaled.

Seeing that, Haruno giggled like she was amused. "For you, Shizuka-chan, you'd have them as a side with drinks, right? Nice, I'd like to have a drink with great chocolates like these, too."

"It's true—I am the type to drink with chocolate…but not today." Miss Hiratsuka shot her a glare, and Haruno puffed up her cheeks with a pouty *boo*.

It was a little surprising to see them talk like this.

Haruno Yukinoshita's actions always seem calculated, and she teases people a lot, too. But the way she'd just reacted to Miss Hiratsuka had seemed completely natural. Of course, maybe she could pull that off because her social mask was like a fortified armor shell.

I don't know Haruno Yukinoshita at all. Yukinoshita's older sister, Hayama's childhood friend, Meguri's senior, Miss Hiratsuka's former student, a Perfect Devil Superhuman with a good social mask—though I could learn of her through such superficial pieces of information, the essential parts of her were completely obscured to me, like a bottomless bog of muddy waters.

Come to think of it, I got the feeling this was the first I'd ever seen Haruno have an extended conversation with someone older than her.

I was taken aback, and as I stared at Haruno in a daze, the surface of that bottomless bog warped.

Haruno's shoulders dropped noticeably, and she slumped over the table to look plaintively up at Miss Hiratsuka. "That's too bad. You should keep me company sometime! We've got lots to catch up on, don't you think?"

It was a careless remark, easily taken as a social nicety.

Miss Hiratsuka responded to it with a serious gaze.

Her hands paused in their task of opening the chocolates, and she quietly folded her fingers together. Looking Haruno in the eye, she told her slowly and kindly, "Haruno. If you…actually have lots to catch up on, then I'll keep you company any time."

The moment that was out of her mouth, Haruno's shoulders twitched.

From where she was flopped forward over the table, her eyes, looking up at Miss Hiratsuka, were colorless like glasswork. But for just an instant, I could almost see a flicker of blue flame behind them.

The time their gazes crossed had to be less than a second, but it seemed much longer, and I even forgot to breathe.

A giggle from Haruno broke the silence, a smile with just the corners of her lips. "Really? Then we've got to check our schedules. Oh, you wanna come, too, Hikigaya? Come drink with some older ladies," she said jokingly, deliberately leaning toward me to look up at me through her lashes.

I smoothly avoided her, backing away. "I'm a minor. I can't have alcohol. Just give me orange juice, please."

Zaimokuza went *bfft* and burst out laughing. Miss Hiratsuka's earlier seriousness evaporated, too, her shoulders trembling.

If something had been communicated between the two of them, that also meant that others wouldn't get it at all.

Totsuka was tilting his head with an apparent question mark, and I don't know if Meguri understood or not, but she was still smiling brightly, while as for Haruno, her eyebrows were in an inverse V as her head remained cocked to the side.

"It's boring if you can't drink. Well, you're a minor, so that's the end of that. What about you, Meguri? You wanna go?"

"Haru, I'm a minor, too. I wouldn't mind some tea, though…"

"Ohhh, huh. Awww, what nooow? Guess I'll call up some classmates."

Watching Haruno click away on her phone, Miss Hiratsuka sighed deeply. "Well, call me sometime," she said, ending the conversation, before thrusting the packages from famous chocolatiers at me. "Hikigaya, Shiromeguri. Distribute these however you like and make sure everyone gets some."

"Okaaay. Um, how many each should I portion out?" Meguri replied, and then we began divvying up the various chocolates onto the paper plates at hand.

Miss Hiratsuka said we could hand them out however we liked, but Meguri really agonized over it for a while, *hmm-hmm*ing until she finally raised her face with a beaming smile. "Then here, Hikigaya. Please do the honors," she said and held out some paper plates to me. It seemed she'd found a way to portion them out that satisfied her, dividing up the sweets from each chocolatier in a well-balanced manner with a variety of colors. She proudly chuckled to herself, and before I knew it, I got Megu☆risshed...

"Sure thing." With a nod, I accepted the paper plates and stood, and Totsuka's and Zaimokuza's chairs scraped as they rose, too.

"Oh, I'll help."

"As shall I."

"Yeah, then let's all go together!" Meguri took up some paper plates and handed them to the others, and we plodded over to each table. But still, the people we were delivering to weren't exactly spread out. If you were to broadly divide them, there were basically three groups.

Meguri headed toward the Kaihin student council, while Totsuka went to the Kawasaki sisters, Yukinoshita, and Yuigahama. Zaimokuza just accompanied Totsuka like a shadow.

Right, so then what's left is the table where Miura and Isshiki are facing off.

As I eyed them from a distance, Miura was giving Isshiki a sharp look, which Isshiki turned aside with a composed smile, while Hayama, caught between them, maintained a charming grin the whole time. Tobe was so busy talking to him and trying to throw him a life raft that he didn't seem to have a moment to spare to try to get Ebina's attention.

Hmm...looks pretty bad. Actually, I don't wanna go anywhere near that situation.

Though I'd somehow managed to approach to their table, I was worrying about how I should talk to them to hand over these snacks when Hayama noticed me.

"Pardon me for a second," he said breezily to excuse himself, then slipped between Miura and Isshiki to come toward me. "Did you need something?"

"Ah, yeah. Miss Hiratsuka said this is, like, a present," I said, and when I held out the paper plate, Hayama's expression clouded slightly.

"More chocolate, huh…?"

"They're supposed to be good."

"…I see." With that short reply, Hayama accepted the paper plate, then strode back to his table.

Well, now it was mission complete. Since I had finished my job of handing over the chocolate, I was about to head right back when I heard a light metallic clink behind me.

The unfamiliar sound made me turn around, and I saw Hayama flicking a canned coffee with a finger. He lightly shook the two cans in his hands, wordlessly asking me with a little smile, *Want one?*

Well, being caught between Miura and Isshiki this whole time, even The Hayama would feel a little tired. Maybe he wanted to use me as an excuse to rest a bit. It wasn't like I had anything better to do.

I gave a little nod yeah, and Hayama sat down at the table one away from where Miura and Isshiki were, offering me a chair as well.

When I sat down, Hayama put down the canned coffee before me with a *clink*. The brand was not MAX Coffee, and it was black. When I scrutinized the can, Hayama smirked at me.

"Would you rather have a sweet one?"

"It's fine." Even I didn't want to be drinking something sweet right then. We were about to have chocolate, after all. Accepting the can and popping open the tab, I took a big gulp.

Hayama also downed some coffee, then blew out a *phew*.

Neither of us had anything to talk about, and the only sound between us was the clink of cans against the table and the call-and-response of the odd sigh, traded intermittently instead of conversation.

Around when the weight in my hand was telling me my drink was nearly done, Hayama suddenly opened his mouth to say, "But anyway. This was a great idea."

"Huh?" I replied with a serious look, not understanding what he meant by this sudden remark.

He smiled kindly, looking very much like the Hayato Hayama everyone knew so well. "With this setup, everyone…everyone can act naturally," he said, then slowly scanned the kitchen. Following his gaze, I could see a number of things.

Miura, glaring at a scale with a serious expression; Isshiki, whistling as she used an oven; Yuigahama with her face covered in flour; and Yukinoshita, watching her and holding her head in her hands.

Eventually, Hayama's eyes returned to me. His expression seemed lonely, a slight wry smile that was very like the Hayato Hayama I knew.

The "everyone" Hayama described.

Who did that refer to? Who was included in his "everyone"? With this vague realization, I looked away from him, drinking down the harsh bitterness of the canned coffee.

When I didn't reply to his monologuing, Hayama suddenly went *pfft* and burst into laughter. "And now Tobe can get some chocolate, too, so he's happy," he said jokingly.

I looked over at Tobe, who had succeeded in getting to taste-test whatever Ebina was in the middle of making, and he was loudly going off about how it was so great and whoa or whatever. *Oh, he's been giving this his all, huh? …Although I think the challenges with Ebina are only going to get harder from here on out. For people like her, there are many stages in opening their heart.* She wasn't the only one; imagining someone else with a similar mental construction, I found myself smiling crookedly.

But for now anyway, I'd give Tobe props for putting up a brave fight. In my own way, though. "Not like I care about chocolate or Tobe, though… Especially Tobe."

"Ha-ha! You're so mean." Laughing, Hayama also tossed his bitter coffee back in one go. Giving the can a light shake, checking if it was empty, he stood to go throw out the can.

Miura must have caught sight of him then, as she called out to him in a plaintive, cutesy voice. "Hayatooo!"

"Coming," Hayama replied. He turned back one last time, giving me a brief "See ya," before he went off to the table where Miura and Isshiki were waiting.

I watched him go, then brought my empty coffee can to my lips one more time.

×　×　×

The highlight of the cooking class was almost here.

The quicker workers had already stuck their batter in the oven or their chocolate into the fridge to chill, entering the final stage before completion.

Despite all of Haruno's chattering, she'd largely finished her process without me even noticing it. And not just her—Meguri, who'd been helping the others along, as well as the old student council members, was also nearing the end. At this point, the only thing left was to pour the chocolate into molds or put on toppings and decorations and whatnot.

What kind of multitasking capacity does she have? She always comes through with accomplishments I can't even begin to understand, in more ways than one…

But even she must have gotten tired of helping out other people, as now she was butting in on Yukinoshita's business to kill time.

"What'd you make, Yukino-chan? Big Sis wants to taste-test, too!" Haruno kept bothering her, but Yukinoshita completely ignored it. Right now, she was supervising Yuigahama and Miura.

Under Yukinoshita's watchful eye, Miura was pouring batter into a pan, while Yuigahama was firmly pressing a cookie cutter into dough.

It seemed Haruno didn't like being blatantly ignored. "Heeey, Yukino-chaaan!" she whined.

"…Haruno. Yukinoshita seems busy right now." Hayama offered the two of them a strained smile, going to Haruno's side to pacify her. You'd expect all this racket would distract Miura, so maybe he was trying to be considerate.

Miura and Yuigahama weren't the only ones focused on their tasks. Isshiki was squeezing out whipped cream, her attention completely devoted to making her decorations cute. As for the Kawasaki sisters, Keika's whole face was covered in chocolate, but she'd finished off some things that looked like truffles, and Saki Kawasaki was busy taking pictures of her. *Uh, just how thoroughly do you plan to record this…?*

Everyone was busy with their work. *Maybe it's about time for my taste-testing job soon*, I thought as I zoned out while watching so as to avoid getting in the way.

That was when Orimoto wandered over. When she found me at loose ends, she said, "Hikigaya. Are there any extra chocolate molds?"

"Y-yeah… Hold on a sec."

The Kaihin group was almost done, too. Considering how much they'd loudly babbled on to each other about what they were going to make, it was surprising they'd made so much progress.

After I told Orimoto to wait, I went to Yukinoshita. "Sorry, do you have extra molds?"

"There's some over there, so if you need them, you may take them."

"Yeah, thanks."

I wasn't the one to make that reply.

The answer had come from Kaori Orimoto, who'd been following behind me.

When Orimoto popped up, Yukinoshita gave her a questioning look and fell silent. Then, since the voice giving instructions had paused, Yuigahama curiously glanced up.

Orimoto's Kaihin uniform stood out a bit among the Soubu High School crowd. She was gathering attention now, but she didn't seem bothered by it as she closely examined each and every mold.

Then suddenly, like it was nothing at all to her, she muttered, "…Oh yeah, have I ever given any to you, Hikigaya?"

The question had been a genuine one, and I couldn't help but make a face. *So she doesn't remember, huh? Of course she doesn't.*

Since middle school, Orimoto had been the sort of person to give obligatory chocolate to anyone, boy or girl, but I, who didn't even count as one of the faceless masses, had not been a recipient.

Indulging in a bit of nostalgia as I tried to remember how I'd reacted at that time, I wound up replying a little slow.

A number of throats cleared during that silence, and tableware clinked restlessly. When I looked over, I saw Yukinoshita with her hand on her chin, gaze focused on me, while Yuigahama was turning away and fidgeting with her hands, and Isshiki was making noises of comprehension as she nodded with deep interest. Meanwhile, Kawasaki was goggling at us, open-mouthed, and Tamanawa kept clearing his throat and blowing long sighs that tossed up his bangs. *Mr. Tamanawa, you're being just a mite obnoxious…*

"Uh…of course not." The memories of ancient history did not dig into my chest, and I think I was able to reply fairly naturally, for me.

Just as naturally, Orimoto cackled, loud and careless. "Oh, then I'll give you some this year."

"Huh? Well, uh, I see…" Her unexpected reply easily unraveled my attempt to handle this smoothly, causing me to stutter. Though you could actually call this my natural state, in a way… Yikes, I'm a creep, aren't I?

"Then once it's done, come have some," she said without hesitation, taking the molds and striding back to where she'd been.

If she's gonna be like that, then I can't refuse out of hand, but maybe she was just being polite… Agonizing over the question, I followed Orimoto's back with my eyes as she left.

Well, I'm sure this was just Kaori Orimoto's typical easygoing attitude, that I was misunderstanding something. It didn't mean anything. Now that I was able to not read into this fact, twist it or misinterpret it, and just accept it, I let out a little sigh along with a smile.

Looking back to the table with a mild feeling of satisfaction, my eyes met with those of Haruno, by the window.

She was grinning broadly, after watching our exchange apparently. Whatever she'd seen, she found it tremendously amusing.

Then that mild smile transformed into something sadistic. Her lips pulled slightly upward, a sharpness entering her narrowed eyes. She turned to Hayama. "That reminds me—a long time ago, you got some from Yukino-chan, didn't you, Hayato?"

She made it sound like she was talking to Hayama, while in fact, she spoke loud enough that anyone there could hear it.

Yukinoshita had committed to ignoring her so well, but now she finally reacted. She turned to Haruno with a startled look that turned into a silent glare.

Yukinoshita was not the only one there speechless; Miura froze on the spot, too. Isshiki mouthed a silent *Yikes*.

I pulled a face. *You didn't have to bring that up in front of Miura and Isshiki*, I thought as I scratched my head vigorously. Or tried to; I'm not sure when my fingers had curled into fists.

Yukinoshita didn't deny what Haruno had said, giving me an uncomfortable look instead. She seemed taken aback and bewildered by this dredging up of ancient history, and she was biting the edge of her lip as her eyes moved around restlessly.

I think I was probably giving a similar impression. Something was lodged firmly at the back of my throat like clogged phlegm, and I had this nasty feeling, like something scraping its way up from the pit of my stomach.

Yukinoshita's face turned down, and I looked away, too. And in the direction I turned, there was an anxious and concerned Yuigahama.

The silence was short, but it felt much longer than it was. I let out a deep sigh to break it, but I couldn't think of the appropriate thing to say.

"Yep, right around the end of elementary school. She gave some to both of us."

The one with the most correct answer for that occasion was Hayama.

With the most wonderful, charming smile possible, he answered smoothly and avoided the issue altogether. Haruno looked a little disappointed.

Miura breathed a sigh of relief, and Isshiki let out a reassured *phew* as well.

But Haruno Yukinoshita's expression turned cold. She eyed Hayama with casual disinterest, then moved away from the window side as if to say she was done here. Hayama watched her go with a tinge of sadness on his face.

Then Haruno came to stand by Yukinoshita. "So who do you plan to give this to, Yukino-chan?"

Her tone was teasing, her smile cheerful. If you weren't paying close attention to this, this would be a cute joke between sisters. The way Yukinoshita turned her face away would be easy to interpret as innocent sulking at her big sister's teasing.

"…It's not really any of your business."

"Aww, you won't give any to your big sis?" Haruno said jokingly with a giggle.

But Yukinoshita gave her a sullen little glare. "Of course I'm not. There's no reason for me to, and you haven't exactly given me any."

"Hmm, true." Haruno nod-nodded, apparently convinced. Then she sighed and smiled wryly. "Well, if you say you're not giving me any, then I know you definitely won't. You've never been one to lie."

I'd had a very similar impression of Yukino Yukinoshita before. But Haruno Yukinoshita's understanding of her was more comprehensive than mine had been then.

"But sometimes you don't say the truth." The temperature of Haruno's look had dropped now, to penetrating cold. She giggled. "You didn't say you wouldn't give them to anyone. So you must be giving them to *someone* after all."

Yukinoshita continued to keep silent, sending icy daggers her sister's way. But Haruno took it resolutely, maintaining her smile. "Well, though there are only a limited few people you'd give any to."

"This is silly. Say whatever you please." Yukinoshita moved her hands instead of her mouth, aiming to end the conversation. She reached out for the empty tray and bowl in front of her, making particularly loud rattling noises as she began the task of cleaning up.

With that little scene between the Yukinoshita sisters done, the kitchen regained its bustle and chatter with a distinct sense of peace.

I sighed, and then there was a loud clanging sound. Looking toward it, I saw a bowl spinning around on the floor toward me. As the noise resounded in the air, a weak voice joined it.

"I-I'm sorry…" Blushing red to her ears, Yukinoshita didn't even raise her head as she hurried over to pick up the bowl.

It's unusual for her to make a careless mistake, I thought as I squatted down to pick up the bowl at my feet.

Then my eyes met with hers, as we squatted down at the exact same moment. We were both frozen halfway, as if we were both trying to figure out whether to reach for it.

Face-to-face with only a few centimeters between us, my fingers almost touched her, and I jerked them back.

Why're you getting rattled? You're gonna shake me up, too.

"Uh…" Adding a brief "Sorry" as I turned away, I yielded the spot to her. Yukinoshita hastily reached for the bowl.

But the bowl was tipped over with its edge on the floor and was wobbling around too much to grab; with another clang, it rolled away.

The ringing sound as it kept rolling away was loud in my ears. Even once the bowl had come to a stop, the sound stayed in my ears and never stopped ringing.

The sound was finally silenced when someone scooped up the bowl.

Looking up, I saw Yuigahama spinning it around her fingers, chuckling smugly to herself. "Heh, you've still got a long ways to go, Yukinon. *I* manage bowls and cooking things perfectly."

Seeing her bright smile brought a sigh of relief from me. The thing that had been stuck in my chest this whole time melted away, freeing up a snarky remark that allowed me to stand. "…Uh, you're a disaster with everything else, though."

"Indeed… Thanks." Yukinoshita smiled, too, showing her appreciation to Yuigahama before reaching out to take the bowl from her. Yuigahama gave her a little nod back. But then after she handed over the bowl, she looked at her own empty palm in a way that seemed sad, and she lightly squeezed her fist.

The reaction bothered me, and I stared dumbly at her. I could have sworn I'd seen that look on her face before.

As I searched my memory, wondering just when that had been, I slid down and slumped into my seat by the wall.

When I groaned to myself, I got the feeling that someone, somewhere, giggled.

×　×　×

An appetizing aroma had begun to fill the kitchen.

There were a few people camped in front of the oven, waiting with anticipation for the baking to be done. Miura was the most serious of that group, continuously staring through the glass window.

Once the baking was finished, it would finally be time to taste-test. I would also be relinquishing my unemployment signboard to finally do my job.

So as to prepare for that time, I was taking a quiet break away from the crowd of people when there was a clap on my shoulder from behind.

I turned around to see Miss Hiratsuka standing there. She held a paper plate with some of the chocolates—there must have been some extras from her gifts.

"This has been a good event," she said, then pulled up a chair beside me and pushed the paper plate at me, urging me to have some.

Accepting one with gratitude, I replied, "Yeah, although it hasn't really made much sense as an event." I didn't even know if this technically counted. It felt like just a bunch of different people thrown together and doing what they wanted.

Maybe Miss Hiratsuka understood that, too, as she chuckled in amusement. Then she surveyed the kids in the kitchen with warm eyes. "That's fine. You don't exactly make much sense yourself. You or the people you hang out with. This was basically inevitable."

"I don't…? Don'cha think that's kinda mean?"

"Well, I suppose you've come to make a little more sense to me than before." Miss Hiratsuka gave a teasing grin, then popped a chocolate into her mouth. "You revise your impression of a person every day, through living and growing together."

"I don't really feel like I've grown, though. I'm always doing the same thing."

"But you still do change, a little," she said as she munched on the chocolate before gulping it down and wiping her lips with her thumb. The gesture was less sexy and more boyish, and it made me chuckle.

It was true; maybe my impression of Miss Hiratsuka had changed a little. So the way others saw me would have done the same.

But in that change, there was a fear I couldn't put into words.

"Have I...changed? Hearing that feels kind of weird," I said.

"Does it?" Miss Hiratsuka tilted her head, then quietly examined my face.

Embarrassed, I jerked my face away as I hurriedly continued. "Uh, it just feels kinda wrong."

When I tried putting that into words, those words actually seemed to fit.

It was something that had been dogging me all this time.

At moments, I'd become aware of it, of this thing that was clearly different from before. Every time I engaged with someone, it'd suddenly well up from the inside, and I'd start asking myself, *Is this right?*

"Kinda wrong, huh? ...I hope you don't forget that feeling," Miss Hiratsuka said with a hint of nostalgia in her voice as she looked far off into the distance. The way she spoke, it was like she was talking to me, but also like it was directed at someone else.

But it turned out she actually was addressing me, as her eyes came back to my face. "I think that's a sign of legitimate growth. Once you're an adult, you get good at pushing that aside. So right now, I want you to take a good look at it. It's something important."

"They say you can't see the important stuff, though," I shot back.

She chuckled. "Don't look with your eyes. Look with your heart."

"What, like, 'Don't think, feel'? This isn't the Force..." *What's she talking about? Why is she smirking? She just wants to be in a* shonen *manga…*, I thought, giving her a dull look.

She seemed a little embarrassed, unsurprisingly, clearing her throat with a deliberate-sounding *gefum*. "It's the other way. Don't feel, think," she corrected, with none of her earlier humor on her face. Her eyes were entirely sincere and gentle as she spoke, slowly and quietly. "Keep on thinking about that feeling, always."

"Always?" I repeated that word, digesting it.

Miss Hiratsuka nodded. "Yes, always. Then you might eventually understand, right? While you're walking, you never look back on how far you've come. But for someone who's stopped walking, the distance you've moved forward will feel like a betrayal…" She cut off there, then gazed out at each of the people in the kitchen in turn. "I'm glad I got to see all this up close, right now," she said, then stood up with a *hup*. She clapped a hand on my shoulder and murmured, "…After all, I can't keep an eye on you forever."

By the time I turned toward her voice, she was already stretching wide with a *hnn*, trying to get the stiffness out of her shoulders and conveniently hiding her expression.

She cracked her neck, and then by the time she turned back to me again, she was the usual Miss Hiratsuka. "All right, time for me to get back to work."

"You're not gonna eat before you go?"

"Nah, I've got work piled up… There isn't much time now before March, so I want to get things dealt with." With a shy *ah-ha-ha*, she scratched her cheek. Then she raised a casual hand good-bye, giving it a flutter before she walked off. Heels clicking on the floor, Miss Hiratsuka jauntily strode out of the cooking room.

As I watched her go, I popped a chocolate into my mouth.

I'd just picked up one at random, and as it dissolved into me like my teacher's words, it left behind a faint bitter aftertaste.

He fails to reach the **"something real"** he's after and continues to get it wrong.

The oven and kitchen timers went off shrilly in succession. When they sounded, the kitchen filled with cheers and sighs, along with sweet, rich aromas.

From what I could see, watching the group clustered in front of the oven, it seemed Miura's wholehearted efforts had borne fruit.

She opened the oven with great trepidation, then took the French chocolate cake out from within to offer it to Yukinoshita.

Yukinoshita checked her work. She took her time—one breath's worth, then two as she examined it meticulously, while Miura was restless and fidgeting at her side, and beside her, Yuigahama was in utter suspense.

Eventually, Yukinoshita let out a short sigh and lifted her head. "…I'd say this is good. I think it's come out quite nicely," she said, and Miura exhaled as the tension in her shoulders dropped away.

"You're amazing, Yumiko!" Yuigahama grabbed Miura in a hug, and Miura gave a faint, soft smile.

"Yeah, thanks, Yui… A-and Yukinoshita." Though Miura's face was turned the other way, her eyes were flicking little glances back at Yukinoshita. It was a really weird way to say thanks, and the response she got back was strange, too.

"I can't say anything until I know how it tastes," said Yukinoshita, "but for now, I suppose I could call it a pass."

She just can't bring herself to say You're welcome, *huh...?* But Yukinoshita made a very reasonable point. The goal of this event was not just to learn how to make sweets.

"Yumiko." Yuigahama gave Miura's shoulder a gentle touch of encouragement.

So prompted, Miura carefully carried her cake over to Hayama, even forgetting to take off the oven mitts. She twisted around shyly.

"H-Hayato...would you mind...taste-testing this?" She examined him with indirect, flickering glances, like she couldn't look straight at him.

Hayama returned that look with a calm smile. "Of course. If you think I'm qualified."

"Yeah...yeah." It seemed like Miura was searching for the right thing to say, but in the end, she just nodded a few times with bright red cheeks.

Nice work. As I was giving her a mental round of applause, someone else nearby was groaning.

"Mmmgh..."

"What're you moaning about?" I said, glancing at Isshiki.

She was staring at Miura with resentment and carrying an assortment of finished baked goods that were prettily wrapped, with little attached cards, too. She was squeezing them tight in her hands. "Miura's doing pretty good, huh...?"

"Yeah, that cake came out surprisingly good," I said.

"Huh?" Isshiki eyed me like, *What the heck are you talking about? Could you maybe stop giving me that look...?*

Isshiki cleared her throat with an *ahem* and animatedly explained what she meant. "No, that's not what I mean, okay? It's, like, the contrast. Normally, she's so bitchy, so where does she get off acting cute *now*?!"

"Oh, that's what you mean..." *As expected of the master manipulator.*

Though I doubt Miura had a single conscious thought in her head about manipulation. That over there is just a girlish heart with a maternal spirit. Isshiki seemed to get that, too. "I mean, she's not *actually* a bitch…," she muttered

Yeah, you're the one with the personality issues here…

Isshiki was still grumbling to herself, but venting had apparently satisfied her. She chuckled. "Well, it's more fun with worthy competition. Some people out there aren't even worth competing with, after all." She sighed as if to say, *Good grief,* then suddenly seemed to remember something. "Oh yeah!" She rummaged around in the pocket of her apron to pull something out and toss it to me. "Have one of these. Since you're here."

Accepting it from her, I saw it was some cookies in a little plastic bag. Aside from the tiny ribbon that tied it shut, it wasn't wrapped at all, and it was a far cry from the elaborate set of baked goods Isshiki was holding.

"What, you're giving this to me? Thanks?" I said.

She'd handed it to me so apathetically, I wasn't sure if I should thank her genuinely or not. Which reminded me—she'd said something about a man's pride and whether he got obligatory chocolate, huh? *What the hell, Isshiki's a good person?! Sorry for thinking you were a jerk before, okay?*

Isshiki giggled at my thanks, then stuck up her index finger and brought it to her lips. "…Don't tell anybody, 'kay?" She winked at me with a devilish smile. "I don't wanna deal with people finding out," she said as she strolled away. She was heading straight for Hayama.

As for me, I was so taken aback by what Isshiki had just said and done, I was standing there, frozen. *That's way beyond manipulative. That's honestly just frightening… The old me might've been swept off his feet, you know?*

As I trembled in fear at the raw power of my manipulative junior, I decided to watch Hayama and his crowd to bear witness to her struggle.

Isshiki had her cutesy ☆ wootsy lashes-batting sweetheart act in high gear as she held out her set of baked goods to Hayama. "Please try these, too, Hayamaaa!"

"Ha-ha, I'm not sure I can eat them all." Hayama's breezy smile never broke as he ate Miura's chocolate cake, and he welcomed Isshiki in a mature manner. He was caught between the two girls yet again.

Then Tobe, who was crunching on some checkerboard cookies, gave Hayama a thumbs-up. "Hayato, if you're having a hard time finishing stuff, I can help any time."

"No, there isn't enough for you, Tobe…" Isshiki's cold tone took all the heat out of Tobe's enthusiasm, and he threw himself on Hayama after the harsh treatment.

"That's so mean! Right, Hayatooo?!"

"I appreciate the offer, but it would be best for you to focus on eating those, Tobe," Hayama said softly in Tobe's ear, and Tobe grinned once again, giving him a thumbs-up.

Ah, I see. I can infer those checkerboard cookies were made by Ebina. That's surprising… I looked over to the one who'd made them.

"Hmm, Hayatobe, huh…? Doesn't quite do it for me…" Ebina bit into a checkerboard cookie with dissatisfaction as she repeatedly tilted her head. I could see a whole 'nother set of difficulties on the horizon…

All right, how about everyone else? I thought as I looked across to the table opposite Miura's clique, where the Kaihin crowd was, and found they were also mostly done. They were chattering away loudly with Meguri and the present and former Soubu student council.

One person from that crowd, Kaori Orimoto, noticed my presence and waved at me. *Ahhh, still waving at me at times like these. She hasn't changed since middle school, huh…? Well, that was a long time ago. No problems here.*

There was some rustling as Orimoto finished up some task on the counter before trotting over to me.

"Hikigayaaa. Here," she said, and she held out to me chocolate brownies on a paper plate. Apparently, this was what she'd said she would give me. *Oh, there's no wrapping or anything, huh…? Still, I'm very grateful to get anything, kind Orimoto.*

"Then…" While quietly intoning my thanks, I munched on the soft brownie.

Then someone popped up from behind Orimoto. "Mmm, this form of engagement is also fortuitous, isn't it? I'm sure leaving the framework of the school and working on seamless relationships will be vital in the future after all."

Just hearing the way he talked, I immediately knew who it was—Tamanawa, the student council president of Kaihin High School.

When Orimoto noticed Tamanawa, she offered a plate to him, too. "Oh, you're here, too, huh, Prez? Then some for you."

"Th-thanks... Might as well give you mine, then." Tamanawa held something out to her: a neatly cut chiffon cake. It seemed this was his group's masterpiece.

Orimoto gave the cake a puzzled look. "Huh? Why?" she asked.

Tamanawa cleared his throat—*ahem, ahem*—and once again did that gesture like he was spinning a pottery wheel as he began his lecture. "In other countries, it's typical for the man to give a gift on Valentine's Day. For this event, I thought it would be a good idea to introduce *globalization*. I suppose this would mean being a sort of *influencer* in Japan."

"Hmm." Orimoto didn't offer him much of a reaction, though, and neither did she offer even a tepid *That could be a thing!*

Her lack of enthusiasm seemed to bother Tamanawa, as he spun his wheel faster and talked some more. "There's a lack of awareness, a *culture gap*, between Japan and other countries, you know. For example, in France, a skirt is worn with someone important to you—things like that."

Oh-ho... So in other words, the reason Totsuka doesn't wear a skirt is, in other words, because of that! I've got to try harder! That could be a thing!

And so with that thought, I renewed my determination as Orimoto reached out to pinch a bit of the cake.

"It's pretty good. Thanks," she said.

"Ah, uh-huh. Well...they're having a *kaffeeklatsch* over there right now, so I guess I'll get back."

"The heck is a *kaffeeklatsch*? That's hilarious." Orimoto cackled, then casually waved at me with a "See you" as she returned to the Kaihin group.

Then Tamanawa glared at me. "Then…may our next engagement be aboveboard." With that mysterious parting remark, Tamanawa briskly strode off.

"Uh, we're not gonna have an engagement, though…," I muttered. But did my voice even reach him? No, I doubt it. I doubt he'd hear anything that's not jargon.

But why was he acting that way just now? Was he making his own go of it? It didn't seem to reach Orimoto at all… Well, it's Tamanawa, so who cares!

Setting aside Tamanawa, I'd make an effort myself, too. Mostly to have Totsuka wear a skirt for me.

Hmm, Totsuka, Totsuka, skirTotsuka…, I was thinking, bursting with energy and drive as I looked for him and found him easily. I knew it—no matter where he is in the world, I'm pretty sure I could sense him right away!

When I sauntered over to him, he was with Zaimokuza, watching Keika. At the table to the side, Kawasaki was briskly cleaning up. The two of them were apparently babysitting while she was occupied.

But just looking at them, I could sense they weren't used to handling kids, as they were both struggling. Zaimokuza was totally frozen.

Totsuka was doing his best on his own, and he was looking a bit flummoxed as he talked to Keika. "Ummm… Nice to meet you, Keika-chan. I'm Saika Totsuka. Let's have some fun today."

"Ohhh. Saika… Saika… Saa-chan? S-Saa-chan…?" Hearing a name similar to her sister's seemed to leave Keika confused about what she should call Totsuka.

Yep, yep, I understand the confusion. Totsuka's so cute, he's made me feel confused, too. Hashtag confusion.

Well, I think I know what I'm doing when it comes to little girls. So I'd switch places with Totsuka here to handle this.

I sneaked up behind Keika, then clapped a hand on her head.

"Ah, Hachiman." Totsuka looked at me with relief, while Keika peered up at me with an angelic expression.

"It's Haa-chan!"

Rubbing a circle on top of Keika's noggin, I turned her head toward Totsuka. "It's Sai-chan. You can call him Sai-chan."

"Mm-hmm. Sai-chan!" That seemed to cure Keika's dilemma, and she identified Totsuka properly. Totsuka gave a little *ah-ha*, seeming glad to have Keika say his name.

All right, then now I guess we've got to deal with the other one, the statue behind Totsuka... "This is Yoshiteru Zaimokuza. You can call him Zai-chan," I said, jabbing my chin at Zaimokuza.

Keika nodded and pointed at him. "Zaimokuza."

"No *chan*?! I'm the only one without?! In our line of work, that's an honor!" Apparently, a little girl calling him straight by his name was surprising, even for Zaimokuza. His jaw had dropped open in shock. Or joy? Well, who cares, it's Zaimokuza, after all.

However, tenderhearted Totsuka would not forget to try to make him feel better. "H-hey, now. Kids are good at remembering strange words."

"H-hmm... But my name is not exactly a strange word...," Zaimokuza said, tilting his head as if he wasn't quite convinced.

Meanwhile, Kawasaki pattered back to us, swiftly wiping her hands on her apron, and Keika leaped on her while calling for Saa-chan.

"Sorry for making you watch her," said Kawasaki.

"Oh, no, it's totally fine. Hachiman came. Are you done cleaning up, Kawasaki?"

"Thanks to you." After showing her appreciation to Totsuka, Kawasaki gave me a hard look. She twisted up her mouth like she was struggling with the words. "Um, we're going back now... I have to make dinner," she said.

"Oh, yeah." Looking up at the clock, I saw it was getting to be about time. That had to be why Kawasaki had been rushing to clean up. She could've just left it for someone else, but she's a surprisingly considerate, good girl, huh? She's got strong housewife skills.

"Come on, Kei-chan. Let's go home." Kawasaki gently patted Keika's shoulder.

"Mm." Then Keika tugged at Kawasaki's skirt and whined, "...Saa-chan."

Kawasaki, being a big sister, could recognize she was being begged. "...Yeah. Hold on a bit," she said, snatching up a bag of chocolates to give to Keika.

Accepting them, Keika looked at the chocolates with satisfaction before holding them out to me. "Here, Haa-chan!"

"Um, she said she wanted to give them to you... Take them," said Kawasaki.

"Oh, thanks. These are well made. You did pretty good, Kei-chan." I rubbed a circle on her head, and Keika came close to hug around my waist. *Ha-ha-ha, you cute thing.* I patted her head more.

"...W-well, I might've made some of them," Kawasaki muttered as she put on her coat.

Now that she mentioned it, I looked at the truffles. "Oh, really? ...I can't tell them apart. Your little sister's amazing."

"Uh-huh! But you know, Saa-chan worked pretty hard, too." Keika praised her sister like she was the older one while puffing out her chest and chuckling smugly, while Kawasaki smiled with some exasperation.

"You've got to hand them over, so let's go, Kei-chan," she said, but Keika was still attached to me and wouldn't leave. Kawasaki gave Keika a glare. I could feel Keika twitch in response.

Uh, you don't have to make such a scary face, okay...?

"Okay, let's go, Kei-chan," I said to her, and with Keika still clinging to me, I walked out.

"Yep, let's go!" Keika started walking along with me. Heaving a sigh, Kawasaki followed.

"Bye-bye, Kei-chan. See you later."

"Aye, fare thee well!"

As Totsuka and Zaimokuza saw her off, Keika waved *bye-byyye*, going straight out the kitchen and down the stairs. As we went,

Kawasaki attentively dressed her, putting on her coat and wrapping her scarf.

It wasn't long before we reached the entrance of the community center, where it was already completely dark out.

"Want me to come to the station?" I asked.

"It's fine; this is normal. You've got things to do, too, don't you?" Kawasaki adjusted her grip on her school bag and shopping bags, and with a heave, she squatted down to scoop Keika up in one arm. Despite the flash of her skirt drawing my attention, I did everything in my power not to look. I get the feeling they were black lace, but I was definitely not looking.

"S-see you." Kawasaki lowered her head slightly as she said good-bye, and Keika, in her arms, responded after.

"Bye-bye, Haa-chan!"

"…Take care," I said to the two of them as they started walking home, watching them go as they grew distant.

The winter sky that night was completely clear, with no wind or clouds, but that just made the chill feel more intense. The two girls were pressed close to each other, so they didn't seem that cold. I kind of regretted coming outside without my coat.

I should've gone back inside right away, but strangely, my feet didn't move from that spot.

I swayed and plopped down on the stairs in front of the entrance and heaved a deep sigh. Though I really hadn't done anything at all, I still felt a little tired. But the sense of fulfillment outweighed it.

We'd heard requests from Miura, Ebina, and the Kawasaki sisters and held the event with Isshiki, then had Orimoto, Tamanawa, and the Kaihin kids—plus Meguri and Haruno—rush over, and even Hayama and Tobe had participated as taste-testers, with Totsuka and Zaimokuza coming, too, and Miss Hiratsuka showing up to bring us snacks.

All this was more than enough.

"This has been fun," I murmured, just to myself.

A stinging itch crawled around the line of my neck, and the corners of my lips drew up and froze there. The cold must have caused my cheeks to spasm.

I gave them an aggressive massage to warm them, then finally got up.

×   ×   ×

When I returned to the kitchen, nobody was cooking anymore; everyone was enjoying themselves eating sweets, drinking tea, and chatting.

And now, this pre–Valentine's Day event was just about done. All that was left was to relax for a while and let it come to a close.

When I headed to my seat, where I'd left my stuff, I found Yukinoshita there. She was setting out a teapot and cups with graceful gestures.

There was a kettle on the built-in kitchen stove, and it was just coming to a boil. Yukinoshita was pouring water from that kettle to make tea.

Arrayed before her were not the familiar cups of varying types, but paper cups. Of course she wouldn't have bothered to bring ours all the way here.

Yukinoshita poured tea into the paper cups, three servings' worth, and sat down. When she noticed me approaching, she called out, "Oh, thank you for your efforts today."

"I didn't actually expend much effort, though," I replied as I sat down.

Yukinoshita held out a paper cup to me, a teasing look in her eye. "Oh? You seemed to be whisking all around the kitchen, though."

"Whisking…"

Because we were baking? Is that the joke? I did kind of feel like the exhaustion from all that brisk whisking was hitting me rather hard. But I definitely had been scrambling, so that was difficult to deny.

"Now we can finally relax," Yukinoshita said as she brought her tea to her lips. I decided to have mine as well and blew on it.

The paper cup wasn't very sturdy, unlike my usual cup, and I could feel the heat going straight into my hand and making me slow down. But still, since I'd been outside just moments earlier, it was enough to warm my chilled body. I took a couple of sips, then let out a satisfied sigh.

Glancing over, I saw Yukinoshita was doing the same, but with more fatigue.

"Thanks for your efforts, too," I said to her.

"Yes. Well… It was a lot of work," Yukinoshita said as her gaze slid to the oven.

The one standing there was Yuigahama.

Oven mitts equipped on her hands, she pulled a baking sheet out from the oven and pattered toward us. *Ahhh, I see.* Yukinoshita hadn't been watching over only Miura's and Kawasaki's work. She'd been guiding Yuigahama's baking, too. Well, that would be exhausting.

"Hikki! Try these!" Yuigahama came over to show off the tray of chocolate cookies she'd made like, *Ta-daa!* It seemed she'd been waiting in front of the oven the whole time they were baking, and the fragrant scent of fresh baking wafted off her cookies.

They looked like normal cookies. Though their shapes were a bit irregular, they weren't blatantly burned, and from what I could see, there were no foreign objects mixed into them, either. So far, so good.

Now then, what remained to be seen was the flavor.

I examined Yuigahama in front of me. Her eyes were filled with sparkling hope, her shoulders fidgeting anxiously, and her smile seemed to be a mask for her uncertainty.

If she's gonna look at me like that, then I have to have one…

I gulped. Of course, I wasn't swallowing any spit. If anything, I was swallowing my determination!

"…Okay, I'll have one." *Take a deep breath in and out and roll up your sleeves!*

When my hand reached out, Yukinoshita, at my side, suddenly opened her mouth to say casually, "You appear to be bracing yourself for the worst, but it's all right. I did make them with her, just in case."

"…Oh, then I'm good."

"Hey, that was mean!" Yuigahama wailed.

The tension in my shoulders slid away with a *phew*, and I tossed a cookie in my mouth with a feeling of relief. After some crunching,

I swallowed. I waited a bit, but no strange effects on my body ever came.

"…Wow, you can eat them like normal." I couldn't help but blurt my honest opinion.

Yuigahama's cheeks puffed up in a sulky expression. "What's that supposed to mean…? Of course you can eat them. They're food."

Uh, knowing your cooking skills, this is high praise, you know?

But I really was surprised. Yuigahama had put genuine effort into this. *Well, I'm sure Yukinoshita's guidance had something to do with it…*

When I looked at Yukinoshita, she was sweeping her hair off her shoulders with pride. "Well, of course. I made sure to monitor you through every single important step."

"You were monitoring me?! I thought you were just teaching…" Yuigahama wilted slightly.

But in the Yukinoshitan dialect, *surveillance* and *education* mean just about the same thing, so there was no cause for concern. It didn't seem Yukinoshita actually cared much about the difference in the two words, and at this moment, she was transferring the cookies from the pan to a paper plate for inspection.

Then she put a hand to her chin and nodded. "It seems there's no problem. And the taste-testing has gone well. I suppose I'll have one, too."

"Like I said before, it's more like testing for poison…," I said. "Why're you giving me the dangerous job?"

"Don't call it poison! And hey, I'm having some, too."

The three of us sat down once again and reached out for the cookies. The texture was flaky, the scent of butter rising to our noses. The soft sweetness and the aftertaste of the bitter chocolate was irresistible.

"…Mmm," Yuigahama said after having one, and Yukinoshita nodded in response. The two of them looked at each other, and then Yuigahama giggled with pleasure, and Yukinoshita smiled at her, too.

Then Yuigahama spun her whole body around to me. "They're good, right? Right?"

"Uh, like I said, they're normal. And that's good." *I already said that, right? Didn't I say that?*

Yuigahama's eagerness had pressured me into an answer, but my response made the girls' expressions darken slightly.

"Normal..."

"Normal, huh?"

Yuigahama's shoulders dropped slightly, and Yukinoshita shot me a little glare.

Um, hold on a minute, what else should I say at a time like this...? I pulled up the *Compendium of Big Bro Hachiman Hikigaya Sayings* from my brain and mobilized all my vocabulary for Komachi-directed use.

"Ahhh...uhhh. Well, they're also just, y'know...really good... Thanks," I said timidly, hesitantly, carefully, and falteringly, and Yuigahama broke into a bright smile, while Yukinoshita's gaze softened.

"Yeah!" Yuigahama answered with energy. Yukinoshita stayed silent as she poured me another cup of tea.

Phew. Komachi, looks like Big Bro managed to pull out the right answer...

Even though I had to use mental Komachi for reference, the cookies were honestly good, and my gratitude was sincere.

Between sweet cookies and warm tea, I was fulfilled. Or I thought I was. So even if it was just under my breath, once more, I whispered to myself, "This was fun."

But there was that feeling that something was wrong.

Just as I noticed it, I heard the click of heels on the floor.

Those footsteps were not trying to hide the sound of their approach, and in fact they seemed to want to be noticed, coming one step closer after another until they finally took form.

Noticing the sound of heels, Yukinoshita flicked her gaze behind me. Her brow knit in a scowl.

That alone was enough to tell me who it was. Haruno Yukinoshita.

"Do you need something?" Yukinoshita asked.

But Haruno didn't reply. She just looked straight at me, without saying a word, then slid a finger over her glossy lips before slowly opening them. "Is this that something real you mentioned before, Hikigaya?" she asked, and instantly, an icy shiver ran up my spine. I instinctively turned away from her.

But she wouldn't let me run, closing the distance between us with a step. "Is spending your time like this what you meant?"

"...I dunno. Maybe."

That meaningless reply was all I had.

Haruno's voice had a coldness to it, but also a purity. Like this was a confession she really just couldn't understand, shoving me away.

"What is this about, Haruno?"

"Y-yeah. Hey, u-um..."

When Yukinoshita and Yuigahama spoke, cracking under the pressure, Haruno gently held up a hand to silence them. I was the one being questioned right now.

The gesture was unnecessary—Haruno Yukinoshita just stared me in the eye as if she had no interest in anything but my answer, watching every single move I made, down to the last breath.

"Is *this* it? ...I don't think that's who you are, though." Haruno paused there, walking up behind me. Her gaze slid from my neck to my face to examine me. "I never took you to be so boring."

She was close enough that I felt her breath, so near it felt like just the slightest squirm might touch my skin against hers, but those words also seemed to be coming from frighteningly far away.

"...If you want someone to entertain you, that's the most popular guy in class," I answered her, with my head turned the other way.

"That's what I like about you." Haruno giggled with genuine amusement, then finally stepped back.

If she would just keep going and leave, it would be easier. But Haruno Yukinoshita wouldn't do that. I was already aware she wasn't so soft.

From her position a step back, Haruno looked down on us imperiously. "...But you guys are all kind of boring now. I...liked you better before, Yukino-chan."

Her words made my breath catch. I felt my face freeze.

Yukinoshita's and Yuigahama's faces were turned down, but I assumed their expressions were similar.

Figuring no one would answer her, Haruno let out a short sigh. Eventually, the clicking of her heels on the floor grew distant.

While listening to her footsteps, I clearly understood what she was trying to say.

Haruno Yukinoshita was implying—that this couldn't possibly be something real.

I agreed.

I did sense something was wrong about this situation, about these relationships.

I'd thought it was just because I wasn't used to it. Because I'd never experienced it before. So that feeling was just that—a feeling. With the passage of time, I would gradually grow into it and accept it.

But she wouldn't let me ignore the dissonance.

That thing that had been stuck in my chest this whole time, like it was frozen there. That restless chill. That discomfort I had kept from showing on my face until this very moment.

Haruno Yukinoshita was taking that thing I'd tried not to think about and shoving it in my face.

Telling me it was not trust at all. That it was something much more cruel, more repulsive.

×　　×　　×

The post-festival mood is always a downer.

And the event in this kitchen was no exception. After Isshiki officially wrapped up the proceedings, everyone cleaned up their things and went off in twos and threes.

As the crowd grew smaller by one person, then two, the energy that had been buzzing in the kitchen settled into quiet. Only the current student council and the Service Club remained.

We were joining the student council in clearing out the garbage as well as some other tasks to put the facility back the way it had been when Isshiki returned from collecting the posters.

"The student council will handle the rest, so it's okay, you know?" she called out to us.

Scanning the room again, I saw indeed there wasn't much work left. We could leave the rest to them.

But we didn't.

"Hmm… Well, we'll keep helping out till it's done."

"Yes, it's perfectly normal."

Yuigahama, Yukinoshita, and I all chose to stay and help.

Isshiki seemed surprised by their answers as she looked over to me for confirmation, but when I nodded back at her, she grinned. "Oh, will you? Then I won't say no to that," she said.

But I was probably the one taking advantage. If I let this end, then I might start thinking, so I was trying to put that off as much as possible.

That kind of resistance didn't last long.

Once we were done cleaning up most everything, the only thing left was the table where we were.

I crushed the paper cup of cold black tea and tossed it in the garbage bag, and once I tugged the mouth of the bag shut, there was nothing else to do.

We finished locking the door and checking to make sure we hadn't forgotten anything, and then we all left the community center. After throwing the garbage away in the designated spot, there was no longer any reason to stick around.

"Sooo see you later." Isshiki bobbed her head in a bow to me at the door to the community center. The other members of the student council returned the gesture.

It had been such a spur-of-the-moment event, everyone was visibly tired. Nobody had the energy left to suggest going to an after-party, and they all started on their own routes home.

The same went for the three of us.

Yukinoshita reshouldered her school bag, plus her slightly largish bag of stuff. The second bag probably had the tea and her personal cooking implements. "…Let's go home," she said.

"Yeah." I pushed my bicycle after Yukinoshita, heading toward the station for now. But Yuigahama grabbed the rear rack of my bike.

"What…?" I asked her.

Yuigahama smiled a little awkwardly. "Ah, ummm, wanna go get something to eat?"

Yukinoshita and I exchanged a look at the sudden offer.

"I don't know," Yukinoshita said. "It's quite late…"

"So, so then…I'm staying at your place anyway tonight, Yukinon, so let's go eat over there."

"You're staying over tonight…? Did she get any say in that?" I said. It was true that Yuigahama often stayed at Yukinoshita's, and I got the impression they'd gone back together before and after events like this.

"Wh-why not? No?" Yuigahama cajoled.

Yukinoshita expelled a small sigh. "I don't mind, though…"

"Yay! Then let's go! Hikki…what about you?" Unlike the way she'd just been pleading with Yukinoshita, that question had a more urgent feel to it.

I couldn't come up with a good reason to refuse, so I nodded. "Let's go. I'm hungry, after all. We're good to meet up at the station?"

"Yeah!"

Once I had approval, I nodded back.

I spun my bicycle around to go the other way and started pedaling immediately.

X　X　X

I arrived at the station right when the two girls came out of the ticket gates.

They'd taken the train, while I'd taken my bike. Of course, the train is faster, but depending on how long you spend waiting, sometimes there's not much of a difference in the total time needed. It seemed we'd synced up just right.

After meeting up, we first decided to head back to Yukinoshita's place for a bit so she could leave her things there. It wasn't that far to the station. The three of us walked, occasionally chatting about nothing, sometimes just passing time in silence.

After strolling along a side road through the big park, a familiar apartment tower came into view. We crossed the street, but when we approached the building entrance, Yukinoshita's feet froze.

"What is it?" I asked, but she didn't react much.

"Oh, nothing…" She was staring at something doubtfully. Tracing her gaze, I saw a parked car. I'd seen that fancy black car before.

By the time I thought, *Isn't that…?* The car door had opened, and a woman was stepping out.

With her glossy black updo and kimono, she struck a balance of glamor and dignified poise. It was Yukinoshita's mother.

"Mother… Why are you here?" Yukinoshita asked.

"I was just talking with Haruno about your future, so I came here to discuss it with you. Yukino. What on earth are you doing out this late…?"

Yukinoshita lowered her head before her mother's worried gaze, and the older woman breathed a little sigh. "I didn't think you were the type to do things like this…," she said.

Yukinoshita raised her chin for an instant, giving her mother a hard look in the eye. But she said nothing, just bit her lip shallowly as she averted her eyes. Those gentle, cold words held her captive. That one sentence was enough to reject who she was in favor of the mold she was meant to fill.

Mrs. Yukinoshita's gaze was not at all sharp. Her tone carried neither anger nor irritation—in fact, the word for it was maybe just *sadness*. "I've given you this freedom because I trust you… No, this is my responsibility, my failure," she said quietly with a shake of her head, not giving anyone room to argue.

"I...," Yukinoshita started to say in a feeble voice, but that was again lost in her mother's next reply.

"Am I the one at fault here...?" she said as if to herself, her voice filled with apology and regret. The words came out fragile, with so much self-recrimination that no one could possibly fight her now—not even Yukinoshita, the one she was speaking to.

Waiting for the pause that came when Mrs. Yukinoshita sighed woefully, Yuigahama ventured, "Um...today was a student council event, um, and we stayed late helping out..."

"Oh, so you came to send her home. Thank you. But it's late now, and your parents must surely be worried...aren't they?" Though she never said so directly, the silent *Go home* was unmistakable in her voice, perfectly kind and gentle, and her soft smile.

And at the same time, her attitude drew a definite line. She was saying we weren't allowed to intrude in this family problem. We had no choice but to back off. Yuigahama and I could both understand intuitively that we wouldn't be allowed to speak here.

As we were both struck silent, Mrs. Yukinoshita approached with quiet and graceful steps and gently touched her daughter's shoulder. "I want you to live freely and be yourself... But I'm worried you'll make the wrong choices... What do you want to do, from now on?"

How much did she care to hear an answer to that question at all? I couldn't tell.

"...I *will* explain. So go home for now," Yukinoshita said, head turned down.

"I see... If you say so..." Mrs. Yukinoshita appeared confused. Then she looked over at Yuigahama and me.

"...Well, we've walked her back, so I'm going," I said, and Mrs. Yukinoshita nodded a bow, and I turned to go. She wouldn't be comfortable with a guy hanging around where her daughter was living alone. It would do Yukinoshita no favors for me to stick around.

"M-me too… See you later!" Yuigahama said, right behind me, then rushed off. She obviously couldn't say she'd be staying over, with things like this.

After getting a few meters away, I glanced back again to see Yukinoshita having a short conversation with her mother. Once their talk was over, Mrs. Yukinoshita returned to her car. Then her daughter, left standing there alone, eventually vanished into the apartment building.

As Yuigahama and I were waiting for the light at the crosswalk, the Yukinoshita family car rolled away. The rear windows were tinted, so I couldn't see the people inside, but I got the feeling they could see us. It made me uneasy.

Eventually, the light turned green, and Yuigahama trotted a few steps ahead. Then she spun back to face me. "I'm going home, then."

"Oh…I'll walk you back," I said.

She shook her head. "It's okay. The station is right over there. And besides, I think it might feel…unfair."

I couldn't ask what she meant.

"…I see." With only that feeble reply, I watched Yuigahama's back as she started to walk away.

It wouldn't be much farther for me to stop by the station before going back home. But still, I couldn't follow her.

After watching Yuigahama go under the shine of the streetlights, I finally got on my bike and started pedaling. The wind wasn't strong, but the cold winter air stabbed at my bare cheeks.

After a while of pumping my legs, the heat began to build, while the inside of my head cooled completely.

Me being myself. Her being herself. Being yourself.

I'm sure everyone has a "self" that is prescribed by another, one that's never quite right. That's true for me, and for her. Another's perception of what is "us" is always in contradiction somewhere.

I didn't need to ask someone else to know that.

I mean, I used to say it myself. The old Hachiman Hikigaya was always howling it. *Are you okay with that? Is that what you want? Is that Hachiman Hikigaya?*

So as to keep myself from hearing those taunts, those yells, those screams, I plugged my ears, closed my eyes. In place of words, a hot, condensed breath left my mouth.

I couldn't even say myself what was "me." So then what about that "something real"? Where was the real us? How could such a person dictate how these relationships were supposed to be?

Now that I'd named this feeling as *something wrong*, I couldn't think of it as anything else.

I'm sure these feelings, these relationships, should never have been defined. I shouldn't have given them names. I shouldn't have found meaning in them. Once they're given meaning, then they lose their other functions.

I'm sure it would've been easier if I could fit them into a mold, but I hadn't done that, because I'd known. I'd known once you give them form, the only way you can change their shape is by breaking them.

And I wanted something that couldn't be broken. So I'd avoided giving it a name.

I kept on wondering if, maybe, she and I had both just been clinging to a bunch of formless words.

If at least one flake of snow would fall, it would cover all sorts of things. Maybe I could have avoided thinking about these things when I didn't have to. But it hardly ever snows around here, and the sky was utterly clear that night. Not a cloud to be seen.

Nothing but the glittering light of the stars, clearly illuminating the person I was now.

Haruno Yukinoshita's eyes are hopelessly clear.

Some time had passed since that pre–Valentine's Day cooking event.

After the clear skies of the other day, the clouds had come in, and it seemed the uncertain weather would continue for the next few days. The chill wasn't supposed to be that severe in the evening, but that was just your typical minor fluctuation. Chiba winters are always cold.

When the sun set after school, that feeling was especially acute.

Fleeing the chilly hallway of the special-use building, I went into the clubroom, and while the heater was getting me comfortable, I spread open my paperback.

As sunset drew near, nothing was out of the ordinary in the clubroom.

On the long table were a teacup, a mug, and a Japanese-style cup that clashed with the other two. Out the corner of my eye, I could see Yukinoshita pouring tea into each. She placed the steaming mug and Japanese cup in front of Yuigahama and me.

The moment I looked up from my book to accept the tea, my eyes met with Yukinoshita's; she was sitting directly across from me.

She quickly dropped her head, then raised it again to glance at me. Then she lowered her eyes again. Her restless attitude clued me in to something out of the ordinary. And it seemed Yuigahama noticed, too.

"Yukinon?"

When Yuigahama addressed her, Yukinoshita gave the other girl a hesitant look, then briefly glanced my way for my reaction, too. Then, with some difficulty, she said, "I'm sorry for the other day… Um, my mother…"

She quietly lowered her head. She didn't say much, but from that gesture and those few words, I could immediately tell what she was talking about. There was no need to bother going back over that incident. I hadn't been able to forget it, and it had been spinning around in my head this whole time—not just that encounter with Yukinoshita's mother. What Haruno had said to me, what Yuigahama had said as she went home, and the cry that had come from inside me—none of it had gone away. It was all still there. It was just that there was no point in talking about it. I couldn't blame anyone else for this, either.

So I replied with just a casual shake of my head and a reassurance that it was nothing.

Yuigahama, sitting diagonally across from Yukinoshita, flailed her hands wide to say, *Don't worry about it.* "It's totally okay! My mom tells me off a lot for coming home late, too."

"Well, that's what moms do. They tend to nag you about stuff. And they clean your room without permission and ask you randomly if you're having fun at school."

Why is it the mothers of the world have such an interest in their sons' living space or their friendships, and even their taste in books…? What is this? Are you a fan of mine? Thanks, Mom, but please don't touch my desk drawer.

Once we gave our responses, Yukinoshita's expression softened. She gave a tiny smile, then swished the hair off her shoulder in her usual manner. "…Yes, your mother would have an especially difficult time."

"Hikki's mom, huh…? What's she like?"

"Huh? I dunno… She's normal. It's like having another Komachi. Entrance exams are coming up, so Komachi and Mom are going at it a lot."

The two of them generally get along, but they do have the occasional conflict. The biggest cause of fights tends to be about how my dad gets treated, though… Dad's so worried about Komachi, he pesters them about something or another, and Mom snaps at him, and

Komachi snaps, too, and then the tension is brutal… Wait, that's not a mother-daughter conflict, huh? That's just them hating my dad. Anyway, it's common enough for entrance exams and postgraduation plans to throw the whole family out of sorts.

When I said as much, Yuigahama nodded along. "Oh, Komachi's entrance exams are already tomorrow, huh? And we've got the day off 'cause of entrance exams, too."

"This is Komachi, though, so I think she'll be all right…" Yukinoshita sounded a bit uneasy.

I nodded back. "Yeah…" That note of unease was in my voice, too.

The following day was finally the day of the high school entrance exam, the big one. It was also Valentine's Day, so basically, no Komachoco. Too bad, so sad, try next year, lad! I wanted to pin my hopes on next year, but who knew what would be happening then. Thinking about what was coming down the line, I couldn't help but feel glum.

Yuigahama must have seen that on my face, as she gave me an anxious smile. "You must be worried about her. After all, you're her big brother…," she said kindly.

"Yeah…" I nodded heavily.

I sighed deeply, and then everything spilled out—the things I'd been trying to avoid thinking about all this time and my cynicism about the future. "Komachi's so cute, she'll have tons of guys interested in her, right? And then I'll have to watch out for them, and worst of all, she'll have to pretend she doesn't know her good-for-nothing older brother. For her reputation."

"That's what you're worried about?! And wait, you're assuming she passes?!"

"I don't know whether that's optimistic or pessimistic…"

Yuigahama was shocked, while Yukinoshita was more stunned. The both of them sighed, then looked at each other and giggled.

There weren't really any visitors that day, so just like always, the atmosphere around us was fairly relaxed. I was a little relieved as I turned the page of my book. Yuigahama was sitting flopped over on the desk with her phone, while Yukinoshita was taking the cozy off the teapot to neatly pour some fresh tea.

And then there was a *tump*. Yukinoshita lifted her bag up to her desk and pulled out from inside it a small, plain paper bag. There was a rustle as she opened it up, and then a mild, sweet scent wafted out. It seemed like she'd brought some cookies as snacks to go with the tea.

Yukinoshita slowly and carefully transferred the cookies to a wooden plate. Looking over, I saw an array of multicolored cookies: chocolate chip, jam flavored, and checkerboard ones, too. Judging from their variety, as well as the paper bag she'd brought, it didn't seem she'd bought them at a store.

"Ohhh, you made those, Yukinon?" Yuigahama's eyes sparkled with expectation as she looked at the cookies.

Yukinoshita's cooking skills were certified. There had been many occasions, including the cooking event the other day, when she had exhibited her ability. And each time, Yuigahama had eaten her cooking with relish.

So this wasn't exactly unusual.

But despite that, for some reason, Yukinoshita couldn't reply to Yuigahama's casual remark. "…Y-yes. I just happened to make some last night," she said as she quietly lowered her face. Her fingertips stroked the edge of the wooden plate as if she needed something to do with them, and then she drew a little breath. She gave me a brief, examining glance.

The expression was diffident; her head was downturned, her shoulders hardly moving at all, just peeking through the gaps in her bangs as if she wasn't sure enough to look directly. It was a gesture that would rattle you, if you saw it.

Yukinoshita's lips parted just slightly as if she didn't know whether to speak or not before drawing a tight line again. They were so innocent, demanding my attention, and I looked away automatically.

The room went suddenly quiet.

"Oh… I tried a bit after the event, too, but it was kinda, y'know…" Yuigahama didn't seem to like the momentary silence, smiling to fill it. She combed at her bun as she tilted her head side to side. "I think the microwave/oven combo at my house is broken. Like, it'll make the batter bubble a bit, but it won't really cook it."

"Then it's probably just a regular microwave…," I said, a little sigh slipping from me. Maybe I was relieved by how some things didn't change.

Yukinoshita hid her mouth with one hand and gave a modest giggle. Then she drew close the bag she'd set down next to her, put it on her knees, and pulled another small paper bag out from within.

She must have planned to give that one to Yuigahama. It was decorated with a cute pink ribbon and cat paw prints. "Here, if you like."

"Can I?! Ohhh, thanks!!"

"It's basically the same things inside," Yukinoshita added apologetically, but Yuigahama was overjoyed to accept it.

"Oh, no, I'm really glad to have it! I mean, your baking is so good." Yuigahama squeezed the paper bag to her chest. And then she held it up in front of her in both hands again to examine it tenderly. She blinked two, three times, and then she was looking timidly at Yukinoshita. "…Um, just for me?"

I got what her question meant and automatically turned my face away. I tried my best to keep reading the book in my hands and not move my eyes, but the lines of words wouldn't enter my brain at all.

Why am I looking away…?

I could hear the clanging of that bowl ringing in my ears. Even if I could avert my eyes, I couldn't plug my ears to the sound inside me. All I could do was crush it with the thoughts in my head.

This was all me—*I* was reading into things, *I* was thinking too hard, *I* was getting my hopes up. Whether she'd made some for me or not, either way, it was weird to expect it to mean anything. There were only three people in this club. If she had nothing, then duh, and if she had something, she was just being nice. Who do you think you are, considering the possibility it might mean something more? If thinking about this stuff is gross and pathetic, it's just as gross and pathetic to have to desperately remind yourself it's gross and pathetic and swallow it down. And something so gross and pathetic is obviously wrong.

But my single-minded attempts to drown out the anxiety with words were unsuccessful, and I couldn't calm myself. I pretended to comb back my hair, and I couldn't keep my gaze under control. It was wandering around aimlessly, without ever landing on anything.

That was why I caught sight of Yuigahama, in the corner of my eye, with her mouth in a firm line. Her thin white throat moved as she swallowed. "…What about Hikki's?"

You don't have to go out of your way to ask that. I mean, it's not like I really want any. I mean, seriously.

That remark did not leave my mouth.

Yuigahama's tone and gaze were the same as usual, and it seemed like she was being careful and timid about it, but her hands—her left hand lying on her lap was squeezing her skirt. When I saw that, my words caught and wouldn't come out right.

"Uh, I mean, I don't really…" That clumsy stutter was all I could manage, and at the same time, I heard Yukinoshita sigh.

She gripped the bag on her lap, then shifted it under her arm. She quietly pushed back her chair to stand from her seat. Leaning against the long desk, she reached out and shifted the plate with the cookies over to me. "…If you like."

"O-okay…," I attempted to reply.

But Yukinoshita wouldn't meet my gaze. The setting sun shone faintly over her profile. Maybe it was the clouds, but the sunset was even redder than usual, and the color seeped into the clubroom.

Her ears and neck were reddish, and she was biting her lip slightly in discomfort. Her long eyelashes blinked restlessly. I almost couldn't look at her directly. I snapped my book shut a bit too hard and reached out to the cookies.

"…They're good," I muttered.

"Yeah!" Yuigahama replied enthusiastically. She grabbed another while she was at it, taking a *nom* out of it as she brought a hand to her cheek in bliss.

Seeing our reactions, Yukinoshita said, "…O-oh? I just made them like I always do, though." The tension relaxed from her shoulders, and she finally sat back down in her chair again.

Our chairs were correctly positioned, and the cookies were placed in the middle. Warm steam rose up from the mug and traditional-style cup.

We exchanged thoughts on the tea and the snacks that day, occasionally falling silent, or reading or looking at phones, and from time to time, conversation would start up again with little smiles.

This clubroom was so peaceful when no one else came.

We passed the time leisurely until the sun just about touched the ocean.

There was no heat to the winter sunset. It might give you a clear view of the sky with its light, but it wouldn't warm you up. If you let it be, it would just keep getting colder and colder.

That's why you force yourself to move so you can warm up.

Even if you can feel that something's wrong.

X　X　X

Nobody came to the clubroom after that, and once it was time to go home, our activity for the day was concluded.

We locked the door and waited for Yukinoshita to go return the key, then walked out of the school. As we picked up the conversation from earlier in the clubroom, we reached the bicycle parking. I wasn't intending to repay them for anything, but I walked with my bicycle to see the girls to the school gates.

We circled around, not to the back entrance I normally took, but to the front gates, which faced the main road that led to the station. The sky above had gone entirely dark. The clouds hung low, foretelling coming rain.

Taking a step out from the school gates, Yuigahama did a full-body shiver. "Urk, cold!"

"You should wrap your scarf properly." Beside her, Yukinoshita attentively rewrapped her scarf for her.

That was a heartwarming sight to see, but it did nothing to actually warm me. It was intensely chilly after sunset, and when I just stood there, it felt like the coldness was surging up from the ground at me.

"I think it's gonna be really cold today…" Thinking about the way home was depressing. *I'm gonna be riding my bike through those violent, frigid winds… I can't take it; I just can't…* I rewrapped my scarf, too, stuffed my hands deeper into my gloves, then raised one casually. "Bye."

"Yeah, see you." Yuigahama did a little wave in front of her chest. I nodded back, and I was about to throw a leg over my bike.

That was when I heard a faint noise like a half sigh.

"…Ah."

I turned around to see Yukinoshita a half step ahead from where she'd been a moment ago, as if she meant to stop me.

I asked with a look, *You need something?* But she didn't react. Her lips seemed like they wanted to say something, but they didn't move. She just squeezed the mouth of the bag hanging from her left shoulder in both hands and stood there.

I met her anxiously wavering gaze, patiently waiting for her to find the words. It would be foolish to ask what it was. As this silent tug-of-war continued, I heard the crunch of a foot on gravel.

"Uh, um… I'm gonna go, okay?" Yuigahama said with a smile, at loose ends, as she took just one step back. She patted her bun with a gloved hand and glanced at Yukinoshita, checking for her reaction.

Yukinoshita answered that look with just the barest shake of her head, then gave her a long, imploring stare.

Yuigahama lowered her gaze for a heartbeat before immediately raising her chin to gently ask, "Um…what should we do?" The tinge of confusion was gone from her voice, and this just sounded like soothing confirmation.

"…Um." Whatever Yukinoshita started to say was lost in the wind. It seemed she couldn't quite find the words, and she blushed and looked at the ground with a pained expression. Her shoulders twitched, maybe from the tension, and she squeezed her bag tighter than before.

We all avoided stepping any closer to each other as we waited for what she would say next. But no voices came, and instead, a hard noise rang out.

A click.

Like a heel hitting asphalt.

The sound of those footsteps approaching, one after another, could be mistaken for a heartbeat. Or maybe it was some kind of auditory hallucination, and only I could hear it. Maybe the constant sense of dissonance in my head had finally manifested in the physical world.

But apparently, I wasn't the only one to hear it. Yuigahama peered in the direction of the approaching sound as well. And then she cried out in surprise, "Ah..."

Eventually, the footsteps stopped. Tracing Yuigahama's gaze, both Yukinoshita's and my eyes widened.

"Yukino-chan. I've come to pick you up."

"Haruno...," Yukinoshita said when she saw who it was.

There was one more click of Haruno Yukinoshita's boot heels as she came to stand before us. She thrust her hands into her coat pockets and tilted her head, smiling boldly as she examined Yukinoshita's face.

"I don't believe there's any reason for you to come pick me up...," Yukinoshita said.

"Mom told me to live with you for a while. Oh, you have a spare room, right? They'll be moving my stuff tomorrow; is that okay? I'll be there in the morning, but I'll be going out in the afternoon, so can I ask you to handle it then?"

Haruno was talking so fast, maybe trying to keep Yuigahama and me out of the conversation. With her taking control so overwhelmingly, there was nothing outsiders like us could say.

Most of all, though Haruno was acting as if this was a hassle, her manner was just too natural. She communicated with both words and behavior that she was simply delivering the news of something that had already been decided, and any chance for argument had long since gone.

"H-hold on. Why this, so suddenly...?" Yukinoshita asked, reproach and confusion in her voice.

Haruno laughed a full and dramatic laugh, shoulders bouncing. Then she leaned an inch forward and teased, batting her lashes, "I think you have some idea, don't you?"

Yukinoshita's shoulders twitched. She glared sharply at Haruno before giving a hostile and flat refusal. "…That's something I'll handle myself. It has nothing to do with you."

Whatever she was referring to—it was probably what she'd talked about with her mother the other day. I seemed to remember she'd promised then that she would eventually answer the question her mother had posed to her. And yet here was Haruno Yukinoshita.

Did their mother not want to wait for Yukinoshita to talk, or was she just so worried about her daughter returning late at night that she had sent over the older sister? I don't know. Haruno was probably the only one who knew Mrs. Yukinoshita's intentions.

Haruno was listening to Yukinoshita in silence.

The amused smile from before was now gone, and her sharp gaze captured Yukinoshita, refusing to let go. Her eyes took in Yukinoshita's expression, her gestures, everything, stony and so piercing it was like she could even see into her mind.

Eventually, Haruno smiled a mirthless smile. "…What 'self' do you even have, Yukino-chan?"

"Wha—?" The unexpected remark confused Yukinoshita. But before she could finish asking, *What are you talking about?* Haruno cut her off to continue.

"You've always tried to do what I would do, so can you even talk about your own thoughts?" Despite the grin on her lips, her tone was far colder than normal, and her gaze was ice.

Yukinoshita said nothing to argue or deny it; she only stared at Haruno, stunned.

Watching her reaction, Haruno gave a little shrug, then sighed in exasperation. "I mean, you've always been allowed to do what you want. But it's not like you've ever decided yourself."

Her tone was kind, even something close to pitying.

The compassionate gaze slid from Yukinoshita to Yuigahama, who was next to her, and then to me, on the opposite side. When her eyes met mine, she giggled. "...You don't know how to act now, either, do you?"

Who was that question really aimed at?

It wasn't just Yukinoshita—my legs were frozen, too. I wanted to keep Haruno from talking, but my voice was caught and wouldn't come out. I didn't know the right way to act or the answer to her questions, either.

"Just what do you want to do, Yukino-chan?" asked Haruno.

"...If you're going to have a family quarrel, could you do it somewhere else?" I somehow managed to say, cutting off Haruno's question.

I was sure Haruno Yukinoshita would say something final. She would shove the truth in our faces. So I couldn't let her say any more. Not for Yukinoshita's sake, but for mine.

Haruno eyed me with disappointment, as if her fun had been spoiled. She gave a me a scornful look that seemed to say, *Is that all you've got? Really?* "A quarrel? This doesn't even count as a quarrel. We've never quarreled, not since we were kids."

"Whatever it is, it's not something to be talking about out here, is it?" I said, and our cold gazes collided. I fervently struggled not to avert my eyes.

"U-um... We'll... We *will* think about it... Yukinon, and me, too." Yuigahama stepped in to defend her. She stood tall by Yukinoshita's side and tried to speak forcefully. But under Haruno's glare, she gradually withered, until she'd lowered her head. Haruno gave her a gentle look that seemed sad.

"...I see. Then I'll ask about it once we're at home. There's only one place for Yukino-chan to go back to anyway...," Haruno added before turning around to walk away. As the sound of heels clicking faded into the distance, I could feel the tension draining from my shoulders.

Watching Haruno leave under the sunset that oozed out over the thick clouds in eerily vivid colors, when I finally heaved a deep sigh, I felt like I could breathe for the first time in a long time.

We couldn't even look at each other once she was gone. Yukinoshita stood there with her face still turned down, biting the edge of her lip, while Yuigahama gazed at her sadly. After a talk like that, all I was thinking about as I looked up at the sky was what I should say to get out of here.

"U-um… I know. Wanna…come to my place?"

So when Yuigahama proposed that with a smile, trying to patch things up, I couldn't come up with an excuse to refuse.

X   X   X

We walked for a while along the main road that connected the school to the station and arrived at a corner with some large apartment buildings standing in rows.

Yuigahama lived in one of these apartments.

It was right around the time of day a lot of people were coming back from school or work, so the streets were busy as we made our way there. Walking in silence, we were grateful for the noise.

Yukinoshita and I only ever opened our mouths to say "Thanks," as Yuigahama was letting us into her home. But when we got to Yuigahama's room, after a while, we could finally find real words instead of sighing.

"Sorry, it's kind of messy in here…," Yuigahama said as she sat down in front of the low table and pushed a cushion toward Yukinoshita and me.

"…Thanks," Yukinoshita said and, with that cushion in her arms, quietly sat down next to Yuigahama. I did the same, crossing my legs on the floor. I sat opposite them with the low table between us. The short-fibered pink rug made the floor warm.

Holding a mushy beanbag cushion, I couldn't help looking around the room.

The shelves were packed with all sorts of cute-looking knickknacks and distinctly Asian-flavor odds and ends; fashion magazines were piled around in disorder, and the study desk that showed no signs of use was functioning as a closet.

As Yuigahama had said herself, it wasn't very tidy, but it was still clean enough. Cleaner than my room, for sure.

It was just that I really couldn't settle down. Her room smelled nice, and that alone made me fidgety. The smell came from the bed, so my eyes were pulled in that direction to a little bottle by the bedside. The bottle had a bunch of thin rods stuck in it, and it seemed that was the source of the scent.

What the heck is that…? I was wondering, peering at it, when I heard an *ahem.* Looking back again, Yuigahama was twisting around awkwardly.

"C-could you not stare at my stuff so much…?"

"Huh? Oh, um, like, there was this fried pasta–looking thing, so?!" I said, my voice going a little shrill.

Yuigahama gave me an exasperated smile. "That's an essential oil diffuser…"

Oh, so it's like a perfume for the room, huh…? I guess those pasta sticks suck up some perfumy stuff and disperse it? Not like I'd know. Huh, there's lots of stuff in girls' rooms, I was thinking, impressed, when I saw out of the corner of my eye that someone's shoulders were trembling.

"Fried pasta…?"

When I looked at Yukinoshita, she was burying her face in the cushion and shaking. *Uh, it's not that funny… Why is her sense of humor so weird…?*

And with that thought, a smile had slipped out of me. Yuigahama sighed with relief.

Once the mood had settled enough for us to have a conversation, Yukinoshita lifted her face from the cushion and shifted in her seat. She quietly raised her head. "I'm sorry… I've been a bother…"

"Not at all! Don't worry about it," Yuigahama said with extra cheer as she waved her hands wide in front of her chest, and while she was speaking, another voice broke in with even more cheer.

"That's right! There's no need to worry at all."

There was no knock, just a click as the door suddenly opened and a woman appeared carrying a tray of tea. Though her attire was subdued—a thick sweater and long skirt—she had a bit of a baby face that gave her a youthful impression. With each bubbly laugh, the bun behind her head bobbed cheerily.

"Mom! Don't just barge in!" Yuigahama huffed.

"Awww," her mom replied, turning aside her daughter's response with a smile. You didn't need anyone telling you to know instantly that this was Yuigahama's mother. The friendly smile and good style were just like her daughter's.

…Well, I'd also believe you if you said she was the older sister. But she's saying "Mom," so she's the mom, right? Mama Yuigahama, Yuigaha-ma for short. That doesn't really abbreviate anything, and it's hard to say.

Yuigahama's mom knelt by the low table and started pouring tea. "Here," she said as she offered me a cup.

"Ah, thanks. Sorry…"

At times like these, is it good manners to say *You shouldn't have* or *You needn't be concerned* or *Your grace much obliges me, my lady*? But I don't have much experience in going over to people's houses, so I just didn't know. And since this was Yuigahama's mom, I was extra-nervous, and my reply came out flustered.

I was a little embarrassed about looking straight at her for some reason, so my head was still bowed down as I heard a rather glad-sounding "Ohhh." Raising my head curiously, I found Yuigahama's mom staring at me.

I was observed for a moment as she kept making those thoughtful little noises.

Not knowing how to respond, I didn't say anything, and Yuigahama's mother giggled. "You're Hikki…aren't you? I've heard all about you from Yui."

"Uh… Uh-huh…" *Oh, wow, I wanna die. This is kinda embarrassing. I actually wanna die.*

"Mom, stop babbling at him!" Yuigahama leaped at her mother in a panicked manner. Then she stole away the tray of snacks and urged her mother to get up.

"Whaaat? But Mom wants to have a chat with Hikki, too!" Mrs. Yuigahama griped and grumbled.

But Yui shoved at her back, chasing her out of the room. "Forget about it!"

Yukinoshita watched the exchange between mother and daughter with a smile, and then her eyes met with Mrs. Yuigahama's as she was being thrown out.

"Oh, yes. Yukino-chan."

"...Y-yes?" Yukinoshita replied, despite her confusion.

Yuigahama's mom smiled broadly at her. "You're staying over tonight, right? I'll put out the futon..."

"I'll do that, too!" Yuigahama gave her mother one last hard shove, then closed the door with a clack. Some talking could still be heard on the other side of the door, but Yuigahama ignored it with a *phew*.

"Ah-ha-ha... Um, sorry. It looks like Mom's glad you're here, Yukinon. She just got a little excited. Ergh, that was embarrassing...," Yuigahama said shyly.

Yukinoshita gave a little shake of her head as if to say, *Don't worry about it*. Then she smiled weakly. "You're close... I'm a little envious." You could see a touch of loneliness and regret in her expression. She had a mother and that sister, too, but it'd be hard for anyone to get along with them. Yuigahama and I didn't know what to say.

When Yukinoshita noticed our silence, she made a hurried attempt to fill it. "I'm sorry—that was a strange thing to say... I'll get going soon," she said and moved to stand, but Yuigahama stopped her and waved her to sit again.

"About that—like, why don't you stay over?" she said brightly. "You let me stay at your place all the time, I mean... Sometimes it can be hard to go home, right?"

"Huh? But..." Yukinoshita seemed confused to hear that out of the blue and hesitated a moment. Her gaze moved about restlessly like she couldn't decide, then shifted over to me.

Uh, don't look at me...

But considering her recent conversation with Haruno, if Yukinoshita were to go back to her place in this situation, the same thing would clearly happen all over again. Besides, Yuigahama sounded confident enough to have some ideas of her own. With that thought, I glanced at Yuigahama, and she gave me the slightest nod so that only I could see it.

Well, when it's hard to face someone, just avoiding them is also an effective tactic for smooth communication. Of course, if you're going to do that, you have to establish a time limit to get closure, or you'll wind up running forever. But still, you couldn't say it would be a mistake to take some time here.

"…Well, I'm sure both you and your sister are worked up right now, so it should be fine for you to think about it for the night. And call, just in case."

"Yeah, I think that's a good idea," Yuigahama agreed.

Yukinoshita hugged her knees, considering for a while, but she eventually gave a little nod. "…Yes, you're right."

Pulling her cell phone from her bag, she started to make a phone call. Probably to Haruno. After a few rings, it seemed she answered. Yukinoshita raised her head as she started talking.

"…Hello. I'm sure both of us are worked up right now, so I'm going to consider things for the night and go over to talk later. I'm just calling to let you know…"

Yukinoshita mostly talked at her sister, with no apparent response from the other end. There was silence. Yukinoshita inhaled with some confusion, while at the same time, I heard a little mutter of "Just now…"

Glancing toward that voice, I saw Yuigahama looking between Yukinoshita and me with a startled expression. I was about to ask what it was when I heard the person on the other end of the line burst into derisive laughter.

"Hmm, fine. Hikigaya is there, isn't he? Give him the phone."

In the quiet room, I could hear the challenge in her tone, even on the other end of the call. Haruno's request made Yukinoshita hesitate a moment. But then I heard a colder "Now" from the other end. Yuki-noshita let out a faint sigh and held out her cell phone to me.

"…My sister says she wants to talk."

I accepted the phone without a word, brought it to my ear, and slowly asked, "…What is it?"

"…You're so nice, Hikigaya." Her mocking giggle was beautiful and enticing. Since I couldn't see her, it felt like a strange spirit was casting me under its spell.

I'm sure the smile I couldn't see would have been lovely in an awful and twisted way. I could imagine her expression vividly. You'd think her features would be a lot like Yukinoshita's, but she didn't resemble her at all.

I heard the sound of a gulp in my own throat, and without realizing it, I was looking over at Yukinoshita.

She was holding her arms idly, standing beside the window. Her back was arched, leaning against the wall, and her gaze was far away.

It would probably rain that night. The streetlamps dotted around and the red lights of the clusters of high-rises in the distance were not enough to illuminate the dark, turning the glass black.

The eyes reflected there were entirely clear but seemed so empty.

$$\times \quad \times \quad \times$$

After that one remark, Haruno hung up on me, ending the conversation.

I gave the screen of Yukinoshita's cell phone a light wipe with my handkerchief before returning it, and then the exhaustion hit me like a wave. I suddenly realized it was getting pretty late.

"Then I'm gonna get going," I said.

"Yeah…"

I snatched up my bag and stood, and Yuigahama rose with me. A beat later, Yukinoshita stood, too. It seemed she meant to see me off at the door.

"Uh, we can just say good-bye here."

"It'd be weird to do that here," Yuigahama said, opening the door and taking the lead.

Instantly, a furball came barreling toward us from the other side of the hallway.

It was Yuigahama's dog, Sablé, charging right in to body slam me.

"Whoa…"

"Hey, Sablé," Yuigahama scolded the dog before scooping him up from where he lay at my feet showing his tummy.

Seeing the dog, Yukinoshita twitched and froze. *Uh-oh. She's scared of dogs, isn't she?*

On our way to the door, Yukinoshita kept three steps behind Yuigahama, doing her best to avoid contact with the furball. Meanwhile, even in Yuigahama's arms, Sablé was sniffing and woofing and flailing around energetically. *Hmm… Will this be okay…? Maybe I should tell Yuigahama to be careful, just in case.*

After putting on my shoes, right when I was about to step out the door, I said, "Hey, Yuigahama. If Yukinoshita's staying over tonight, then Sablé—"

"Hikigaya." Yukinoshita cut me off harshly. Her lip jutted out slightly, arms folded as she flicked me a glare.

Are you that determined not to admit you're scared of dogs…? Well, maybe she just couldn't bear to say she didn't like something her friend loved so much. She'd probably feel bad about making Yuigahama do extra for her when she was already letting her stay over. If that was it, then I should respect her wishes.

But as always, once something has started coming out of your mouth, you can't put the words back.

Yuigahama was tilting her head with a blank expression. "Ummm, Sablé? What about him?" she asked me again, and I didn't know how to answer.

"Mmm, uhhh… I'm sure Sablé gets lonely, but part of training is teaching him restraint. It's extra-important," I said, making it up as I went along.

"Yeah, we've taught him that!" Yuigahama nodded emphatically.

Oh-ho, I didn't think you'd be so confident about his training… Strangely confident, though, given he doesn't listen at all to what you say…, I was thinking, when Yuigahama's shoulders slumped.

"…'Cause when we're inside, Sablé always sticks with Mom."

"Ah, I see…"

Doggies have a strong sense of hierarchy, so he had to have zero respect for Yuigahama. But then he wouldn't be approaching Yukinoshita very much, either. And this could be an opportunity for her to get acclimated to dogs.

"Then I'm going home," I said, giving the dog in Yuigahama's arms a little pet on the head.

"Yeah, then see you later."

"See you."

With the two of them seeing me off, I went outside. Even after stepping onto the outside walkway, I heard Sablé whining for a while like he was lonely. I left Yuigahama's home, but I was quite reluctant to.

×　×　×

After coming home and finishing dinner, I slid into the *kotatsu* and focused entirely on lying around and reading.

My parents had come home early for once, and they'd already gone to bed. Now it was just Kamakura and me in the living room. The cat was curled in a ball on top of the table the whole time, though, and I was the only one awake.

Then there was a click as the living room door opened, and Komachi came in, wearing her pajamas and a sleep cap for her hair.

"You're still awake?" I said to her.

"Yeah. Komachi's gonna sleep, but just one thing first," she replied, circling around to the kitchen.

"Whatever, but go to bed soon," I said, while on the inside I was in quite an anxious tizzy. *But tomorrow is your exam—should you really be awake this late?*

But her reply was particularly laid-back. "Hmm." And then before long, I heard the *tik-tik-tik* sound of the gas stove being turned on.

What, is she cooking or something? I wondered, and next I heard the sound of her fishing around on the shelves. *Is it that she can't sleep because she's hungry?* I thought, and then Komachi came over to the *kotatsu*.

"Here, take this."

"Hn. Oh, thanks."

What Komachi had come to offer me was a MAX Coffee. When I took it from her, it was warm and toasty. It seemed she'd bought it before and warmed it in hot water. She's good.

"Your feet are in the way, Bro," she said, kicking my legs as she wiggled her way into the *kotatsu*. Then we both started sipping at our warm drinks.

Komachi let out a satisfied sigh. "*Pfew...* It's finally tomorrow, huh?"

"Yeah. Once this is done, go to bed early. Tomorrow's exam day."

Well, a warm Max can before bed will give you a good sleep. I'm terrified of when they inevitably certify these things as a prescription drug. If you say *Heh-heh, this is the good stuff...* as you drink it, the unnatural sweetness will make it feel like something naughty. I very much recommend it.

But it seemed that wasn't what Komachi was trying to say. "...Not that. Valentine's Day. A boy should be all excited about it, you know?" she said with an *agh*. She seemed exasperated.

Bringing that up, before entrance exams... The princess of this household really has some nerves of steel. Apparently, I wouldn't even need to bother asking, *Have you prepared yourself?*

"I'm not gonna get all excited about it. Actually, I've got my head full thinking of you."

"'Cause you're too sweet on Komachi. It's creepy. You should try pampering yourself for a change."

"I do pamper myself."

"That's not what I mean; I mean you do, but...," she said while shaking the Max can, then snorted.

...Hey, did you casually say something really mean just now?

If you say your bro is creepy, then Big Bro really will do something creepy. For starters, I decided to try banging on the *kotatsu* and acting like a spoiled brat. Yeah, maybe I am creepy.

"Oh yeah, if you're gonna talk about sweet, then, you know, give me chocolate. Come on."

"I gave you something close, didn't I?" Komachi jabbed her chin at my drink.

No, no, it's not at all close. I mean, this is barely even coffee. I'm not feeling the love here!

"...Komachi, do you love your big brother?"

"Not really, no."

She just had to answer instantly with a nonchalant smile, huh?

"Wahhh..." So mean... Well, I guess we're close enough that she can say it to my face.

Even if it was jokingly or half-teasing, we could say we loved or hated each other and, regardless of the answer, could honestly reveal the real feelings beneath those words.

The fifteen years of time we've shared are not for nothing.

So then what about those sisters, that mother and daughter?

If you could be together over fifteen years, spending your time in the same spaces, sharing memories and recollections, and having similar values in life—and still fail to understand each other, still be at odds, then how could you get along with a stranger?

Our sibling relationship works entirely because of Komachi. I truly can be thankful to her for so much.

...But that's one thing, and this is another. Chocolate is chocolate.

"Give me chocolate, come on..." I broke down into teary wails as I twiddled my fingers.

With a beleaguered sigh, Komachi got out of the *kotatsu* and pattered off somewhere.

I... I despaired, flopping face-first onto the *kotatsu*, when Komachi rushed back to me with another pitter-patter.

"Hnn." And then she poked at my slumped back and handed me something.

Turning around to look, I saw some prettily wrapped chocolates.

"...What, you're giving this to me?"

"Well, it's just basic stuff. Since you told me to give you some...," Komachi grumbled, looking displeased for some reason.

Hugging the chocolates with tears welling in my eyes, I thanked her over and over, "Thanks so much...so much..." *She went to the trouble to get this for me, huh? What an upstanding sister...*

As I was sobbing, Komachi made a face at me. "Komachi wishes you could learn to ask for things from other people, too, though."

"How could I say something so embarrassing to anyone but you? ...Plus, anything you get from asking for it is worthless," I said.

Komachi gave me a dull look. "If you're gonna be like that, then Komachi's chocolates are worthless, too..."

"...Mm, ahhh, well... That's not true? Your chocolates are different. Special. Komachi's the super-ultra-cutest."

"That doesn't sound very sincere, Garbro." She breathed a deep sigh, and her face was clearly annoyed. "...But if you could get some from someone who doesn't deceive themselves, Komachi might be a little happy about that," she said, smiling with an expression far more mature than usual. Leaning her face on her hand, elbow on the *kotatsu*, she cocked her head, looking up at me with a direct and warm gaze.

The kindness in her eyes was embarrassing, and I let out a rough snort and looked away.

That seemed to embarrass Komachi a little, too, as she snickered in a particularly deliberate way. "Or whatever. Did that score a lot of Komachi points?"

"I keep telling you, that stuff doesn't score points..." My ultra-sweet coffee had gone lukewarm, and I finished it with a bitter expression. It was so sweet, my lips relaxed into a smile.

Komachi tossed back the rest in one go and stood up with a *hup*. "Okay then, I better go to bed."

"Yeah, do." Shaking the now-empty can, Komachi went to throw it out in the kitchen garbage. When she came to the door, Kamakura twitched and got up, then padded after her.

"Oh, hey, kitty. Wanna sleep together?" Komachi asked.

Kamakura didn't reply with a meow, rubbing his head against Komachi's leg instead. With a satisfied chuckle, Komachi lifted up the cat and put her hand on the doorknob.

I called after her. "Komachi."

"What?" Hand still on the knob, she turned back halfway.

"I'm rooting for you. Night."

"Yeah, thanks. I'll do my best. Night." Her words were few, but her smile was calm. Adjusting the cat in her arms with a *hup*, she went back to her room.

I watched her go, then folded my hands behind my head and flopped back down.

"Not deceiving yourself, huh…?"

Komachi might say I didn't, but right now, I couldn't say with confidence that was true.

I wasn't going out of my way to approach myself, but I also wasn't the one to back away, either.

I was aware of it and drawing a clear line, flatly putting a lid on it, making myself duller than usual, deciding not to think about it, as I have quite consciously continued to take the position of the coward in an attempt to be the canny observer.

I'd been trying to maintain a distance, to avoid recognizing that feeling that something was wrong for what it was.

This act was performed solely to avoid mistakes, and I understood well that it was not the only correct answer. But I was trying to swallow that down.

That had to be why she'd seen through me.

Once again, that voice torturing me came from inside.

Is that Hachiman Hikigaya? Is that what you wished for?

Shut up, stupid. Stop talking bullshit when you don't even know me. Shut up.

After that, I didn't say another word.

Interlude
@ Yui's room

Yui Yuigahama

Yukinon...are you still awake?

 ...I am.

 ...Yukinon, what d'you want to do?

 I...

 I have something I want to do.
I've made up my mind.

Wanna go on a date tomorrow?

 ...Pardon?

Y

ukino
Yukinoshita

Yui Yuigahama's gaze is always gentle and warm.

On that day, for once, it snowed.

It doesn't snow much in Chiba. The wet clouds coming in from the Sea of Japan are blocked by the many mountain ranges that run through Honshu like a backbone, and the snow falls there. On the Pacific side, particularly over the flatlands of Chiba, the winds are typically dry.

But once in a while, at odd moments such as these, it will snow. In my seventeen years of experience, we've had sudden blizzards on New Year's Day, on Coming of Age Day, and also at the end of March.

This snow unfortunately came exactly on Komachi's exam day.

Fortunately, it wasn't very windy, so the snow was just fluttering down like flower petals.

Equipped in her usual uniform, plus coat, scarf, gloves, and boots, Komachi was all ready to go out the door. This was quite a bit earlier than planned, but considering public transport was bound to be crowded, that was probably best.

"Did you bring your examination admission ticket?" I asked her. "How about your eraser, handkerchief, and five-sided pencil?"

The five-sided pencil is something our dad bought when he visited the Tenjin Shrine, shaped like a pentagonal cylinder. Well, aside from that, it's a normal pencil. Frankly, I think a normal round pencil might be easier to write with. Most entrance exam students will write the letters

A to *E* on each side of one of these pencils, or 1 to 5, or the vowels, and then every time they run into a multiple-choice question where they don't know the answer, they wind up praying and rolling it for dear life. In fact, you could say this pencil was created as a kind of five-sided die.

Komachi scanned the inside of her bag one last time and nodded cheerfully. Then she raised her umbrella and gave a snappy salute. "I'll be okay! Then, Bro…time for departure!"

"Yeah, see you later. Watch your step."

"I will! Urk, so cold. Sine, cosine, tangent… Oh, wait, that's not on the test." With a shiver, babbling and *hmm*ing to herself, Komachi trudged off.

I felt a touch of anxiety as I watched her go. *Is she gonna be okay…? She hasn't studied too much and wound herself too tight, right…?*

But anyway, it was finally the day of her entrance exams.

At this stage, there was no point in kicking up a fuss. The apocalypse was still a ways off, but exam days and deadlines will come, no matter how you struggle and fight it. It's the way of the world.

All I could do now was just to pray, and I looked up at the sky.

It really looked like the thick, low-hanging clouds would not clear, silently dropping white snow from the sky. That snow might continue all day.

A shiver ran through me from head to toe, and I took a step back inside. That was when I felt a different kind of shaking.

Reaching into my pocket, I found my cell phone was getting a call. The display read ★☆ *Yui* ☆★. It was Yuigahama. That entry hadn't been changed since she'd put in her contact info. It had remained the same, all this time.

I waffled for a few seconds about picking up. But the ringing didn't stop, and my phone kept vibrating. Bracing myself, I accepted the call and brought the phone to my ear. "…Hello?"

The moment I said it, I heard an inexhaustibly cheery voice from the receiver. "Hikki, let's go on a date!"

"…Huh?"

The first thing that had come out of her mouth, with no hello or anything, was the last thing I expected. The sound that left my mouth was particularly shrill and silly sounding, if I do say so myself.

×　×　×

After that call, I slowly got ready to go out.

As I was leaving the house, I checked the transit info on my phone and found that the crowds on the line I was about to ride had eased a bit. I didn't have to worry that I wouldn't reach the place where we were about to meet up, at least.

The fact is that the Kanto public transportation network really can't handle snow.

With Chiba prefecture, the Edo and Tone rivers are at the prefectural borders, so it's not just an island on land—it winds up being an actual isolated island. There's even a risk that Chiba could secede and declare independence.

Going outside, the weather looked about the same, and the snow was starting to accumulate like a faint frost fallen on the asphalt.

There wasn't enough snow on the ground to catch your feet, but the snow was slushy and slippery. Tracing the bicycle tracks and footprints, I slowly walked to the bus stop.

I transferred from the bus to the train, then gazed out from the train car window at the sea for a while.

The snow out the window fell lightly, from right to left. The sun was already fairly high, shining whitish light through the cloudy gray sky.

The train line running along the ocean was a little packed—not just because of the weather. This line generally gets crowded every time there's an event. For example, when there's the Tokyo Game Show or the Tokyo Motor Show at the Makuhari Messe, or Comiket at the Big Sight, or a live concert at Shinkiba—that's when it gets really crowded.

But the biggest reason was that this line has the station for the top-class domestic amusement park Tokyo Destiny Resort, or TDR for short.

Not to mention that day was Valentine's.

Even with the snow, business was booming. Listening in on the chatting of the couples on the train, they were all saying it was romantic or whatever. They actually welcomed the snowfall.

True enough, it was hard to complain about this setting for a Valentine's date.

Eventually, the white castle and the smoke-spewing volcano came into view up ahead of the train. The announcement told us we were stopping at the station, and the train car gradually decelerated. There was a dull swaying before the train came to a complete stop, and then the doors opened with a *pshh*. Cold air and snow blew in, and then the couples in my train car rushed to get off.

Then the bell rang to announce the doors closing. The special station ring, a clip from Destiny music, played as the train's departure melody.

Listening to the tune, I leaned against the door inside the now much-emptier car. The white castle and the smoking volcano both disappeared toward the left, growing distant.

This was not the station where I would be getting off that day.

At some point, it had crossed my mind that we'd come here together eventually, but that hadn't happened.

That promise you couldn't even call a promise was being fulfilled, even if it was with some changes.

The meeting spot for the newly made promise was one station over.

The train went over a big bridge, and after crossing the river at the prefectural border, a giant Ferris wheel came into view. I seemed to recall it was hailed as the largest in Japan.

I remembered the phone call from that morning. It hadn't been just confusion and surprise that had kept me from refusing that unexpected invitation. I'd been the one to make the original invitation. I'd just kept putting it off.

There wasn't really any reason to refuse.

But I wondered—*Am I okay with this?* Doubts rose in my mind.

As I was searching for the answer, the train slowed, and whether I wanted it to or not, it gave one last shake and came to a complete stop.

×　　×　　×

When I came out from the ticket gates, the big Ferris wheel immediately came into view.

You could see that attraction from the fountain square in front of the station. Being celebrated as the largest in Japan, it left an impact when you saw it up close. As the snow fluttered around, it continued to turn in a relaxed circle.

With the big Ferris wheel in the corner of my eye, I began to trudge along.

I'd come here before with my family when I was little, so I didn't get lost or anything. Referencing my memories and the info on the signboard, I hurried to my goal.

I went down the long main road that led to the beach, and eventually, a dome-shaped building came into view on my left. Beneath that was the entrance hall of the aquarium.

That was where we were meeting.

I went under the roofed area, closed my umbrella, scanned the area. It was a weekday, so maybe that was why there weren't many people around. So I was immediately able to find Yuigahama, who was in a blue coat.

"Hikki!"

She'd probably arrived on the train right before me. When she found me walking toward her, she called my name and slowly waved the pale-pink plastic umbrella in her hand.

I nodded back at her, heading over at a mild trot.

But then my feet stopped.

"…Ah."

Behind Yuigahama fluttered the hem of a gray coat.

The girl who'd been standing directly behind Yuigahama turned to me, and her eyes widened in surprise.

"Hikigaya…," she muttered. It was Yukino Yukinoshita.

Wondering, *Why is she here?* I stood before the both of them.

"So you're here, too…," I said, stating the obvious. I couldn't quite digest what was going on.

It seemed Yukinoshita felt the same. She squirmed uncomfortably and glanced at Yuigahama. Then she said anxiously, "U-um…if that's what's going on, then I'll be going…"

"It's okay! Let's hang out, the three of us!" Yuigahama said, hugging the other girl's arm. Yukinoshita seemed ready to leave at any moment.

Yuigahama took my arm, too. Holding both of us, she squeezed our arms tight against her chest and let her head hang. "I want the three of us to go…," she said in an almost inaudible murmur.

She was looking at the ground, and I couldn't see her expression. But the pleading in her voice got it across well enough.

Yukinoshita and I were speechless, looking at one another.

Yukinoshita's gaze continued to wander around, and she sighed as if confused. But Yuigahama picked up on that, raising her chin to give her a kind look, and Yukinoshita nodded with another little sigh.

Then Yuigahama's eyes turned to me.

If neither of them had any objections, then neither did I.

But I did want to ask just one thing. I found it hard to look straight at Yuigahama while I said it, and my eyes shifted away. It seemed incredibly pathetic to be saying something about it at this stage, and the words wouldn't quite leave my mouth smoothly. But I did manage to wring them out. "You want it to be here?"

"Yep," Yuigahama answered instantly—and directly, without averting her eyes, with a hint of urgency in her expression.

I hadn't meant my question in the general way, and I think her answer probably didn't mean it in the general way, either. Or wait, was it? Maybe there was nothing else to the meaning.

Whatever it was, it didn't matter. I had no reason to oppose the idea, if that was what Yuigahama wanted. "All right…"

"Yeah! If we come here, it's okay if it snows! I figured if we were all coming to hang out, then this would be best," she answered, standing proud and tall.

It's true that if you're hanging out with a group, this was better than Destiny. It'd be a bit of a hassle to go there as a group of three. So then, well…maybe another time? The day may yet come when I could fulfill that promise.

"Then let's go," I said.

For today, all three of us.

×　×　×

I'd seen the glass dome from a distance, but going inside made me realize how bright the sun was. The dome, made from countless pieces of glass put together, gathered the light even under cloudy skies. That plus the high ceiling made it feel quite bright.

On the other hand, the long escalator that led down into the aquarium got darker the deeper you went.

The way the light from ground level gradually grew distant was like a movie theater before the film starts, and the sense of anticipation made my heart race. And then, after descending the long escalator, there was a large tank just like a movie screen.

Huh, pretty impressive, I thought while gazing at the tank, as Yuigahama pattered off.

"Sharks!"

As she said, there were sharks in this tank. It seemed this kind was called a *tsumaguro*, a blacktip reef shark. The *maguro* part of the name made me think of tuna sushi, but it's not. It's a shark. Very much a shark.

Though there were not in fact sea bream and flounder dancing, aside from the sharks, the tank had rays and pilchards swimming around. Yuigahama peered excitedly into the tank and snapped several photos.

Next, she turned to her side and giggled as she pointed at the tank again and repeated, "Sharks!"

"…Indeed." Catching up to her, Yukinoshita gave Yuigahama a confused look. She sounded a little exasperated, too.

Yuigahama laughed an embarrassed *ah-ha-ha*, combing at her bun, then stepped right in to lean against Yukinoshita. "Yukinoooon, sorry I didn't say anything. Let's have some more fun with this!"

"I'm not going to have fun just because you told me to…"

Ignoring their conversation, I went to stand in front of the tank, too.

I didn't need Yuigahama telling me. That sure is a shark, all right. Sharks are cool…, I was thinking as my mind drifted absently, when a particularly composed and graceful silhouette swept into view.

It was a scalloped hammerhead. Because of its characteristic shape, I knew what it was called without having to read the sign.

Every boy will be into sharks at some point in his childhood.

I mean, like, everyone's got that period where you're all over picture books of dinosaurs and sea life and stuff. Every boy goes through a phase where he'll say, *I'm Hachiman Hikigaya and I'm three years old and my favorite dino is triceratops and my favorite deep-sea fish is barreleye.*

Eyes boring into the tank, I gave an appreciative and involuntary "Ooh." I was now totally like a boy in front of the trumpet in the show window. Like, *tutti!*

"Oh, a hammerhead shark… Huh, whoa, can we take pictures?" I asked Yuigahama beside me as I pointed at the sharks, and Yuigahama nodded *yep, yep* with a big sisterly expression. *Wow, you're allowed to take pictures…!*

As I was snapping photos, in the corner of my eye, I saw Yuigahama shuffling over to Yukinoshita. Then she whispered in her ear, "Look, Hikki's having fun."

"Agh…" Yukinoshita sighed in resignation. I didn't hear any whispers after that. The strange silence bothered me, and when I glanced over, my eyes met Yukinoshita's. She had her hand on her temple, and she was watching me.

She was staring pretty hard, so I got embarrassed. "…Wh-what?"

She swished the hair off her shoulders, then smiled a little teasingly. "Nothing. I was just surprised… I'll take a picture of you with the shark," she said and held out her hand. If I handed over my cell phone, I'd get a proper souvenir photo with the scalloped hammerhead shark.

"For real? I can show it to Komachi." Taking advantage of her offer, I handed over my cell phone carefully so that no fingers would touch the screen. "The hammerhead shark, okay? Press the button when it comes by. And if you can, get it right when the hammer part is sideways and you can get a good view of it."

"Those are surprisingly particular instructions…" Yukinoshita's eyebrows came together, but she tried taking a number of photos for me. Yuigahama, beside her, was grinning wide with amusement.

"How is this?" Yukinoshita asked.

I looked at the cell phone when she handed it back to me, and there it was, just as I'd asked, a photo taken at the perfect moment. The hammerhead shark looked about to bite me.

"Ohhh… This is good."

"Is it? All right, then." Yukinoshita sighed. She sounded a bit tired but also relieved.

Clinging to Yukinoshita, Yuigahama squished right up against her and tugged at her arm. "Then let's move on!"

"…Sure." Smiling back at her, Yukinoshita walked after Yuigahama. At first, Yukinoshita had been reluctant to go along with this, but now she was actually getting into exploring this aquarium.

Though I was sad to leave it behind, I said my farewell to the hammerhead and followed after the girls.

× × ×

Perhaps because it was a weekday, the visitors in the aquarium were sparse.

The crowd was more on the quiet side: elderly husbands and wives and calmer-looking couples, plus I saw a few with babies, as well as young women with female friends. If this had been a weekend or holiday, it would have been awash with kids and families.

The area was dim, and many of the tanks were lit up. It was like a movie theater, making everyone naturally talk quieter.

The same went for us. The giant tank with the Pacific bluefin tuna was impressive, and we just sighed in wonder, and also at the next one, in a group of tanks titled "Oceans of the World," which was divided into a number of different areas. The brilliance of the tropical fish section made me stop and stare.

Seeing the grandeur, strength, and beauty of nature up close, all we could say were things like "Wow" and "They're so beautiful" and "Looks yummy." *Wait, yummy...?*

But of course, there were exceptions.

When we passed in front of the tank of a certain fishy, Yuigahama's feet froze. And when she stopped, so did Yukinoshita and I.

At a glance, the tank was dark and plain, nothing to grab your attention like the fish tanks around it. There was no light shining into it. There was mud piled in it, with one thin tree sticking up alone.

And in the water was a rather vacant-looking fish that seemed kind of dumb, swimming around lazily. No, maybe it wasn't quite accurate to say it was *swimming*. The thing wasn't moving much, just bobbing aimlessly, almost drifting.

"Whoa, gross...," Yuigahama muttered carelessly. Then she looked at the sign for it. "It says it's a nurseryfish."

"'It lives in muddy rivers and doesn't swim around very much'...?" Yukinoshita read the explanation, then looked at me.

Why's she looking at me? I thought, and then my eyes slid over to the sign to see there was more. *Oh-ho... So when a shrimp or something comes by right in front of it, it'll swallow it in an instant, huh...?*

"Sounds like the life...," I blurted out.

"You can sympathize with it?!" Yuigahama was shocked.

Yukinoshita's lips quirked into a smile as she listened to us. "Now that you mention it, this fish does look quite similar to someone, doesn't it, Fishigaya?"

"It's not similar at all. And that nickname is kinda weak..."

Why's she smiling at me, come on... Well apparently, the nurseryfish is also called the *komori-uo*. The *komori* there is probably supposed to mean "babysitting," but if this were a *hikikomori* fish, I guess it would be kind of similar to me… Well, I am pretty good at child-minding, you know. I love kids!

At some point in the course of our idle chatter, Yuigahama started ignoring it and leaning forward to gaze into the tank. Expression entranced, she giggled, then said gleefully, "Wooow, so gross."

"Don't call it gross; it's doing its best." *It's our friend on Spaceship Earth, isn't it? Hey, why does she seem kind of pleased…?*

As Yuigahama continued to stare at the nurseryfish, Yukinoshita came up beside her and squatted down. The two of them kept talking to each other and discussing how gross and creepy it was.

But suddenly, Yuigahama got a smile on her face. "But…maybe a little cute."

"Possible cuteness aside, it does have its own kind of charm," Yukinoshita said, and then she and Yuigahama looked at each other and giggled.

"If you're calling it creepy, then how is it cute…?" I grumbled.

Bottom line, the nurseryfish was just ugly. How can you call something like that cute?

I don't really understand girls' sensibilities. This is just that thing, right? Like that stuff you say to boys when introducing your friend at a mixer, like *Her gestures are cute* or *Her hair is cute* or *Her voice is cute*, right? It's what you say when you're indirectly communicating her looks *aren't* cute, right? I've seen that on the Internet, you know.

It really is true what they say: You can't trust what girls call cute.

X X X

Porcupine fish and clown fish. Seahorses and leafy sea dragons. Lefteye flounder and righteye flounder. And even largehead hairtail and Japanese sea lilies…

Walking around, looking at the many fish from the oceans and deep seas of the world, we continued along the route as it led outside.

After being in the dark for a while, the light of the sun was dazzling even beneath a cloudy sky. When we passed through the automatic doors and reached the outside walkway, the cold ocean wind stroked my cheeks, and at the same time, the strong scent of sea salt hit my nose.

It looked like there was a reproduction of a tide pool here. They had a whole bunch of beach creatures, like crabs, acorn barnacles, and sea stars on display.

Go a little farther, and you'd leave the roofed area so you could look up at the sky.

There was a lull in the snowfall, and it was just a mild flutter coming down now. I'd heard the recent cold wave was causing weather fluctuations, so you couldn't say how it would be later. But regardless, it seemed like we didn't have to worry about the weather at this time of afternoon.

"Oh, there's a bunch of people over there."

As I was considering the weather, Yuigahama turned back to us and pointed ahead. There was a little crowd gathering down the way, calling out excitedly.

"Guess we should go check it out," I said. Heading over to this little hotspot, I found a tank like a small pool extended in a long line along the outside walkway. Unlike the other tanks, it didn't have a lid on it, and the water was exposed to the air.

Looking over at the sign, it read, TOUCH GENTLY WITH TWO FINGERS. So this was like a petting-zoo experience.

What sort of ocean creatures are here for the petting? I wondered as I peered into the tank.

Sharks.

That was what was there.

Small sharks and rays drifted around. I looked at the sign, which read, BROWNBANDED BAMBOO SHARK (ALSO KNOWN AS THE "DOG SHARK"); BULLHEAD SHARK (ALSO KNOWN AS THE "CAT SHARK"); RED STINGRAY; and PITTED STINGRAY.

"Hey, Hikki! It says this is called a dog shark!" Yuigahama smacked at my upper arm excitedly before taking a closer look. Then she poked at the creature with her finger.

The so-called dog shark didn't really react, calmly letting itself be touched. Eventually, Yuigahama nodded like she was convinced of something. "...I think it's a little like Sablé!"

How? Like the fact that it's light gray? This shark is literally nothing like a dog; are you okay? Like, if you're so sure it's similar, are you certain your dog is actually a dog? Not a shark?

Anyway, why would they call these things dog sharks...? I wondered, tilting my head, and it seemed someone else had a similar question in mind.

Yukinoshita was right beside me, hand on her chin with her eyes locked on the bullhead sharks.

The bullhead sharks, or "cat sharks," were a size or two smaller than the dog sharks, with characteristic striped patterns on their bodies that made them easy to identify.

"Cat shark...," Yukinoshita muttered as she stared hard at the bull-head sharks swimming around. "Inscrutable... Just what about these is catlike...? If they're naming them cat sharks, then something about them should be similar..."

Oh-ho, so she feels compelled to react to anything with cat *in its name, huh? She's really got the friskies for kitties.*

Yukinoshita rolled up her sleeves as if she'd made up her mind, then cheerily reached out to a bullhead shark and petted it for a while. Then a satisfied smile broke on her face. "...I think it feels a bit like a cat's tongue."

"That's just shark skin," I said, but Yukinoshita wasn't listening. She was utterly absorbed in petting the "cat shark."

"Here, kitty, kitty, kitty shark... *Meow...* No, perhaps it's *sheow...*"

"I strongly doubt that's the sound that shark makes..." *I mean, sharks don't make noise at all...I think.*

That was when Yuigahama began looking for a new target after the shark, her hand wandering around in the water. "Oh, there's rays, too!" Yuigahama said, ever a *ray* of sunshine herself. Eyyy! …Fine, so it wasn't my best.

"Eeep!" But then she immediately cried out and yanked back her fingers. "It was slimy! Yuck!" She sounded like she was on the verge of tears.

Yukinoshita, who'd been entranced by her cat sharks all this time, rushed up to Yuigahama's side and said with concern, "What did you touch? Hikigaya? You should hurry and wash your hand."

Hey? Could you not treat a person like a sea creature? There's no mucus coming out of me, you know. Admittedly, when I'm touching a girl, I definitely get sweaty hands, so maybe we're not so different. All girls, if you touch me, make sure to wash your hands!

But you don't get a chance to touch sharks or rays and stuff every day. I rolled up my sleeves as well and petted them with my fingers.

As I was enjoying the roughness and sliminess, Yuigahama drew back her hand. She just watched the sharks with a loving gaze.

"What, you've had enough?" I asked her.

"Yeah, I don't want to tire them out."

"Ah. That's very you." I couldn't help but smile. It's true—from the animal's position, getting petted excessively by thoughtless humans would be pretty stressful. Like when I pet my cat, he swats at me and stuff. It genuinely feels nice to me when Yuigahama shows consideration like that.

That was all I'd meant when I'd said that. But Yuigahama's shoulders twitched, and she glanced away, her gaze trending down. "…What is?"

My eyes followed her gaze to see what she was looking at. Snow was fluttering downward, making ripples on the surface of the water.

She slowly lifted her head to examine me. "…I'm not as nice as you think I am." There was a delicate, wistful smile in her eyes, as if she were telling me of our parting, and those whispered words sounded more for her than for me.

Hearing that, my breath caught. What, exactly, was I pointing to when I said that gesture was "like Yuigahama"?

That feeling like something was wrong once again crawled out from inside me, slithering around in my chest and disturbing the peace as I wondered if I wasn't overlooking something serious. I clenched my fists.

I opened my mouth anyway—because I had to say something—but the right answer wouldn't come out. Yuigahama just looked at my trembling lips, smiled sadly, and lowered her eyes.

Without our voices and words, the noises around us sounded that much louder.

And among them was a shrill cry. *Nooot!*

Yuigahama's head jerked up, and she jumped to her feet. "Oh, that's a penguin! Hikki, Yukinon, let's go!" she said in a cheery voice.

When I looked at Yukinoshita, she was regarding us with a vacant expression, but then she snapped out of it with a gasp. Her eyes wavered between Yuigahama and me, as if she was worried about us.

"Let's go?" said Yuigahama.

Yukinoshita replied to Yuigahama's excitement with a weak smile. "Y-yes… Let's."

Had she been listening to our earlier exchange? Maybe she'd gotten a glimpse of the expression on Yuigahama's face.

Yuigahama took Yukinoshita's arm, then marched off for the rocky mountain. Her steps were light.

From what I could tell from behind, along with her extra-cheery attitude, she seemed to be saying that talk was now over, and we were all going to have fun.

Letting out a sigh and trying to change gears, I followed after them.

×   ×   ×

After walking awhile, we came to a wide rocky mountain.

On it were a whole bunch of penguins *merp-merp*ing at each other, splashing as they jumped into the pool or pressing up against each other in the shadow of the rock to keep warm.

"Wow, so cute!"

"...They are."

Yuigahama was bouncing around, taking a whole bunch of pictures, while beside her, Yukinoshita was smiling. Though she was more reserved, she snapped the shutter a few times, too. Girls really love penguins, huh?

I was also madly in love with their plump yet streamlined bodies, their cute, round eyes, and the way they waddled. "Aw, what the hell. They're so cute... I've gotta send pics to Komachi." Getting as close to them as I could, right up to the fence, I snapped a bunch of photos.

As I was doing this, an idea struck me.

If I showed a picture to Komachi after she finished her exams, she would most definitely be like, *Komachi wants to go too!* and then if I said, *Okay, then how about we go together?* she would easily agree, and then I'd be able to have a legal date with my little sister, *shleh-heh-heh-heh.*

As I was wickedly scheming, Yuigahama and Yukinoshita had already gone on ahead. *Ah, oh no, they're about to leave me!*

I abandoned my photo taking and chased after them. They were following the standard route, down the stairs that led to the semibasement.

In the penguin zone, in addition to the standard route, there was also a space where you could see into their big pool from the side and watch the penguins swimming in the water.

The penguins here had a totally different vibe from the slow, pengy waddles they did on land.

In the water, they made fine turns and swam with incredible guiny speed, almost as if they were flying.

Watching them, Yuigahama cried out in wonder as she kept tugging on Yukinoshita's sleeve. "Wow! Wow! Look at 'em swimming! They remind me of birds like this!"

"...Penguins *are* birds, though," Yukinoshita said, sounding exasperated. She pressed her temple with her free hand.

Yuigahama's mouth dropped open dumbly, but she snapped out

of it with a start. "...Huh. I—I knew that," she hurried to add. Yuk-inoshita smiled softly at her, and I cracked a wry smile, too. Oh well, it's not like I can't understand the feeling.

After enjoying the penguins elegantly swimming around, we continued to the stairs that led up from the semibasement.

From there, we headed to the rock mountain where the Humboldt penguins were. You could get a good view of the busy little huddle.

There were two penguins in the group that happened to catch my eye. They pressed close in an intimate way, grooming each other and constantly making those *merp, merp* noises at each other.

Feeling rather charmed as I watched them, I looked at the sign ahead that had explanatory notes. When I read it with interest, the girls both leaned in around me. "Lemme see, lemme see." I took half a step back to yield the space to them as I traced the sign text with my eyes.

The sign said the two cuddling penguins were a mated pair. Generally, with Humboldt penguins in captivity, so long as one of them didn't die, they would continue to stay with the same partner.

After reading that, I looked at the pair of penguins once again and saw Yukinoshita in front of me. She swayed a little, and then her breath caught. Then she quickly left.

"What's wrong?" I asked, curious as to why she was rushing ahead.

Yukinoshita turned halfway back. "...I'll be waiting inside," she said briefly, and then without looking back again, she returned to the aquarium.

The penguin zone was outdoors. Considering the weather, it was a good time to go back inside.

I was turning around, about to say we should move on, too, when I saw Yuigahama still watching the two Humboldt penguins. Her eyes were soft and gentle.

"...Wanna get going?" I asked her.

"Oh, yeah... I'm gonna look a bit more before I go... I-I've got to take a picture of those tiny ones, after all! ...I'll go soon," she said, pointing to the fairy penguins and holding up her phone for me to see before turning back to the pair again. It didn't look as if the cell phone in her hand was being used—she was just squeezing it tight.

"…Okay." I couldn't bring myself to say anything more. With that brief reply, I went on inside.

Behind me, the conversation between the two penguins sounded a little sad.

×　×　×

Perhaps because we'd been outside for a while, when I went back indoors, the warmth drew a sigh from me.

Following the course onward from the penguin zone led down the stairs to another floor.

There was bigger size tank there. The sign called it a "seaweed forest," with large waterweed and giant kelp, and even from a distance, I could see the giant kelp's arms reaching wide, drifting to and fro.

This floor was darkened, and aside from the pale-brown kelp, there were also various red and green sea anemones and coral under brilliant illumination.

They'd gone to the trouble of setting out benches in front of that tank, just like a little movie theater. But it was deserted.

Meanwhile, the light seeping out from the other side of the tank dimly brought into view the figure that stood in front of the glass.

The one standing there couldn't be mistaken for anyone else.

It was Yukino Yukinoshita.

Under the pale light of the tank, she looked like a painting, and I couldn't call out to her. The breath I'd need was stuck in my chest. So I just stopped there.

She must have noticed my footsteps halting, as she turned back to me. Once she gave me something resembling the barest nod, I was finally able to start walking again.

"Where's Yuigahama?" she asked without looking, still gazing into the tank as I came up beside her.

"She's taking pictures of the fairy penguins. She said she'd come soon, so we can just wait here."

"I see…"

After that, no words were exchanged. We just stared into the tank in front of us. At the giant seaweed beneath the light, with multicolored fish swimming all around.

Countless fish came and went among the unsteadily wavering kelp. Tiny fish with bluish scales hid behind the seaweed, while particularly attention-grabbing red fish sailed around, fearing no one.

Eyes following the fish, Yukinoshita suddenly spoke. "…Some are free, aren't they?" she said quietly, like she was talking to herself and not anyone else. But she was probably looking at the same fish I was.

So I naturally responded. "Mm. Yeah, those fish are big, after all."

She let out a faint sigh.

"If you have no place to go, then you can't find where you belong… You just hide, follow the current or whatever else there is to follow… until you hit an invisible wall." She started gently reaching out her hand to touch the glass. But before long, her hand lowered weakly, soundlessly. When I examined her with a sidelong glance, her eyes weren't focused on anything. They were just pointed straight ahead.

"…Which fish are you talking about?" I asked. I didn't know what she was looking at.

She didn't answer immediately, sighing peacefully.

"…I mean me," she said, cocking her head a smidgen as she smiled sadly and touched the tank with a gentle hand.

With her arm extended, she looked as if she would be sucked into the water, but the wall prevented her from going back to the home she'd found.

She looked so delicate and ephemeral, as if she were about to turn into bubbles and vanish.

That floor was utterly silent. The glass prevented the bubbles popping and welling up inside the tank from sounding on this side.

As I watched Yukinoshita gazing into the tank, thinking about that separate world, there was the tap of a foot on the floor.

When I turned around, there was Yuigahama, watching Yukinoshita with peaceful eyes. Her expression was utterly gentle, maybe even close to tearful.

"Sorry to make you guys wait!" When Yuigahama noticed me, she waved an arm wide and called out to me with her usual smile.

×   ×   ×

After going through the floor with the giant kelp display, it got suddenly bright inside.

Perhaps for the sake of lighting, the upper parts of the walls were glass, and the ceiling was high. In place of the earlier black carpets, cream-colored floorboards lay under our feet.

The tapping of Yuigahama's energetic footsteps sounded cheerful on them. Those footsteps suddenly stopped as she discovered something. "Oh, hey, c'mere, come on!" she said, beckoning to me and Yukinoshita.

The place she called us to had a number of cylindrical tanks. Pink, purple, marine blue. The tanks were lit up in all sorts of colors, and inside were jellyfish, wafting and drifting.

Yuigahama grabbed on to Yukinoshita's arm, and the two of them gazed at the fish, side by side. The tank was like a round window, a little small for all three of us to look at, so I peered at it from a step farther away.

"They're kinda like fireworks, huh…?" Yuigahama murmured fondly as she gazed at the undulating jellies.

"…You think?" I said.

But a jellyfish is a jellyfish. I gave them a good look, wondering just what about them was like fireworks.

Yuigahama turned back to me and pointed to one part of the tank with a *hnn*. "You can't see it? Look, like that one, it's all *zoooom, baaang…*"

The jellyfish where Yuigahama was pointing folded and then spread its star-shaped body, folded and then spread it, over and over. It did kind of look like fireworks.

"Huh, I get it. I kinda see it, when the round things spread out," I replied.

But Yuigahama gave her head a little shake, and then she tried again, this time tapping the glass with her finger. "Not that one, this one...," she said. The jellyfish Yuigahama pointed to was a long-armed one at the back.

It brought its long tentacles together for an instant, then opened them all up again in a burst. Under the lights of the tank, it traced sparkling threads that then dangled down and spread out in the water like a fall of golden light.

We had seen fireworks like that before.

Back in the summer. In a park teeming with crowds, there had been a bunch of giant star mines reflecting in the half mirror of the tower. I seemed to remember they'd fired up those golden rain fireworks for the finale. They'd sparkled in the night sky, leaving droplets of light that lasted forever.

Yuigahama leaned on Yukinoshita's shoulder. We were all remembering that sight as we looked into the tank.

"...Okay, that's enough." Yukinoshita squirmed around like she didn't know how to deal with it.

"Eh-heh..." But Yuigahama didn't seem to care. She tugged Yukinoshita's arm to bring her close, taking up position in front of the tank. Eyeing my reflection in the glass, she made sure I was behind them.

And then Yuigahama closed her eyes for just a heartbeat. "I'm glad the three of us could see this together..."

Those words were like a sigh of relief.

Strangely, they felt right. Yukinoshita drew her chin back slightly, too, and nodded.

I wanted to believe that even if it went unsaid, the feeling we had in our hearts that moment was probably not all that different.

X   X   X

We went down a bright corridor and came out on a floor with a restaurant and a shop. Turn left there, and it leads outside. It seemed the course ended here. Continuing on up the stairs would lead to the exit.

Glancing farther in, if we went right from the earlier floor, that was the tank with the hammerhead shark we'd seen at the beginning. In other words, now we'd done a full circle.

"Goal!" Yuigahama hopped energetically and turned back to us. "Hey, let's do another round!"

"No…there's no point in circling around the same stuff," I said.

"Y-yes… And I'm a little tired…" Unlike Yuigahama, Yukinoshita was lacking in energy. We'd walked around quite a bit, and Yukinoshita, who had difficulties with endurance to begin with, seemed worn out.

I gave Yuigahama a look that said, *See how she's doing?*

Yuigahama fiddled with her bun, looking down the path we'd come. She didn't want to go. "I guess… I think it'd be fun, though… And besides, we still have…," she said as she checked the time.

Then it seemed something caught her eye.

"Ah!" With a cry, she pointed to the big Ferris wheel that rose up in the distance.

X   X   X

The Ferris wheel was the biggest in Japan, and it earned that title.

When I pulled the ride ticket out from my breast pocket, it read, *Diameter of 111 meters, total height of 117 meters.* I can't think of a precise example to describe how tall it actually was, and it's difficult to express, but if I had to say it in a word: tall. And scary. Scary enough that I needed to add it to my one-word summary.

We didn't have to line up long for this Ferris wheel we were going to ride on Yuigahama's whim, and we were able to get on soon after buying a ticket.

And I was immediately assaulted by fear.

Thinking about it, it had been ten years since I'd last ridden a Ferris wheel. *Were they always this shaky?* I wondered as the floor underfoot started to wobble.

The gradual rise in altitude felt just like a bizarre adventure. With every gust of wind, the car swayed slightly, and I really worried that this might be the end of the road for me.

"This is terrifying…," I muttered without thinking.

But I kept that to just a whisper because I couldn't be losing my cool in front of two girls: the act of a gentleman. If I'd been riding this thing alone, I would've been curled in a trembling ball.

As for how those two were doing, they were sitting side by side in front of me.

"Wow! So high! Scary! And, like, this is swaying a lot!" Yuigahama was practically standing, pressed up against the window as she gleefully enjoyed the ride. Thanks to her, my quiet, fearful mutter was drowned out.

Meanwhile, Yukinoshita was white as a sheet, avoiding looking at the scenery outside as she focused her gaze at her feet.

"Look, I just asked you, didn't I? I said you didn't have to go if you didn't want to," I said carelessly, smirking at her reaction.

She gave me a little glare. "Th-there's no problem… We're all together, after all," she said, then jerked her face away. That must have brought the view of below into her field of vision. She choked silently and reached a hand over to where Yuigahama was standing, seeking her help. Firmly grabbing Yuigahama's hand, she forced her to sit.

"Yuigahama. Did you not read the caution sign saying that you shouldn't jump around on the Ferris wheel?"

"Yukinon, don't glare at me like that! S-sorry, I was just having fun…" Yuigahama apologized with an *ah-ha-ha*.

"I don't mind if you enjoy yourself, but…in moderation, please." Yukinoshita chided her coldly but showed no indication that she would let go of the hand in her grasp.

Yuigahama noticed Yukinoshita holding her hand and squeezed

back tight, scooting closer to Yukinoshita with a smile. Then she pointed to the right, from their perspective. "Look, over there! Your apartment is probably around there. Oh, maybe we can see if we lean more that way."

"…I'm fine. I can see it just fine from here." Yukinoshita stubbornly stayed in her spot. But she did, with trepidation, peek out the window.

Then, a satisfied-sounding *ahhh* slipped from her lips.

Still leaning my cheek on my hand, I looked at the scenery outside, too.

Spread out below was Chiba, with the snow falling on and on. Crystals sparkled under the light peeking out from between the clouds, and from a distance, you could get a good view of the townscape sprinkled with a white layer of snow.

"It's so beautiful…," Yuigahama said.

I nodded my full agreement. "Yeah, that's my Chiba."

"When did it become yours?!"

"We're actually in Tokyo right now, though…," said Yukinoshita.

"If you're around Kasai, that's basically like Chiba. People don't treat Edogawa like Tokyo, right?" I said, making Yuigahama giggle and Yukinoshita smile in exasperation. Then we gazed out at the scenery spread below, without ever tiring of it.

It was our usual conversation, with an air of the mundane, and I think you could say it was like us. But the floor under my feet was uncertain and wobbling.

The Ferris wheel slowly came down.

Hiding its instability, it continued to slowly circle around. Never moving onward, just going around and around the same place, forever.

But even so, in the end.

"…It's just about over, huh?" she said quietly.

Spring is made and begins to bud underneath the snow.

Even after we got off the Ferris wheel, snow was still fluttering around. It wasn't enough to warrant an umbrella, reflecting in the light as it blew in the wind. The park lawn had a faint layer of white, quietly informing us of the passage of time.

We hardly spoke as we walked through the park. Yuigahama took the lead, while Yukinoshita and I followed.

Eventually, the side path merged into the long main road that came from the station. Turn left here, and it would lead to the train station, while if you went right, it would take you to the beach.

Yuigahama didn't hesitate. She turned right.

"Hey…" I called out to her to ask if she meant to stop by somewhere; she spun around back to me and pointed down the road without a word.

She was indicating a glass-walled building, and the sign said it was called Crystal View. It was probably an observation tower where you could look out over Tokyo Bay.

When I glanced at my phone clock, it was still early enough that I didn't have to go home yet.

"Let's go," Yukinoshita prompted me, and she started walking to catch up to Yuigahama, who was waiting ahead.

I followed after the two of them for a while.

The observation deck was closed by now, but the part that was like a terrace was open. We could still get a view of Tokyo Bay from there.

Snow was falling on the quietly rolling sea, and the setting sun blurred out from between the clouds.

A colorless white sparkled among the rose and azure.

"Ohhh!" Yuigahama cried out in excitement at the view.

Yukinoshita, a few steps behind her, pressed down her hair as it blew in the wind, gazing into the distance. The sight was affecting her, too.

There was nobody but us, with the sea sprawled before us and the dots of the city lights in the distance.

This view could only be seen right here, right now.

That moment was peaceful, leisurely.

Which was exactly why it wouldn't last long.

Yuigahama pulled back from the terrace fence she'd been leaning over and turned to us again. "What should we do now?"

"Go home," I said, half-joking.

Yuigahama quietly shook her head. "That's not what I meant..."

There was an earnest weight in her tone. She took one soft step up to Yukinoshita and me and looked straight at both of us. "About Yukinon. And about me... About us."

The words I'd been running away from made my heart jump. The feeling I'd had all this time, that feeling that something was wrong, rapidly rose inside me and took shape.

Yukinoshita paused hesitantly, then asked, "...What's that supposed to mean?"

Yuigahama didn't answer. She just gave us a serious look. "Hikki. This is thanks for before," she said, then drew something out of her bag. Offering with both hands, she held up a package of prettily wrapped cookies.

I heard someone's breath catch upon seeing that. In the corner of my eye, Yukinoshita clutched at her bag and gave a barely perceptible shake of her head. Then her head dropped, and she stared down at her feet.

Yuigahama passed by her side then, coming up before me. "Do you remember my request?"

"...Yeah," I replied with a voice that was hardly there.

There was no way I could forget; it was the first consultation that I—that the Service Club—had taken. Back then, though, I'd just wound up saying something dumb to muddy the waters. The matter was far from resolved or canceled.

But despite that, Yuigahama had been trying to bring closure all by herself. She was trying to indicate that clearly now.

I was still bewildered, unable to force myself to move, so she took my hand and pressed the cookies into them. There was a definite weight in my hand.

The cookies I could see through the cellophane were uneven shapes, and some of them were a little burned or off-color. Nobody would call them pretty. But that was how you instantly knew they were homemade.

She was such a bad cook, their workmanship spoke to me of her effort and seriousness.

Yukinoshita, who'd been staring blankly at the cookies in my hands, opened her mouth with a sigh. "Homemade cookies... You made them yourself?"

"I sort of screwed them up, though." Yuigahama smiled shyly to cover her embarrassment.

As if to say, *That's nothing*, Yukinoshita gave a little shake of her head. "Yuigahama. You're...amazing." There was longing in her kind tone, or maybe it was something like admiration. Yukinoshita was looking at Yuigahama with awe.

Yuigahama returned that gaze with a happy smile. "...I said I'd try it myself. And that I'd try doing it my own way. That's what this is."

And Yui Yuigahama came up with her own answer.

"...So it's just a thanks," she said, standing proud with a bright smile.

If she was calling this a thanks for that time, that matter had already been dealt with. What had happened in the past had already been squared, and I wasn't going to dig it up now. I'd already gotten more than enough thanks, over all the days up until now. So it wasn't logical to accept this as gratitude.

We'd started off wrong, but I'd thought we'd put a proper end to that. That we'd made a new start.

So then maybe the feelings, or the answer that had been in that new start, could change.

…If…just supposing… If those feelings were something special…

Without averting my eyes from Yuigahama, I found the words in my tightening throat. "…I've already accepted your thanks."

It wasn't like I actually wanted to make sure what she really meant. But I couldn't just nod along and accept this without considering it at all.

But the moment I said that, I regretted it. As she stood in front of me, she looked like she was going to cry.

"But still…it's just a thanks, okay?" she said, her voice sounding stifled, then bit the edge of her lip as her face scrunched up. And then she spun away, as if to hide the light in her eyes.

"I want everything. Now, and in the future, too. I'm unfair. I just don't have the guts," she said at the sky, sounding a tiny bit sulky. That seemed like an answer, and also like a monologue that asked for no answer or refutation. So all I could do was gaze at her back and at least listen closely so I wouldn't miss anything.

When she was done talking, a white sigh rose up to melt into thin air.

And then she turned back to fix a direct gaze on us.

"I've made up my mind." Yuigahama's eyes were no longer moist, but determined and strong.

"I see…," Yukinoshita muttered with something like resignation, and I couldn't even come up with a meaningless response.

Yuigahama smiled at us a little sadly. "I think once both know how the other feels, you can't keep going along the same way… So this'll probably be my last request. Our final request is about us."

She didn't say a single concrete thing. Since once she'd said it out loud, that would define it. We had been avoiding that.

She spoke gingerly, vaguely, without giving a name to that truth. So there was no guarantee at all that the truths Yuigahama, Yukinoshita, and I pictured were completely the same.

But when she said we couldn't stay like this, that was the one thing that did seem to be the truth.

This was the doubt that I'd continued to hold in a corner of my heart all this time, and Yuigahama was deeply aware of it, too.

And then there was one other.

Yukinoshita's face was downturned, eyes closed. Though I couldn't quite see her expression, she didn't argue, and she didn't question Yuigahama, either, listening in silence. I think she was probably feeling it keenly, too.

"Hey, Yukinon. That contest is still going on, right?"

"Yes. Doing whatever the winner says...," Yukinoshita answered as if she was confused to be asked something so unexpected.

Yuigahama, standing right in front of her, gently touched Yukinoshita's arm and said in her encouraging voice, "I know the answer to the problem you have right now, Yukinon." And she slowly rubbed Yukinoshita's arm.

Yukinoshita's problem—that had always been there, in her behavior, in her words.

And Haruno Yukinoshita had stated it explicitly. That Yukino Yukinoshita didn't know what to do. Do about what? Her mother, her sister, or these relationships? Any of them, maybe all of them.

"I..." Yukinoshita hung her head weakly, utterly lost, then murmured in a near whisper, "I don't know."

Yuigahama nodded gently and released her. "I think probably... that's our answer."

Not knowing, ultimately. Me, or them.

Once you comprehend it, then it will break. If you put a lid on it and ignore it long enough, then it will rot away bit by bit. So no matter what you do, it'll come to an end. You can't avoid losing it.

That was the answer, the conclusion that awaited where we were headed.

Yuigahama paused there a moment, then gave a little shake of her head. "So…," she began, looking right at Yukinoshita and me. "If I win, then I'll take everything. Maybe it's not fair, but…that's all I can think of… I'd like things to stay like this forever."

That was why Yuigahama had gone with the answer first. She had ignored the hypothesis, conditions, equations, and everything to start with making the conclusion explicit.

She was saying that no matter what process you went through, no matter what sort of situation it was, even if it was an equation that was impossible to balance, the answer was the one thing that wouldn't change. This fun time wouldn't go on forever.

"So…?" she asked.

I didn't know how to answer. "So…? Well…"

Normally, that couldn't be done—working backward from the conclusion, even if it twisted the formula a bit or falsified the evidence, to bring it to that answer. But the compulsion to "do whatever she said"—no, it was only possible to grant that wish if you rationalize and say we were being compelled.

If she gave us an excuse like that, then I was sure I could convince myself, too.

I might even start thinking that if we could keep doing what we did today, even if it felt a little wrong, then wouldn't that also count as happiness?

Most of all…

…Yuigahama probably wasn't wrong. I felt like she was the one person who'd been looking at the right answer the whole time. I was sure it would be easier to accept that. But—

Was it right to leave something distorted without trying to fix it? Was that the true nature of the thing I'd been wishing for?

As my teeth were gritted, unable to reply, Yuigahama looked at me kindly. And then she reached out beside her and gently took Yukinoshita's hand.

"Are you okay with that, Yukinon?" Yuigahama asked her, like a mother questioning a small child.

The question made Yukinoshita's shoulders twitch. "O-oh, I…" She averted her eyes but put together the words in a weak, faltering voice, compelled to respond.

The moment I saw her like that, my intuition spoke to me.

Ah, this is… No, this is wrong.

Yukinoshita couldn't entrust her future to someone else. That would never be okay.

And Yuigahama was being unfair—letting her say something like that would never be okay.

"I still…"

"No." I took a step in to keep her from saying any more. When I raised my voice, Yukinoshita looked at me, eyes filled with surprise.

"I can't go along with your proposal. Yukinoshita should resolve her own problems herself." Clenching my fists tight, I fixed my gaze on Yuigahama, who stood in front of me.

Her mouth was drawn in a hard line as she stared at me with an unusually cold and dignified expression.

Yui Yuigahama is a kind girl. That was what I'd assumed.

Yukino Yukinoshita is a strong girl. That was the ideal I'd forced on her.

With those in my mind, I'd continued to take advantage. But that was exactly why I couldn't leave this to her. I couldn't repay her kindness with lies.

I mean, after all, Yui Yuigahama is a kind girl, and Yukino Yukinoshita is a strong girl.

"…Besides, that's just phony anyway," I spat, and the words disappeared in the surging ocean waves. The rolling water just washed in, then out, over and over.

Nobody spoke.

Yukinoshita's lips trembled, eyes wet, while Yuigahama gave a warm little nod, waiting for me to continue.

"I...don't need vague answers or shallow relationships of convenience."

What I wanted was something else.

I think I'm an idiot.

I know something like that doesn't exist. I know that even if I obsess over it, I'd get nothing out of it.

But.

"But still, giving it the thought it deserves, suffering...and struggling... I..." The words I wrung out lost all voice.

I knew something like this wasn't right. Maybe if I could say I was fine with this, that would have been okay. If I could have spent that time thinking of different futures and beautiful possibilities, then nobody would have to suffer.

But even so, I want to force my ideals on them. I'm not strong enough to live on in slumber. Because after all that doubting myself, I don't want to lie to someone I care about.

So I wanted to get a proper answer. No falsities or equivocation. The answer I want.

I let out a hot breath, and when she realized nothing else was coming, Yuigahama looked me right in the eye.

"...I thought you'd say that, Hikki." She smiled kindly. That instant, a drop trailed down her cheek.

What about me? I hoped I didn't look like a mess.

Yuigahama and I looked at each other and traded little nods.

Our wishes could not be seen with the eye. But their forms were probably just slightly out of sync, unable to perfectly overlap.

Still, it wasn't like they would never be the same thing.

Now that it was out, it would come that much closer into view. Surely a part of it would be connected somewhere. And I turned to Yukinoshita.

Yukinoshita squeezed at her chest, looking between Yuigahama and me with teary eyes. Her anxious gaze wavered like something fragile. But when she realized I had been waiting for her answer the whole time, she took a little breath in and out.

"…Don't assume how I feel," she said a little sulkily, then wiped her eyes. "Besides, it's not the end. There's still your request, Hikigaya."

I tried to reply, *My request?* But Yuigahama's faint smile cut me off. She nodded at Yukinoshita like, *That's right.*

With just a look, the two of them traded smiles like a secret just for them.

"…And one more thing." Yukinoshita tucked away her smile and pointed her beautiful face at the two of us.

As we waited for her to continue, she took one step forward.

Toward us.

One soft step.

"…Could you hear my request?" Yukinoshita asked shyly, like she was embarrassed.

Yuigahama's mouth split in a smile. "Yeah, tell us," she answered, taking another step to bring them closer, and she reached out a gentle hand.

Eventually, the rays of the twilight sun that had sunk into the sea cast shadow puppets on a white canvas.

It was dim and wavering, its warped form with an unclear outline.

But the shapes had clearly connected into one.

If what I wish for would have a form…it would be—

Afterword

Good evening, I'm Wataru Working.

Before you know it, the season has completely turned to early summer, and it's gotten all hot. But there's still the occasional day when it suddenly gets chilly, and every single time, at this time of year, it's like I have no clothes to wear.

When they can't make it clear if it's going to be hot or cold, you ultimately want to choose the option of not leaving the house, but since I'm a corporate slave, that is not to be so.

And so every day I think, *Is this outfit okay...? Tell me, Piiko!* as I choose clothes to wear and head to work.

Well, there is no absolute correct answer when it comes to selecting clothes, but still, it seems there are still wrong answers. This is also true when it comes to weather or temperature, like I mentioned earlier, but aside from that, there are also standards for business manners and dress codes for stores. Fundamentally, it's also true for the way people see you, too.

When you're very unsure in your fashion sense, even just walking around town, you get weirdly anxious like, *Just now, that person looked at my clothes and laughed... A-and that person... And the sun is laughing, too... And the puppies are laughing! Luulululu luu ♪* and I think such mental suffering is possible. Or not.

The objective angle aside, there's also those moments when you yourself are not really satisfied with how you've dressed.

Following that nagging sense that something is wrong with him, being at the mercy of options of right/wrong and subjective/objective, at the end of it all...what should he wear?

And so on that note, this has been *My Youth Romantic Comedy Is Wrong, As I Expected*, Vol. 11.

And below, the acknowledgments.

Holy Ponkan®. You pulled another god move! The cover is Gahama-san again after so long—it's lovely! It's whoa. So cuuute. Poggers. Thank you as always!

To my editor, Hoshino. Ga-ha-ha! Ohhh, I'm real sorry, man! Ga-ha-ha! Um, I really am sorry for having caused you trouble. Thank you very much. Hey, I can get the next one in on time easy, ga-ha-ha!

To everyone involved with the media franchise: I'm very sorry for all the trouble I've caused you with the TV anime and other things. I'll continue to do my best in the future, so I'll be looking forward to working with you moving forward as well. Thank you very much.

To all my readers: As usual, it's been a string of mistakes and spinning around in circles and continuously wandering off course, but finally, we're at Volume 11. I think this story may finally be reaching the climax. I'd be really glad if you could support me to the very end of the end of the end, and the anime and manga as well. Thank you very much.

Now then, I've run out of pages here, so I'll lay down my pen for the time being.

Next time, let's meet in Volume 12 of *My Youth Romantic Comedy Is Wrong, As I Expected*.

On a certain day in May, while drinking MAX Coffee no matter what,

Wataru Watari

Chapter 1 ⋯ Once he's aware that **winter** has begun, it has already passed.

P. 3 **"According to the lunar calendar, the day of Keichitsu was less than a month away."** Keichitsu is in mid-March, the day in the Chinese calendar when the sun's celestial longitude is exactly 345 degrees. It's a day when hibernating insects are thought to emerge from the ground.

P. 8 **"There is also the example of flowers and storms; life is naught but farewells."** This is from a poem by the famous Chinese poet Li Bai called "Offering a Drink" that was rather poetically and liberally translated into Japanese.

P. 11 **"…is she as swift as the *Shimakaze*?"** The *Shimakaze* was a real Japanese navy vessel, but this is almost definitely referring to *Kantai Collection*, of which Watari is a big fan. The card for Shimakaze includes the quote "swift as the *Shimakaze*" (*shimakaze* means "island wind"). This is a reference to *fuurinkazan*, motto of the warlord Shingen Takeda, adopted from Sun Tzu's *Art of War*. It goes, "As swift as wind, as gentle as forest, as fierce as fire, as unshakable as a mountain."

P. 11   **"...I wasn't sure if Isshiki's presence here meant membership... some people even build a collection!"** The original text here read, "[Yukinoshita] was offering her surprisingly legitimate hospitality. There are so many types of hospitality in the world, it makes you want to make a collection!" The pun is on *kantai* (hospitality) and *kantai* (navy fleet), referencing the game *Kantai Collection*.

P. 14   **"The Heart-Pounding ☆ All-Girls Witch Trial in Absentia! With added snitching!"** This fake title is a reference to *Doki! Marugoto Mizugi! Onna Darake no Suiei Taikai* (Heart-pounding! All-swimsuits! The all-girls swimming show), a spin-off of the *Swimming Show* idol pop star variety show that began in 1970, with swimming as a theme.

P. 15   **"...for when I'm making obligatory chocolate."** The tradition in Japan on Valentine's Day is that girls give guys chocolate, but there are two types. The first type is meant to convey a crush, while the second kind is given out of social obligation.

P. 16   **"The end of a lemon is the closest I'll ever get to sucking the golden teat anyway..."** The Japanese wordplay here involves the idiom "suck the sweet juices," which means "to make money without working." Hikki follows up by saying, "It's always nothing but bitter juices." Yukinoshita shoots back, "You don't suck bitter juices; you lick them," referencing the idiom "lick bitter juices," which means "to have a bad experience." Then at the end, Yukinoshita says, "What you were licking was not bitter juices, but life..." *Nameru* (to lick) also means "underestimate" or "to not take seriously."

P. 18   *A Sister's All You Need.* is the name of a light-novel series by Yomi Hirasaka.

P. 18   **"Komachi? Who's that? The rice girl? ...Or even down here in Chiba."** Akita Komachi is a brand of rice. *Komachi* in fact means "town beauty"; Akita Komachi rice has a picture of a beautiful woman on it. In the original, Hachiman refers to the agricultural cooperatives of the northern Akita prefecture and Chiba prefecture.

P. 20   **"…a baseball manga (which is a little light on the baseballness for a baseball manga), okay?"** Hachiman is referring to the baseball manga *H2* by Mitsuru Adachi.

P. 21   **"Like how the sun lances into your eyes, specifically."** The original wordplay here was on *nikkori egao* (bright smile) and Nikkari Aoe, the name of a famous Japanese sword.

Chapter 2 ⋯ And so begins the **all-girls battle** (with boys, too).

P. 26   **"…you and Hayama should share some guy chocolate, too!"** *Tomo-choco*, or friendship chocolate, is nonromantic Valentine's Day chocolate. In the original, Hachiman references the children's anime *Chibi Maruko-chan*, where the main character's grandpa is named Tomozou Sakura.

P. 27   **"…girls attempting to settle the score…"** The original Japanese wordplay here was on *hatten* (develop, as in "develop into conflict among the girls"), using the word again to mean a relationship developing, and then the slang use of *hatten* meaning "sleeping around," finishing it off with *reiten* (score of zero).

P. 28   **"…her bluish-black ponytail did a hop-hop here and a hop-hop there, here a hop, there a hop, everywhere a hop-hop."** This was originally from a tongue twister about frogs.

P. 31   **"…lately that jagged-hearted Yukinon-ness, sharp edges hurting everything that touched her…"** This is a reference to the song "Lullaby for a Jagged Heart" by the 1980s pop band Checkers. The lyrics include the line "I was pointed like a knife, hurting everyone who touches it."

P. 34 **"Potato is a good name for a cat, so there is something cute to it."** The original name for this dish is *satoimo nikkorogashi*, which is taro root (a purple tuber that tastes a little sweet-potato-y) parboiled and then simmered in sake, sugar, and soy sauce. It's called *nikkorogashi* because it's boiled (*niru*) while rolling (*korogashi*) the pieces of taro in the sauce as all the water boils off to keep them from burning. Yukinoshita comments that *nikkorogashi* sounds like *nekkorogashi*, which isn't a word, but sounds more catlike.

P. 37 *"We can still save it, we can still save it, we can save it save it please don't make us corporate slave it!"* This is a double-layered joke—this reference is to a sketch by comedian *Gor☆geous* where he repeats *mada tasukaru* (we can still be saved) and finishes off with "Madagascar!" rather nonsensically, but the word sounds similar. Here Hachiman finishes with "Tasmanian devil!" instead, deliberately getting the reference wrong with a word that sounds nothing like the original.

P. 42 **"I didn't care if it was *Crows* or *Worst* or *QP* or what..."** All of these are manga by Hiroshi Takahashi, with the same setting. They're about delinquents.

P. 42 **Doraemon** is a robot cat from the future in the children's anime of the same name, and he lives in the protagonist Nobita's closet.

P. 43 **"Though in this case, with Miura and Isshiki feeding him chocolate, he might be biting off more than he can chew."** The original wordplay here was on "feeding him chocolate" (*choko kuwaseru*) and "deceiving him" (*ippai kuwaseru*).

P. 44 **"We've got to double-time it, or they'll be booked out!"** This is a quote from Nike in *Magical Circle Guru*.

Chapter 3 ··· Unexpectedly, what **Iroha Isshiki**'s absence brings is...

P. 47 *My First Errand* is a TV show that features real children going out to perform their very first errands. It's common for Japanese children to be sent out on errands at very young ages, like four or so, and a child's first errand is a bit of a celebrated event.

P. 51 **"...I might even wind up squeaking like a Chibull alien."** The Chibull alien is an enemy in the Ultraman series that shows up and is immediately defeated with hardly any fight—it's comically weak. The original pun here was on *bibiru* (get scared), *chibiru* (wet yourself), and *chibiru seijin* (Chibull alien).

P. 55 **"I was just like an ARMS with the core knocked out of it."** This is referencing the manga *Project ARMS* by Kyoichi Nanatsuki and Ryoji Minagawa.

P. 57 **"Not at the face! At the body!"** The original context for this quote was "Don't [look] at my face, [look] at my body." This is a famous quote from *Sannen B-gumi Kinpachi-sensei* (Mr. Kinpachi from class 3-B), a TV drama about a middle school teacher and his ninth-grade class that originally began running in the 1970s. This particular quote is from the character Reiko Yamada, a delinquent girl.

P. 59 **"...you're seriously jooshy polly yey party people every day..."** Jooshy polly yey, a slurred version of "juicy party yeah," is a greeting coined by Chiaki Takahashi, a voice actor, singer, and gravure model. It has no particular deep meaning. "Polly peepoh" is also slang for "party people."

P. 60   **"Like, a blue ribbon around your chest will accentuate it in a way that's sure to get everyone talking about you! Your popularity will explode!"** Hachiman is probably talking about Hestia from *Is It Wrong to Try to Pick Up Girls in a Dungeon?*, who wears blue ribbons both above and below her boobs.

P. 65   **"Will the day eventually come when Wakame-chan talks to Katsuo like this…? The Isono family bathwater would probably taste really good."** Wakame and Katsuo are characters from *Sazae-san*; Katsuo is Wakame's older brother. They're also words for broth ingredients—seaweed and fish flakes, respectively.

P. 65   **"…the smart, cute Komaachika…"** "The smart, cute Eliichika" is the motto of Eli Ayase from *Love Live!*

P. 65   **"But if this were the Sengoku era, I'd be a success!"** Hachiman is referring to the saying "A child who is loathed will be successful in the world." It's a very old saying that appears in *Heike Monogatari* and generally means that a naughty child has the gumption to succeed later in life. It's sometimes said of Oda Nobunaga, the famous Sengoku-era warlord.

Chapter 4 ⋯ And so begins the **boys' emotional roller coaster** (with girls, too).

P. 68   **"It'd be more accurate to call them jumbo-sized hand-drawn pop signs."** Hand-drawn pop signs are little cards with handwritten notes that are taped besides products at stores. They're ubiquitous in Japan, and you often see them at bookstores with messages like *Staff recommendation!* and then a paragraph about why a certain staff member likes it, with a decorative border and simple illustrations.

P. 68   **"This was not just a company run by black-hearted executives, but Black Company RX…"** Hachiman originally uses the term "black company," which is a term for an exploitative business that drains its employees dry, while Black Company RX is a play on *Kamen Rider: Black RX*, a rendition of the *sentai* series from the 1980s.

P. 73   **"What's with that greeting? Is he gonna show off his Walk the Dog like we're in elementary school?"** Tobe's original slang greeting was *choriisu*, which also sounds like *chorizo*. Hachiman says, "Is he a sausage?"

P. 75   **"And so, the next work begins..."** Every episode of *Sound! Euphonium* ends with the line "And so the next piece begins..."

P. 77   **"He's not gonna say *Gather round for a round of cheers, whoo!* or anything, right...?"** The original pun here is "He's not gonna say that since this is a circle formation [*enjin*], let's get our engines running, right...?"

P. 77   **"*'You don't have nothin'?'* Look, this isn't an ad for Ajigonomi... and I'm not your mom."** Ajigonomi is a brand of *arare*: mixed rice crackers and peanuts. The old ad slogan from the 1990s was "You don't have nothin'? You don't have nothin'? Hey, Mom?"

P. 79   **"Where the heck is Tobe from...? He says *dude* way too much."** Tobe's verbal tic is to add *be* at the end of everything, which is a northern Japan thing. But he doesn't have any other northern elements to his speech, so it sounds weirdly fake. Through this series, it's mostly been translated as "man" or "dude" or "whoa."

P. 80   **"...Kawashima, Kawaguchi, Kawagoe, Kawanakajima, Sendai, or Sendai..."** *Kawa* is the character for "river," a common kanji in names. The first Sendai is also written with the "river" character (though has different pronunciation), while the second Sendai is pronounced the same, but it doesn't have the "river" character and is in fact the name of Sendai city.

P. 83   **"I am not the one called sale-immune."** The original pun here is "The participation fee is also a pretty cheap list price [*shoubai kakaku*] and *shoubai* rock *pyuru*!" *Pyuru* is the verbal tick of Moa, a character in the anime *Show by Rock!!*

P. 83   *Quiz Derby* is an old quiz show that ran from the 1970s to the 1990s. The scoring system involved multiplication from 1x to 10x, and whenever there was a multiplier, the announcer would go, "Multiplication bang!"

P. 85   **"Are these nin-nin ninjas or what?"** *Nin-nin* is the verbal tic of the titular protagonist of *Ninja Hattori-kun*.

P. 86   ***Haru* here didn't particularly refer to a hostess who works at a hot spring."** Hachiman is referring to the 1980s manga *Haru-chan* by Yuusuke Aoyagi. It's about a young hostess at a hot spring in Ishikawa.

P. 87   **"Kind? You mean kinda scary?"** The original gag here was "It feels less kind [*yasashii*] and more *yashashiin*." In the 2014 adaptation of *The Heroic Legend of Arslan*, Persian is used for a variety of scenes, most of which is incomprehensible to Japanese audiences, but one word, Japanized as *yashashiin*—meaning "Commence the attack!"—stuck out among fans.

P. 88   **"She's so good, I bet she could win over not just humans, but fairies, too."** This line is written mostly in hiragana, a characteristic of the fairies in *Humanity Has Declined*. They're particularly attracted to sweets.

P. 88   **"Just like her name, she exposes things under the light of the sun."** The first character in *Haruno* means "sun."

Chapter 5 ··· Suddenly, **Shizuka Hiratsuka** lectures about the present continuous and the past.

P. 92   **"…you can bet your 'sweet' bippy…"** In Japanese, Isshiki puns on sweet again with *kangae ga amai* (your thinking is sweet), an idiom that means "you're naive."

P. 95   ***"So sweet and bitter, I feel like my head will spin!"*** This is a line from the ending song to *Blood Blockade Battlefront*, "Sugar Song to Bitter Step."

P. 101   *Unagi Pie* does mean "eel pie," but it's neither eel nor pie. It's a small, dry, sugar-covered pastry that's like a long strip wrapped into an oval. It apparently has eel powder in it, but it doesn't taste like eel.

P. 102   *The Man Without Talent* was the last manga by Yoshiharu Tsuge, an avant-garde manga artist and cult figure. At one point, the protagonist, a failed manga artist, tries to make a living by selling rocks picked up from the riverside.

P. 103   **"No financial return. I'm at the point of no return. Sixth layer of the Abyss. Unpaid in Abyss."** The original line here is "The Service Club is unpaid all year long [*nenjuu mukyuu*]! …*Mukyuu*." Usually, *nenjuu mukyuu* means "no holidays all year long"—in other words, "open 365 days a year," and this instance deliberately uses the wrong kanji. *Mukyuu* is also a meaningless moe noise often said by Patchouli, a Touhou character.

P. 105   ***"Pi, Pie… Pierre Taki? Jean Pierre…Polnareff?"*** Pierre Taki is a Japanese singer / actor / TV personality, and Jean Pierre Polnareff is a character from *JoJo's Bizarre Adventure*.

P. 106   A **fortified armor shell** is the name of the mecha suit from the manga *Apocalypse Zero* by Takayuki Yamaguchi.

P. 106   A **Perfect Devil Superhuman** is a bit of a cross between the Perfect Superhuman and Devil Superhuman, (or "Chojin" in the localization), a fictional race in the manga *Kinnikuman*, which is localized as *Ultimate Muscle*.

Chapter 6 ··· He fails to reach the "something real" he's after and continues to get it wrong.

P. 130   "**You seemed to be whisking all around the kitchen, though... *Because we were baking? Is that the joke?*"** In Japanese Yukinoshita says he was *chokomaka* (restlessly moving around) and Hachiman thinks, *Because it's* choko [chocolate].

Chapter 7 ··· Haruno Yukinoshita's eyes are hopelessly clear.

P. 162   "**Apparently, I wouldn't even need to bother asking, *Have you prepared yourself?*"** This is part of the *Go! Princess PreCure* group speech: "Oh dream, trapped in a cold cage, we shall have you returned! Have you prepared yourself?" It's a bit more obvious from the Japanese wording.

P. 164   "**I said over and over, 'Thanks so much...so much...'"** *Arigatee* is from an iconic scene in *Gambling Apocalypse Kaiji* where the protagonist is stuck in an underground labor debt camp and finally gets a cold beer and freaks out over it. The beer is just part of a scam to get him in more debt.

Chapter 8 ··· Yui Yuigahama's gaze is always gentle and warm.

P. 177   "**The *maguro* part of the name made me think of tuna sushi, but it's not. It's a shark. Very much a shark.**" *Tsuma* means "tip"; *guro* means "black." Thus, *tsumaguro* = blacktip reef shark. *Maguro* means "tuna."

P. 177 **"Sea bream and flounder dancing"** is a line from an old children's song, "Urashima Tarou," which is about the folk story of the same name.

P. 178 **"I was now totally like a boy in front of the trumpet in the show window."** This is from an old JACCS credit card commercial. The narrator talks about how "back then, I could never get that trumpet." "Tutti!" is the ending theme song for *Sound! Euphonium*.

P. 183 **"She's really got the friskies for kitties."** The original line here is *maji neko daisuki furisukii*, a sort of grammatical double-wordplay. It sounds like he's starting off saying "Yukinoshita really loves cats," but then slides into a cat food slogan instead.

P. 183 **"Oh, there's rays, too!"** *Ei* means "ray" in Japanese, but it's also the sound one makes while stretching, so there's a bit of wordplay here. The original line is "'Oh, there are rays, too!' she said and reached out her hand with an *ei!* 'cause it's a ray, *ei*. Whoops, I mean *ee* [mm-hmm]."

P. 187 **"...shleh-heh-heh-heh..."** *Nuru-fu-fu* is the laughter of Koro-sensei from *Assassination Classroom*.

Afterword

P. 207 **Piiko** is a TV personality and fashion critic.

P. 207 **"And the sun is laughing, too... And the puppies are laughing! Luu-lululu luu ♪"** These are lyrics from the opening to *Sazae-san*.